MAFIA SAVAGES

A DARK MAFIA REVERSE HAREM ROMANCE

STEPHANIE BROTHER

Mafia Savages © STEPHANIE BROTHER 2025

All Rights Reserved. This book or any portion thereof may not be reproduced or used in any manner whatsoever without the express permission of the publisher except for the use of brief quotations in a book review.

This book is a work of fiction. Any resemblance to persons, living or dead, or places, events or locations is purely coincidental. The characters are all productions of the author's imagination.

Please note that this work is intended only for adults over the age of 18 and all characters represented as 18 or over.

PRINT EDITION

1

MAGGIE

"Why did you become a barmaid, sweetheart?"

If I had a nickel for every time someone had asked me that, I'd be rich. Or, at least, I'd have more than I made from my lousy wage and meager tips.

Not that all of the customers at the Rusty Bucket were jerks. Far from it. There were mostly hard-working men, and the occasional bored retiree, like Burt here who was sitting at the bar. Though he had to be closing in on eighty, there was often a twinkle in his eye when he spoke to me.

"Just lucky, I suppose."

He sipped his beer. "A pretty girl like you could do a lot more."

I frowned; not sure what looks had to do with it. The truth was, I'd tried to go for more. I'd completed a year and a half of college with money my mom had saved for her whole life.

But now she was gone, and the money had long since run out.

"You could get a beauty license," Burt said, as if this was secret knowledge. "You could do hair and nails and not have to deal with the vermin who come in this place."

I mentally rolled my eyes. Burt was harmless, and usually pretty good company, but he'd just revealed himself to be both sexist and classist. And it wasn't the first time.

"Or you could be a weather girl on TV. You're pretty enough to be on TV."

I set a fresh bowl of peanuts in front of him. "I think they hire meteorologists for those jobs."

"Right," he nodded sagely. "Too much schooling involved."

Some men at the far end of the bar flagged me down, and I was glad to get away from the older man even though I usually liked chatting with him. He was harmless in general, but his assumption that I wouldn't make it in school bothered me. My dream had been to finish college and then go to law school. It had been money, not brains, that had stopped me.

As I took drink orders, I noticed a huge man sitting by himself at a table in the back. He had a whiskey and a plate of fries, so one of the waitresses must've served him. He caught my eye because of his size, but also because he was alone.

He was called Rock, and that seemed appropriate because he was the size of a boulder. He had muscles on top of muscles, which was an interesting contrast to his tan skin and dark, Italian eyes and hair. Most of the Italian men in the neighborhood were on the slimmer side, but Rock looked like a bouncer.

Usually, he came in here with his two buddies, Julian and Slater. I didn't know them, but I'd served drinks to them plenty of times, and they always tipped well. It was strange to see the big man in here by himself tonight. Something about the set of his shoulders made me think he wasn't in a good mood. But somehow, I knew he wouldn't give me any trouble. He never did.

I tended bar for another few hours, giving Burt a sincere good-bye when he toddled on home to his wife. He meant well. Probably when I was in my late seventies, I'd be out and about talking the ear off younger people, too. I just hoped my views would be a little more enlightened.

The dining area emptied as people headed home. This was a working-class neighborhood in Brooklyn, and a lot of our customers had to get up early. Besides, there were other options for those who wanted to stay out all night.

Rock seemed to be in that category. He nursed his drink, occasionally scowling at his phone.

I took advantage of the lessening crowd to clean up behind the bar. Maybe, just maybe, I'd get out of here at a reasonable time tonight.

Two men in their twenties were seated at the bar, and a group of two men and four women at a table fifteen feet away. Rock was still there, reading a newspaper that someone had left. I popped the register open to put some more money in, my gaze on notes piled on top of one another. Just as I shoved a twenty-dollar note into the correct pile, the distinct sound of a gun cocking filled my ears. I froze, my gaze still on the cash register. Another, identical sound sent shivers of fear down my spine. My heart jumping in my throat, I looked up. The two young men were standing in front of me, their guns pointed at my head.

"Give us the money, gorgeous."

My frozen mind wouldn't thaw, and I just stared at him. He looked hardly old enough to grow a beard, let alone rob a bar.

"Now, darling," the other one said. I got called things like that a lot while bartending, but not usually while guns were pointed at me.

Smugness filled both men's faces. Clearly, they

thought they had me right where they wanted me. That they could do whatever they wanted by virtue of having guns.

And that pissed me off. The desire to knock the smug looks right off of their faces somehow made my brain kick into gear, and I knew what to do.

"Hey assholes."

A deep voice from behind the men made them turn and look. Rocco came to a halt behind those two, his dark eyes flashing red in the dim illumination.

As he did so, I ducked under the counter.

Not for protection, but for the double barrel shotgun my manager kept there. She'd trained all the staff how to use it.

I pointed it at the men while their attention was Rocco. He looked pissed as hell. Suddenly, I was afraid. Not for my own safety, but that he might do something stupid and get himself thrown into jail.

"Hey assholes," I said firmly, echoing Rock's words. They turned back to me, one man's mouth dropping open as he saw the gun in my hands.

They'd made a mistake in turning their back on a man like the Rock. He moved up behind them and slammed both their heads into the bar. Hard.

One man's gun skittered away. The other guy held onto his pistol, and it was pointed at me. Shit.

I changed up my grip on the shotgun and brought

the butt down on his wrist. He yelped and dropped the gun. I batted it away from his hand.

"Call the police," I shouted toward the people at the nearest table as I trained my gun on the men who were now bleeding from their noses and looking dazed. My plan was to hold them there until the police came, but that plan was ruined when the shotgun was wrenched out of my hands.

Astonished, I stared as Rock tossed my shotgun out of the way. "Go back in the kitchen," he growled. "I'll take care of these two."

What the hell?

He didn't even work here. What right did he have to snatch my gun away? I opened my mouth to say as much, but the murderous look in his eyes stopped me.

The smaller of the two men rallied and tried to throw a punch at the big man, which he easily deflected. Then he decked him, sending him slumping onto the bar again. The Moron #2 tried it and got the same result.

I picked up an empty beer stein and started to bring it down on the punk's head, but again, Rock stopped me. "I got this," he repeated gruffly.

Who the hell did he think he was, our bouncer? This place couldn't afford one and usually didn't need it.

But if we did, Rock was clearly up to the job. He

took swings at each man in turn since they were too stupid to give up. It almost looked like he was having fun. He'd shove one, then punch the other. Then turn back to deal with the first.

"Does your mom know you're out this late?" Rocco growled, his voice rising over their groans. "Does she, you fuckheads?"

"Stop," one cried. Yeah, that did a lot of good.

"What are you hassling us for?" the other one sounded stuffy, as if his nose was broken.

"What are you hassling her for," Rock countered with a growl, gesturing toward me.

"We just wanted the money," the first one said, sounding whiny. "Then the cunt got in the way—"

I gasped, but not from the word they called me. Rock's expression changed. If I'd thought he looked dangerous before, he looked downright deadly now. He punched the guy who'd said that in the face, knocking him out. That made me think that I'd been right before, that he'd been toying with the guys and pulling his punches.

He grabbed the other guy so hard that he made him cry out. Then he dragged them toward the door, one conscious, the other unconscious. The other customers and I watched until he'd manhandled them out the door.

Then all was quiet as I stared in disbelief at the door the powerful man had just exited.

What the *hell* was that?

Why had Rock taken it upon himself to take care of those guys?

I was still shakily contemplating it when a customer from the table called out. "Miss? Can we get another pitcher of beer?"

2
ROCCO

Ron Keeler and Simon Portis.

Those two delinquents had made a mistake.

A *serious* mistake. As I dragged them down the dark alley, I wondered if they'd gotten that message left.

About two months ago, they mugged some old lady three blocks away. They'd been lucky I wasn't anywhere near that spot. If I were, I would have beaten the shit out of them. Then this would never have happened tonight. Maggie would have locked the place up and gone home, without worrying about a couple of assholes trying to earn their stripes.

Keeler and Portis had been desperate to get into the Gambini family. They thought they deserved to be part of a crew, because they thought they were so big and bad. Yeah, right. I'm pretty damn sure I proved otherwise to them tonight. Hell, Maggie had been on the path to proving otherwise. I never thought I'd see the pretty barmaid with a shotgun in her hands, but she looked like she knew how to use it.

If nothing else, she'd scared those two assholes. Well, if they'd been able to see past my fist connecting with their faces. When it came down to it, those two were tiny. Not in size—they were each around six feet tall each. But they just didn't have what it takes to enter this world.

Guts.

It takes guts to take on some of New York's arch criminals. Stealing from an eighty-year-old lady? Robbing a pretty barmaid? That was the opposite of gutsy. Even a high school kid with a gun could have done that shit. Alone. With no backup.

Yet somehow, these two assholes thought it would impress Michael Gambini. If that wasn't fucked up, I didn't know what was. Don Gambini had been running the family for almost thirty years. During that time, he had had a lot of people working for him, tough bastards who would eat those two for lunch.

Keeler clawed at my hand, trying to break the iron grip I had on my shirt, but I wasn't letting go unless it was to drop him off a cliff. And I had to admit, I liked having their blood on my knuckles. Dishing out brutal beatings was part of my job. They had to know this was my turf. That the Rusty Bucket was my favorite place to relax. To drink whiskey. Catch a game. And to enjoy the sight of the sweet young thing behind the bar.

The image of Maggie swinging that shotgun around was still inside my head. She didn't seem the type. Sure, she could shoot the shit like any good bartender, and she poured a mean drink. Still, there was something about her. She was always kind of... delicate. Yeah, that was the word. Even though she shoved her hair in a messy ponytail and wore flannel shirts, there was no getting around that she was a petite, feminine woman.

Except tonight I'd seen a different side of her. Growing up in the foster care system, I'd met plenty of girls who were tough as nails. They'd had to be. We'd all had to be.

It made me wonder what in Maggie's past had made her develop that steely streak.

As I contemplated it, I smashed Keeler and Porter's heads together for good measure and then released them. They collapsed on the trash-covered pavement with a groan. Or one was groaning. The other appeared to be unconscious.

Served them right. They couldn't just walk into a moderately respectable dive like the Rusty Bucket and think they can do whatever the hell they wanted, especially mess with a working girl like Maggie. Her life couldn't be the price for their admission into the

Gambini family. She had to be left alone, or else Keeler and Portis would soon find out what staring down the barrel of a gun was like. Either mine, or shit, maybe I should sic Maggie on them.

Instead, I hoisted one man after the other into a filthy dumpster. The stench when their bodies slammed against the garbage was an assault to my nostrils, but hey, at least I'd taken out the trash, like the fucking model citizen I was.

I half thought about going back to the Rusty Bucket. The scent of greasy burgers and the sweat that men got after a long day of work would be heaven compared to the smell of the dumpster.

But first, I had to find my buddies.

Julian and Slater had promised to meet me at the Rusty Bucket, but hadn't shown, which wasn't like them. In another world that might make me worry, but they were tough men who could take care of themselves.

That meant that if they got delayed, it was probably because of their own doing, not someone else's.

They were my best friends, but that didn't mean they couldn't be fuck-ups sometimes.

So it was time to find them and figure out what the fuck was going on. And if that meant knocking their heads together the way I had to those two punks, so be it. At least I wouldn't toss them in the dumpster.

Julian had texted a few times, saying that they were

stuck in traffic and that they'd be there soon. The last text had been over an hour ago.

The day before, Slater had sounded pretty excited on the phone. He'd hinted that something big was going on. Something life-changing, even.

I'd believe that when I saw it, and maybe not even then. Slater was too goddamn reckless sometimes. Not so long ago, he suggested sneaking into the police impound to "liberate" his old Charger. That Dodge was a fucking sweet car, but we'd still have to take care of the eight cops on shift in that impound. I wasn't *that* crazy to start a shootout with all those cops, just because Slater had missed the feel of roaring down the interstate in his Charger.

I walked into Bella Marina's, a dive bar that made the Rusty Bucket look like a five-star hotel. As I scanned the dark room for my buddies, I was almost ready for a second tonight. I hated being stood up—those two should have known better than to keep me waiting like some chump. Two waiters were wiping down ripped tablecloths that looked only marginally cleaner than the dumpster I'd just left. Marina herself walked toward me. Though *bella* wasn't the right word to describe her plain, pock-marked face, she was another tough woman. As opposite of Maggie as you could get, but tough as nails.

Our eyes met. "Men's room!" she said, giving me the

information I needed. Striding past the tables, my ears picked up a weird sound. The sound of someone gagging. Unless my cock was stuffed down a pretty woman's throat, it wasn't a sound I enjoyed hearing.

I barged into the men's room, already pretty sure of what I was going to find. Julian's tall figure outside one of the stalls, and he looked apologetic as I glared.

The groans were coming from the stall, and it didn't take a genius to know who was in there.

"Where the fuck have you two been?" I demanded, closing the gap between us.

"Sorry, Rock." He looked away and gestured toward the closed door of the stall. "It's Slater. He, uh…" He faltered. "He got a little fucked up while we went over his little plan."

The sound of a flushing toilet didn't allow me to speak. Once it had faded, I rolled my eyes at him. "He's drunk off his ass? *Again*?"

"You know Slater, man," Julian's tone calm and steady, not frustrated as fuck like I was. But then again, nothing ever rattled Julian. "Every time he gets excited about something, he can't get enough tequila in his system."

"I already know that he doesn't use his head," I snapped, flashing him a nasty glare. "But you're supposed to. Why the hell did you let him get like this?"

"I'm not his fucking babysitter," Julian said, but again, without heat.

The creaking of the stall door turned our heads in its direction. Slater staggered out, eyes red, his brownish hair a huge mess and stinking like a distillery. I almost preferred the dumpster smell.

"Sorry about tonight, babe," he spoke in a wobbly voice, his body swaying back. "I didn't mean to stand you up."

I took a few moments to figure out if the "babe" part was worth wiping the floor with him, but it wasn't like he was in his right mind at the moment. Though he did sometimes enjoy trying to get a rise out of me.

"So much for being stuck in traffic," I shook my head in disapproval, turning back to Julian. He was the only one sober enough to yell at. "You should have told me Slater was getting shitfaced. Or strapped on a pair and stopped him."

"I didn't think it'd get this bad," Julian said. "Two shots. That was the plan, until Marina bought us the next round."

"And then, let me guess, Slater told her to leave the bottle." I shook my head in disgust. "So tell me more about Slater's fabulous plan. Because clearly, he's a man you want to listen to." Slater chose that moment to spit up at least a shot and a half of Tequila into the sink.

With bleary eyes, he turned to me. "Well, see—"

"Move," I cut him off. "I don't want to have that conversation here."

"I like it," Julian's last words made me look back at him in confusion. "Not... *that.*" He gestured toward the wreck that was our friend. "His plan, I mean. It's smart."

"Outside," I demanded, twisting the handle on the door.

"First, explain to me how you got those," Julian stated, pointing down at my bruised knuckles.

I sucked in a deep breath, remembering the sweet moments when my fists slammed into those two asshole's faces.

"Keeler and Portis," I began, the two of us reaching the table across from the men's room entrance. "They decided to rob the Rusty Bucket."

"Assholes," Julian muttered. "Was Maggie tending bar?"

I grunted, nodding. None of us knew her well, but we had eyes. She'd be hard not to notice. "She actually pulled a shotgun on them."

"Seriously?" Julian grinned. "I'd have liked to see that."

Yeah, it'd been quite the sight. "I took care of them for her."

"Ouch." Julian cringed. "That had to hurt. Them, I mean."

"It did," I confirmed with a nod. "If I ever see them

again anywhere near the Rusty Bucket again, they're dead. You tell me if you see them, okay?"

"Will do," Julian nodded in agreement, Slater joining in a few seconds late. He all but fell into the corner booth we chose. With another groan, he leaned his elbows on the sticky table and palmed his face.

"Damn..." he croaked. "That hangover's killing me. Julian, you tell him the plan."

"Rocco's right," Julian uttered in an annoyed voice, tossing a sideways glare at him. "I should have stopped you before you got drunk out of your fucking mind."

"Ah, shit..." Slater muttered, his eyes shut as his fingers raked through his spiky hair. "Just tell him."

"Whatever," Julian spoke, shifting his focus to me. "All right, here goes. Rocco, you remember North Haven, right?"

I nodded. "Rich suburb—takes a while to get there. Why?"

"Slater had been checking it out for a while," Julian continued. "There's a police station there, but it's understaffed. There are like two cops on shift, twenty-four-seven. Locals don't rely much on police anyway. They've got the money to employ security firms."

"I'm still waiting to hear what we're going to do up there." It would be nice if he got to the fucking point. "Police stations are understaffed pretty much everywhere outside of the city. You don't see people shooting each other on the street, though."

"No shooting," Julian assured, waving his hand in front of his face. "At least, I hope we won't have to shoot anybody. We've all been looking for a way out of the organization, Rocco. This might be it."

The words hit me hard. They weren't the kind of thing guys like us should even think, let alone say. And we wouldn't have, years ago when we worked for Emilio Roselli, he was the head of the family. He was a good man. Okay, there were a bunch of cops, judges, and city officials who probably didn't think so, but Emilio had lived by a code.

But he was dead, and his son had taken over. Nicolo Roselli. Nick was the kind of guy who stationed drug dealers outside of fucking middle school to get the kids hooked early. They'll be our customers for life, he'd say.

Yeah, right. For their very short lives. Loyalty was everything in my line of work, and I'd had it for Emilio. I would have given my life for him—we all would have. But his son? His son could go fuck himself. Nick was our boss, but it wasn't like we could just hand in a two week notice. But the longer we worked for that asshole, the more I wanted to get as far away from him as possible.

Except trying it would likely end with the three of us six feet underground.

Julian was still talking, and I'd missed part of it. "It's what we do afterwards that's the real problem," he continued. "No one's going to hire guys like us, unless we're willing to work for bum paychecks."

"Bum paychecks are better than being dead," I pointed out. Though, it wasn't like I'd be content to work a fucking nine-to-five. "So is North Haven supposed to be some kind of golden opportunity for us?"

"Yes, actually." He cocked his head to the side. "Forget breaking into one of those mega-mansions up there. Like I said, there's private security watching them all the fucking time. I'm talking about a bank. Palmer's Savings and Loan branch is easy pickings. It's about four miles from the police station. Slater knows this hacker, Eddie. He can disable its alarm system remotely. The cops won't even know we're there."

"So that's the plan? We knock over a bank?" My tone was sarcastic, but the gears in my head were turning. "Those private security firms you mentioned—they won't engage us in a firefight, but they *will* call it in if they notice us. What's their patrol schedule? How many ways in and out?"

"A security van passes by that bank once every hour," Julian's response was fast, as if he anticipated my query. "Three ways in and out. This is what makes this so goddamn irresistible, Rocco. Even if the hacker fucks up somehow and the bank alarm goes off, the cops won't be able to corner us. We'll just drive away. By the time backup gets there, we'll be miles away."

"Easy money," Slater said, but he sounded so goddamn miserable that his words didn't instill much confidence.

We talked it over in low voices for a while longer. Finally, I sighed. "It does sound pretty tempting. But we can't forget Roselli. What the fuck is he going to do if he finds out we pulled a job without telling him?" And that was just part of the problem. If we actually used the money to obtain our freedom, there'd be a huge price on our heads.

"He'll be pissed—that's for sure." Julian grinned at the thought. "Like I give a shit about that. Hopefully we'll be sipping cocktails on some beach in Cuba before he finds out."

"You think he can't reach us down there?" My question wiped that smile right off Julian's face. My friends knew that the organization could locate anyone they liked. "That's what I thought," I went on. "I tell you what. Let's go over to North Haven tomorrow night. I want to see for myself how easy it would be to rob that bank. And Slater?" I looked at my suffering friend. "Make sure you're sober, or else I'll kick you out of the fucking car." I meant it, but he was one of my two oldest friends. I'd be sure to stop it first.

Giving Marina a wave, I strode out. Despite the many details to work out, Slater's plan intrigued me. Sure, the millions were part of the appeal. But to get out from under the thumb of a prick like Nick Roselli? That was priceless.

It could be our ticket to a better life. A life where we wouldn't have to work for a fucking idiot—and would never have to worry about money again. Still, until I saw the bank with my own two eyes, I couldn't reach a decision. No matter how much I trusted my boys, I wasn't going to put my neck on the line for something that I hadn't even seen.

3

JULIAN

THE WHOLE TIME I'd been playing nursemaid to Slater, I'd been trying to anticipate Rocco's reaction to the plan. There'd been just one question I'd been dreading, hoping he wouldn't ask it.

He had.

We'd all heard of stories of wise guys turning up in the most unlikely places, thousands and thousands of miles away from the US. Some had gone all the way to India or Japan to get away from the people after them. It all depended on how careful they were. On how well they'd managed to cover their tracks. Somewhere along the line, most of those poor bastards got sloppy and made a mistake. After that, their fate was sealed. Their bodies were found in pools of their own blood.

The men in our line of work hated getting double-crossed. Upsetting a powerful Don equaled a death sentence, and that death was quick and brutal. One shot to the head and a few more in the face, which was even more despicable. They did that so that the dead guy's family couldn't have an open-casket funeral. So that his loved ones got even more horrified...

Not that that was much of a concern for us. None of us had families. All three of us were the product of New York's abhorrent foster care system. All we had was each other, but that was enough.

I felt relieved that the plan was now in Rocco's hands. As I'd anticipated, he wanted to do some recon. That was smart. Slater was good with coming up with the ideas—and drinking Tequila—but Rocco was the man with a plan. I helped. I researched, I analyzed. But Rocco was the one who'd make the call.

The next night, the three of us drove to North Haven in my ancient, rust-covered clunker. The clattering engine had been something like a fourth passenger for the past hour or so. It was hard to miss, especially whenever I decided to push it a bit faster.

"That thing ain't going to explode, is it?" Slater asked as my wheel hit a pothole and the whole vehicle shuddered.

I stared him down through my rearview mirror. "I liked you better drunk."

"Look at that," Rocco's remark had me look across the street. He was pointing at a huge estate. Surrounded by stone walls, it featured an arched entryway with an iron gate like the fucking drawbridge of a castle. Beyond the gate, a sleek black Lamborghini was facing the street. "I'm telling you, guys. If I don't like the bank set-up, I'm going to break into one of these mansions and empty the motherfucker."

"Trust me, you will," I said with a smile. "Besides, I don't know about you, but I don't want to shoot some poor security guard to get away with a Ming vase and a fancy espresso machine." Growing up in the foster care system had given us all a healthy disregard for rich assholes. Sure, they gave to charity once a year, but other than that, they were pretty useless.

"You and I both," he maintained, as we watched a red Ferrari belting down the street in the opposite direction.

Slater whistled at the supercar. "Goddamn. I've *got* to get me one of those." He'd been in love with expensive cars since he was a boy.

I sighed, taking the last left turn. I had to admit that I'd had a few daydreams about the money, too. Slater was just the only one who'd said out loud what he wanted to do with his money.

"There she is." I pointed at the Palmer's Savings and Loan up ahead on the left side of the street. I pulled over and switched off the lights and the engine, my eyes on the blue sign over the entrance.

"Three ways in and out," Rocco confirmed, squinting at the bank. It was on the corner with free access from either side of the intersection. "That's good. Are we sure your friend can take out the alarm system?"

"He can do it, Rocco," Slater replied, his tone low as I spotted an oncoming van in the rearview mirror. "I don't know tech stuff, but he showed me some of the jobs he's pulled, and I got a good bullshit meter. He's been a hacker for years."

I was only half listening as I watched the white van approach. The rumble of its engine made Slater whip his head around to check it out. It pulled up right behind us with its headlights still on. The driver jumping out, making tension tighten the back of my neck. I shoved my head through my open window and looked back as he flipped around. He had white, spiky hair and was about 5'6". Adrenaline flooded me as I recognized the son of a bitch.

"Down!" I shouted and I crouched down in the driver's seat as best I could. A moment later, a tremendous blast rocked the car, the street, and possibly the whole damn state. The white van behind us had exploded and the back window of my car exploded inward, shards of glass flying everywhere.

The noise from the blast was deafening, so it took my ringing ears a moment to realize that a dozen car alarms had gone off, as well as an ear-splitting one from the bank itself.

"We have to get out of here." Slater's voice broke through the clamor. "Can you drive?"

Shaking off glass shards, I nodded. My hands were bleeding, but I could grip the steering wheel. The side mirror was missing, but I pulled out into the street, tearing recklessly through the intersection. "You guys okay?" I called out, my ears still ringing.

"Yeah," Slater spat. He'd been closer to the blast than us, but he'd had more room to duck behind the protection of the back seat. "What about Rock?"

My heart sank as I looked over at the passenger seat. My friend had been thrown forward, his face resting on top of the dashboard. Shards of glass were lying around his head. A larger chunk had been lodged into the side of his neck. Blood was spilled out, disappearing under the collar of his white shirt.

"Rocco!" I shoved his shoulder, panic filled me.

His groan was barely audible, but at least it reassured me that he was alive.

Slater leaned forward, cussing as shards of glass cut his hands. "Rock, can you hear me?"

There was another groan.

"Fuck!" Slater said. "What the hell happened?"

To my surprise, it was Rock who answered. "Ambush," he said weakly. He pushed himself away from the dashboard.

"Easy," Slater cautioned, reaching forward to guide Rocco back into his seat. "What the fuck do I do about the glass?"

"Just pull it out," Rocco said with a groan.

"Don't!" I warned him.

Fortunately, Slater was in his right mind today. "You're bleeding like a stuck pig, man."

"We should get him to a hospital," I said.

"No," Rocco said, his voice stronger. "The police have to be on their way. Just get us out of here."

Yeah. That was a good plan—or it would've been if he hadn't been actively bleeding. He'd banged his head, too. Not sure if this ancient car still even had airbags, but they sure as hell hadn't deployed.

"We'll drive a few towns over and then find someone to patch you up," Slater said. He had his hand on Rock's shoulder, holding him still. "No way are we taking you back to your family in a body bag."

"Hurts like a son of a bitch," Rocco admitted.

I made a turn and in spite of my concern for my buddy, I slowed down. People had come out of their houses and were looking toward the source of the blast.

If I drove slowly, hopefully they'd think we'd just been caught in the blast and were not, in fact, the target of it."

Slater had noticed the onlookers, too. "Motherfucker," he cussed under his breath.

We needed to get undercover somewhere and get Rock fixed up, but where?

The porchlight was on at the house at the end of the street. Two women were on the front porch, looking in the direction we'd just come from. Shock flickered through me. Without thinking, I turned the corner and parked by the side yard, not near any streetlights.

"What the fuck are you doing?" Rocco moaned.

"Getting you some help." I turned to Slater. "Come on, let's get him out of here."

A cascade of glass shards poured out of my car when I opened the door. Slater was already pulling Rock out of the car when I joined him. Together, we half dragged, half carried the big man into the yard.

"What the hell?" The voice that carried across the yard was full of shock and surprise, but also something deeper beyond recognition.

Though I'd only caught the briefest of glimpses of her before, I'd known deep inside who it was.

Maggie Owens. She was miles from the bar at the Rusty Bucket, and she was the last person I expected to see out here, but somehow, it was her. A blonde followed in her wake.

"Rock's been hurt," I said, groaning a bit with the weight of supporting him.

"There's a hospital on the other side of—" the blonde began, but Maggie put her hand on her arm, stopping her.

"I know these guys," she said. Then she motioned to us. "Come inside."

The blonde didn't look convinced, but she didn't say anything as we limped past.

Slater immediately shut the door behind us once we were all inside of a small, old-fashioned living room.

"Bring him in the kitchen," the blonde said, not sounding happy about it.

"She's a nurse," Maggie said as her friend disappeared further into the house. "What are you guys doing out here?"

"Bleeding," Slater said sharply, and Maggie's eyes were full of concern as she gazed at Rock.

"It wasn't those guys from last night, was it?"

Rocco scoffed, which immediately made me feel better. He wouldn't care about wounding pride if he were at death's door.

Or, well, this was Rock. Maybe he would.

We carried him into the kitchen, a room covered in floral wallpaper. Maggie pulled out a chair at an ancient Formica table.

The blonde came back in as we got Rock settled.

She frowned as she looked at the shard of glass in his neck. "At least it didn't hit the carotid artery."

"How can you tell?" I asked. The woman was taller than Maggie and had a mane of dark blonde hair that spilled around her shoulders.

"Because he's alive."

Oh. Shit. I was torn between relief that it wasn't worse but also shaken by how close I'd come to losing my friend.

"What can I do, Piper?" Maggie asked her friend.

The nurse, Piper, was still examining the shard in Rocco's neck. "Get some rags and wash his arm. Then find a tweezer, sterilize it, and pull out some of those little fragments."

Maggie's face turned paler which made her dark eyebrows and lashes look even darker. "I'll do it," I said. "You just get me the stuff."

She gulped and nodded, hurrying off. It was almost funny. Rock said she'd pulled a shotgun on those assholes last night, but apparently, she didn't do well with blood.

Piper seemed to know what she was doing as we worked on Rock. After a while, she pulled her eyes away from her patient and spared me a glance. "You should get cleaned up, too." I looked down. My left arm was covered in blood as was Rock's right arm. There was a foot of space between the two front seats, and it hadn't offered much protection. Slater had some glass in his hair, but he looked mostly unscathed. He stood behind Rock with his hands on his back, holding him still while Piper worked on his wound.

Jesus. He could've been killed.

"Julian?" Maggie's voice cut through the chaos in my mind. "I'll show you where the bathroom is so you can get cleaned up."

I followed her down the hall, still bemused to see her here. I'd never seen her outside of the Rusty Bucket, let alone so far from the city. What she was doing here in a house that looked like it was owned by someone's great-grandmother was beyond me.

The bathroom was tiny, but Maggie didn't take up much room. The bartender couldn't have been more than 5'5", and I could see the top of her glossy black hair as she adjusted the water temperature at the sink.

My hands stung as I washed them, but it felt good to get the blood off. Maggie picked up a hand towel and wet it, using it to clean spots on my arm. Her body was warm, and I got a whiff of some kind of floral scent. It smelled good.

"What happened out there?" she asked quietly, causing me to do some quick thinking.

"There was some kind of blast," I said. "We were caught in it." Involuntarily, the image of the man I'd seen in the van behind me flashed across my mind. Sean Baxter, that cowardly motherfucker.

He'd pay.

Maggie was studying my face, and I wondered if my expression had shown my thoughts. She bit her lip, as if biting back questions she wanted to ask. She wasn't part of the dark world the three of us inhabited, but she was from the neighborhood and knew better than to ask too many questions.

She was silent as she helped me, fishing a few small shards out of my skin. Her touch was light, only occasionally making me wince. And I nearly smiled as I heard three voices drift toward us from the kitchen. Rocco's sounded stronger than before.

The last thing I wanted to do was to cause trouble for Maggie and her nurse friend, but at the moment, I felt nothing but gratitude for the pretty young woman next to me. She had a level head and a gentle touch. Hopefully the nurse who was helping Rocco did as well.

4

MAGGIE

NORTH HAVEN WAS the last place I expected to run into Rock DeLuca, Julian Knight, and Slater Winslow. Then again, it was the last place I'd expect to hear the sound of an explosion, yet that had happened.

The teapot Piper had put on the stove had rattled a half-second before we heard the noise of the blast. For a few moments, Piper and I had stared at each other in shock. Though the small house was in the poorer section of town, this was a quiet, sleepy community that was nothing like where I lived and worked in Brooklyn.

Julian's tall form looked out of place here, especially in the hall bathroom. The pastel wallpaper and pink sink didn't at all fit the profile of the owner of the house, my friend, Zoey. She'd recently inherited it from her great aunt and had been gone so much that she hadn't had any time to redecorate.

When Piper and I said we'd come house-sit this weekend, we hadn't known we'd be walking into a shrine of the fifties. But we fit in here amongst the fussy floral patterns better than Julian.

His dark eyes flashed as he examined himself in the mirror. There was a cut on his forehead, but it didn't look very bad. I made a mental note to get Piper to look at it, however.

Something in his short beard caught the light, and I reached up, dabbing with my towel until a small sliver of glass fell into the sink. "That stuff really went everywhere," I said.

"That stuff used to be the rear window of my car." He sounded pissed. When he and his buddies came into the Rusty Bucket, he always seemed like the level-headed one. He never drank too much. He never raised his voice. Then again, all three of them kind of kept to themselves. They only spoke to each other, and were polite but not overly friendly when I served them drinks. They just came in, ordered, paid, and left. I'd hardly ever get anything more out of them than "hey," "evening" and "goodnight."

"Sorry about your car," I said.

He sighed. "It definitely could've been worse."

"What—" I bit back the question I'd been wanting

to ask since the three of them got here. I'd learned early on at the bar that there were some things you didn't ask about.

"I'd like to know what happened, too." Though his voice was steady, there was a look in his eyes that made me take a step back.

He caught my movement and his expression softened. "Sorry, Maggie. You're about the last person I should be bitching at right now."

I gave a short laugh. "Who's the first?"

"Long story." He heaved a deep, long sigh. "Maybe I should go tell Slater to leave her alone to do her job."

"If necessary, she'll do it herself," I told him, and it was true. Piper was a quiet introvert at heart, but when there was a medical emergency, she turned into a different person. A very competent, focused person.

"Piper's pretty experienced. She's my best friend." I wasn't sure why I added that, but it was true. She, Zoey, and I were close. As close as these guys seemed to be. "You and your buddies... you seem pretty tight."

Julian nodded, still looking in the mirror. He tilted his face one way and then the other, wiping away the rest of the glass from his hair.

"In the bar, I've never even seen you three talking to anyone else." It was something I'd always wondered about.

"Yeah, we *are* tight," he confirmed, his gaze dropping down to his feet. "Like brothers."

It wasn't a lot of information, but it was more than I'd known about them before. I also knew that he was worried about Rock. He kept poking his head out and glancing down the hallway.

Each time he did, it gave me a chance to examine this mysterious and hot-as-hell man.

He was the tallest of the three, at least 6' 3" with brown hair and a short, well-trimmed beard... His upper body seemed to be suffocating in that tight, blue shirt. It was tight around the arms and across the chest. Perhaps Julian should have considered a bigger size when he bought that one, but it wasn't like I was going to complain about the view. Nor about those dark green eyes that sometimes seemed to look right through you.

My throat went dry as I stared up at him. He was so damn handsome and so damn close. I didn't know him, but his concern about his friend touched me.

But then *my* friend appeared. Piper paused in the doorway, pulling off rubber gloves and leaning close to Julian to throw them away. "Your friend is going to be just fine," she announced, bringing a broad smile to Julian's face.

"Thanks, Piper." He offered her a warm glance, his smile widening. "Can I go see him?"

"You can, but I gave him a strong painkiller. He's on

the couch and likely to be out for at least a couple of hours."

"Where's Slater?" Julian questioned, craning his neck.

"He's standing guard," she said, rolling her eyes. "In case Maggie or I attack your sleeping friend."

Piper rolled her eyes, and I nearly laughed out loud at the way she spoke to a stranger like Julian. Clearly, she was still in her take-charge nurse mode. It would be amusing to see what she thought about being around these three, big strong guys when she returned to her normal, shy self.

"Thank you for fixing him up," Julian said, his voice warm and sincere.

Piper's eyes widened—she must've finally noticed his looks. "You're welcome. Are you two okay in here?" She squeezed his hand as she examined the cuts and scrapes on his arm.

"Just fine. Maggie took good care of me." Julian turned his gaze back to me and winked.

Piper went to get cleaned up, and I followed Julian into the living room. Rock was stretched out on the rose-colored sofa, looking far too big for it. Slater sat on the floor, his head leaning against the arm of the little sofa. Like Rock, he was out.

"Oh for fuck's sake." Julian rolled his eyes and shook his head in disapproval at Slater.

"You guys have been through a lot tonight," I said. Slater was the one who came into the bar the least, but I already knew he was an interesting character. Always doing something out of the ordinary. Like sleeping on the floor next to his injured friend. The tip of his tongue poked out of his open mouth as his head lolled back.

"He's an ass, but he's like a brother to me. They both are." Julian sat in the pink and white armchair across from the sofa. He looked ridiculous with his long limbs sticking out. Ridiculous but somehow still handsome. He wasn't as muscular as Rock, but he was still shredded. All three were.

"How long have you known them?"

He leaned back in the chair. "Since we were kids. We were all in foster care together."

Since he didn't seem to mind my questioning, I asked more. "In the same family?"

His face darkened. "No. There weren't a lot of people who wanted to take in rambunctious boys. Rocco's the oldest. Just by three years. I know it doesn't make much difference right now, but, believe me, it made a big difference when Slater and I were twelve and he was fifteen. He used to rough up everyone who tried to give us a hard time. That occasionally included a foster parent or two—when we had one."

His confession shut me up for good.

The good news about his friend probably helped

him relax enough for him to disclose something this personal. And all I could do was just stand there, mouth agape, trying to force another word from my throat.

"Jesus..." I gasped. "I'm sorry."

"It's all right." He interrupted me with a hand raised up to his chest. "We probably wouldn't be as close as we are without the crappy upbringing."

I wasn't sure what to say to that, so I focused on something else he'd said. "I didn't even know his name was Rocco until just now. I thought they called him Rock because of his size."

Julian smiled. "That, too. But yeah, he's Italian. Very few people call him Rocco, though."

It was still jarring to see such a big, powerful man lying on the sofa. The living room already felt crowded with the four of us in here, and there was nowhere for me to sit. I could hear Piper cleaning up in the kitchen, and I knew I should join her, but I didn't want to leave Julian. There was something almost intimate about talking to him quietly while his friends rested.

Still, I was tired. Not physically tired, but sort of emotionally tired. In my line of work, I witnessed a lot of bar fights, but most weren't as epic as the one last night. That, on top of the injuries today, had kind of taken a toll on me.

Julian either noticed me eyeing the seating

arrangements or looking tired. "Want to sit?" He started to push himself up from the armchair.

"No." I put my hand on his good arm, stopping him. "You're the injured one. You stay there." That made me think of something. "Can I get you something to drink?"

"You and your friend have already done enough." He shook his head. "Just sit here with me." He patted the arm of the chair and scooted over, though, there wasn't much room for him to do so.

I hesitated for just a second and then perched on the arm of the chair, my knees angled inward so that my ass wouldn't be in his face. Unfortunately, the arm of the chair was narrow, and I immediately started to slide toward his lap. He wrapped his arm around my waist, holding me steady, but I still felt unbalanced. "Zoey really needs to get some new furniture."

"Zoey?"

"Our friend who owns the house. She's a singer on tour, so Piper and I said we'd come out for the night. Water the plants and such."

Julian grinned. "I bet the plants will seem easier after dealing with the three of us." He arched an eyebrow as he looked around the room. "So your friend is a singer? I didn't know a ninety-year-old went on tour."

I laughed softly. "She just inherited this place from a ninety-year-old."

"That explains it."

I shifted, trying to keep my balance. Julian's hand was still around my waist, all steady and warm. Like a seatbelt. Only a sexy seatbelt.

Piper appeared in the doorway. When she saw how Julian had his arm around me, she hesitated. Then, without comment, she checked the dressing on Rock's neck, checked his pulse, and went out.

"She's good," Julian said.

"She really is." I felt a little tongue-tied, but there was something about Julian's calm presence that made me feel comfortable. He'd always seemed like the most approachable of the three. Rock was so big and sometimes a bit grumpy. Slater could be charming and funny one moment and then do something completely wild the next. But Julian was always polite and steady. "I'm glad Rock's going to be okay. I never got a chance to thank him for taking care of those two guys last night. He told you about that, right?"

"Yes. He'd hate to see you get hurt. We all would."

"Next time you're in the bar, you all get a round of drinks on me."

"I'd say that you and your friend made up for it tonight by helping us out."

I tilted my head at him. "You'd really turn down free drinks?"

He grinned. "Probably not. Especially not ones

delivered by you." His gaze flashed briefly to my lips, and for the first time, I wished I was wearing something nicer than jeans shorts and a halter top. It was strange because at the bar, I deliberately dressed down to discourage men from hitting on me—which was pretty much an exercise in futility given all the alcohol served. But now I resisted the urge to take my hair out of the messy bun.

Oh, what the hell. I reached up, pulling a long pin out of my hair and letting it cascade down my shoulders. Unfortunately, when I had my arms up, I lost my balance and slid down onto his lap. My hands flew out, trying to catch myself, and my palm landed on the warm bulge in his pants. It twitched and grew harder.

I snatched my hand away as if it burned. "I'm sorry," I gasped. I tried to hop up, but Julian had his hands on my hips.

"You're fine."

What did that mean? That I hadn't hurt him? That he liked me being on his lap? It felt weird being so close to him with his friends in the room and Piper out in the kitchen. It was like we were alone together—and also like we had several unknowing chaperones.

Our gazes locked in the silence, his lips parted. I could tell he was trying to phrase his next sentence.

Only, all of a sudden, I didn't want him to speak. His lips were mesmerizing, full and flushed above his short beard. I felt an insane urge to trace them with my fingertips. His startling blue gaze flicked between my eyes and my mouth. I could feel his powerful thighs underneath me and his strong grip on my hips. Everything else faded away and it was like only he and I truly existed.

He stared at me, as if trying to make a decision. Then his head tilted down. I bit my lip as he neared, all thoughts leaving my head. He came closer and closer—and then at the last second, he changed course, kissing me lightly on the forehead.

"Thank you for your help tonight," he said huskily.

I nodded, my gaze falling. Now my brain kicked in again, and all kinds of thoughts filled my head.

Chief among them was disappointment.

5

SLATER

WHAT A FUCKING CRAZY NIGHT.

We drove back to the city slowly, Julian's wreck of a car limping along. First chance we got, we'd ditch it. Julian was surly about that. Rock was surly in general. I couldn't remember the last time when we spent hours together and talked so little.

Nobody was willing to speak. We all knew what a close call that had been.

I really wanted to blame shock for this weird silence, and yet, I couldn't. We'd all come close to getting killed, more than once. In our line of work, we'd been shot at and stabbed, but this sort of gloom was a complete first. After a gunfight, we'd all mention this or that about our enemies and brush it off. Bullets and guns were part of the life. We got to suck this up, long before that goddamn van blew up right behind Julian's car.

The next morning, I woke up feeling better. The night was behind us. We'd survived. Rocco was too thick-headed to be laid out by an injury like that. It was over.

At least until the text came from Don Roselli.

"Get ur sorry asses down to the pier. I wanna know what you fuckers were up to last night."

Shit. That wasn't good. And Rocco was going to go apeshit crazy. How could anyone have known that we were casing that bank? Well, except for the guy who'd blown up the van behind us. That thought stopped me in my tracks, but then I realized that Julian would probably be all over the implications of that. His massive brain was always eight steps ahead of mine. My brain was simpler. It liked tequila. And pretty barmaids. I'd seen Maggie sitting on Julian's lap last night. Lucky bastard.

But none of us would be lucky today. Roselli was going to be all over us. He and his squeaky voice would be pissing us off for a while, in his attempt to hear about what had happened in North Haven. Like I had a clue why that asshole Sean Baxter had been there in the first place, let alone blow up the van behind us. Julian had been pretty silent on the ride home, but I'd heard him and Rock muttering that it had likely been more of a warning than a serious attempt on our lives. Yeah, right. Tell that to the giant shard of glass the pretty nurse had pulled out of Rock's neck.

Today, I'd let them do the talking, but that was mostly so that I wouldn't be tempted to wring Roselli's scrawny neck. Killing your Don was frowned upon in our line of work, but god the guy was an ass. I'd been a fuck-up my whole life, but I looked like a responsible, upright citizen compared to Nick.

He'd inherited the family business from the real boss of the family, his father Emilio. The man who had taken in Rocco, Julian and me. He'd taken us—Rock especially—under his wing and had been almost like a father. He'd been a fair boss, and he rewarded our service handsomely, unlike his son. But then he died and left his asshole son in charge. Nick had to be the stingiest, and one of the stupidest Dons in history.

Mainly, though, his worst quality was his experience.

Or, rather, his *inexperience.*

Before Emilio's death, Nick didn't give a shit about the family business. All he did was squander his daddy's money in Miami, Monte Carlo and every other place his kind loved to visit. He would party up with whores, cocaine, thirty-year-old scotch and post pictures of that shit on social media. Needless to say, anything illegal stayed out of those photos.

I stewed about it as I walked toward the pier. But it was hard to stay pissed off. The sun was shining, the weather was perfect, and a pretty girl at the coffee kiosk gave me a flirtatious look. I tipped an imaginary hat at her and went on my way with an extra spring in my step. Maybe, once we were thoroughly chewed out, I'd swing back this way to see her. Except then a face popped into my mind. That of the gorgeous bartender who'd saved our asses last night. Was she interested in Julian? She sure looked content to be on his lap last night.

I spotted Roselli and his weaselly face on the pier fifty yards ahead of me. My boys were there already. Rocco and Julian were on his flanks, their gazes on me. The Don himself was staring at the bandage around Rocco's neck.

Asshole that he was, he reached out to poke at it, but Rock grumbled and slapped his hand away. Only Rock could get away with crap like that around Roselli.

"Morning, boss," I spoke, my heavy footsteps drawing his attention.

"Nice of you to join us. Fucking finally," Roselli complained. "Now, I want to hear what you idiots thought you were up to last night."

"Sure." I said the word easily, but then I paused. Conversations with Roselli never went well when I took the lead.

When no one spoke, Roselli pursued his thin lips. "This is the part where you explain to me what the hell you were doing in North Haven last night."

I glanced at Rock, who was being uncharacteristically quiet. Maybe his neck still hurt. He caught my eye and nodded.

Shit. They wanted *me* to do this? Then again, it had been my idea. "We were staking out Palmer's Savings and Loan there. It's easy pickings, and we thought you might want to hit it. We thought—"

"You *thought*?" Don Roselli's face turned red. "No one pays you to think."

The way he stressed the word you pissed me off, but I kept my cool. Mostly. "We weren't going to do anything without your permission, Don Roselli. We just did some recon. I think you'll find..."

"Recon?" His annoying voice rose up another octave. "What the fuck? Are you in the Army or something?"

"No," I said. Very early on, I'd ruled out that line of work. Too many orders to follow.

"In our line of work, we don't do recon," Roselli continued. This from an asshole who did lines of cocaine off stripper's bodies in Miami while the three of us collected loan shark debts.

"Don Roselli..." Julian cut in respectfully. "What Slater's trying to say is that we were checking out the area for possible escape routes. Of course, we were going to report this to you today, but my car was in such bad shape that we barely got back last night."

"It's amazing that piece of crap lasted as long as it did," Roselli snapped. Then he actually asked a relevant question. "So who blew up the fucking van?"

"Sean Baxter," Julian said immediately.

"Baxter? How can you be so sure?" Roselli asked, furrowing his brow.

"I'd recognize Baxter's freaky white hair anywhere."

"We were about to go out looking for him when you rang, sir," Rocco chimed in. "Meaning, Baxter's part of Gambini's crew, but he made a direct strike at us."

"You'd kill him without asking for my permission?" Roselli asked, anger creeping into his tone.

"We wouldn't kill him," Rocco saved us the trouble of tackling that one. "But we'd rough him up pretty bad and bring him to you."

The Don brought his gaze back to Julian. "Why the fuck didn't you nab him last night?"

"Because Rocco was hurt," he explained. "I wouldn't let him bleed out just to hunt down that little prick."

"Did you take him to the hospital?" Roselli's question was a dangerous one.

"No, they patched me up with a first aid kit," Rock said, and I was glad that he hadn't mentioned Maggie and the nurse. Not that I'd thought he would have.

Luckily, Roselli moved on, turning back to Julian. "Baxter had to have been on your tail since New York. How come you didn't spot him?"

"He wasn't." Julian's steady, confident tone once again not leaving much room for doubt. "I checked my mirrors all the time. We had no tail. I only saw that van right before it pulled up behind us."

Roselli nodded, his little pea-brain lost in thought. Finally, he shook his head in wonder. "Knocking over a bank. It's been a while since we've done something like that." He thought for a minute longer, something that was probably hard for him. "Some friends of mine have cased North Haven before. Those rich bastards have got a lot of valuable items in bank safe deposit boxes. But how you three fuckups think you'll get into those boxes, let alone the vault, is beyond me. You don't have the skills—or the balls."

Anger filled me. We definitely had the balls—far more than he did. As for skills, if there was something we didn't know how to do, we'd find someone who did. Or learn it ourselves.

"Forget about the bank," Roselli said, and my heart sank. "It's an unnecessary risk. You got me?"

"Sir, think about the revenue if we could just—" Julian began, but Roselli cut him off with a wave of his pudgy little fist.

"Don't make me say it again," Roselli snarled. Just

because he was a total fuck-up didn't mean he couldn't make our lives miserable—or end them. "If I hear about a bank robbery in North Haven, you're going to be in deep shit."

"All right," Rocco said curtly. He didn't treat Nick with the same reverence he'd treated his father, but he still knew the chain of command. We all did. "What about Baxter? What are we going to do about him?"

"Rocco, look..." The Don lowered his voice, softening his stance. "You want revenge; I can understand that, but, if you whack Baxter, it's war between my family and Gambini's. I'm not prepared for that war. It's going to fuck up business, too. I'll arrange a sit-down with Gambini to sort this out with him."

"Sort this out?" Rocco was clearly pissed, but he kept his temper in check and his voice steady. "He tried to blow us to pieces."

"I made the decisions, not you," Roselli said angrily. His father would never have said that—he wouldn't have had to. Emilio had been the boss, but he'd ruled fairly and had always shown good judgment. The same could not be said for his son. "This conversation's over." Roselli's tone was blunt. "Now, get the fuck out of my face."

Shit.

Roselli strode away, on boots that likely contained lifts. His bodyguards joined him, flanking him as he moved through the crowd. He was probably trying to look important, but with his stiff little waddle, he mostly looked constipated.

Shit.

"This was my fault," I began, words that didn't slide very easily from my mouth. Roselli waved me off.

"We all agreed to go up there."

Julian shoved his hands in his pockets, his brow furrowed. "I just wish I knew how Baxter knew. I know he didn't follow us the whole way up there."

I believed him. Checking for a tail was second nature to us. And now, Julian had lost his car. It was a shit heap, but he'd loved it. Guilt was another emotion that I wasn't used to, but I felt it now. "I'm sorry, guys."

No one responded, but they didn't need to. They were my best friends, practically my brothers and I knew they weren't going to hold this against me.

"What do we do about Baxter?" Julian asked. Roselli had just told us to leave him alone, but I wasn't surprised by my friend's question.

"We find out what we can," Rocco said. "Discreetly."

"Want to meet at the Rusty Bucket the night after next to talk about it?" Julian asked. "I know a certain bartender who said she wants to buy us drinks."

Rocco grunted. "We owe her, not the other way around."

Julian grinned. "She seemed pretty impressed by your fighting skills."

Rocco didn't say anything, but he didn't exactly look displeased. But then he sighed. "I got plans."

I exchanged a glance with Julian, but we didn't ask. Rocco often kept things close to his chest, but he let us in when he needed to.

"Want to grab some hot dogs for lunch?" I asked, since it was clear the meeting was over.

"Yeah," Rocco said, and Julian nodded.

As we walked through the park, my good mood returned. The weather was mild. Kids were playing ball and shouting as they chased each other around the playground. We got our dogs and sat on a park bench, talking about nothing in particular, but that didn't matter. These guys were my family, and that was what mattered.

When we were done, and parted ways, I passed by the coffee kiosk without looking at the girl manning it. Instead, I kept seeing the image of a dark-eyed beauty the killer figure.

Last night, Julian had his hands on her slender hips, the lucky bastard. If our positions had been reversed, it would've made almost getting blown up worth it.

Almost.

6

MAGGIE

I READ the text for the third time.

Hey, Maggie. Rocco here. Can you meet me at my place tonight at seven?

The third reading didn't enlighten me any. It also made me wonder how Rock had gotten my number, but I didn't spend too long dwelling on that. Clearly, the guy had connections. But he also seemed to have communication problems. He seriously couldn't have spared another sentence or two to explain what he wanted?

Mystified, I looked up the address he included. It was an apartment building a couple miles away from the tiny studio I rented.

So getting there wouldn't be a problem, but I'd really like to know what was up. Had his wound reopened? If so, I sure as hell was the wrong person to contact. Unless he'd been so out of it that night after the explosion that he'd gotten me and Piper confused?

Or it could be a booty call. That thought made my stomach do a funny little flipflop, but that didn't seem to be Rocco's style. If I even knew his style. But he'd never done anything flirtatious at the bar, though I'd caught him watching me a few times. That came with the territory of working at that kind of place.

I set my phone down and paced the length of my small living room. It didn't take long. Sighing, I tugged on the end of my ponytail. A new thought hit, one that almost made me laugh. Maybe Rock was pissed that I'd sat on Julian's lap and almost kissed him while Rock had been passed out on the sofa.

Somehow, I didn't think that was it, but the memory of being that close to Julian's strong, lean body wasn't exactly an unpleasant one. Far from it.

The trio had been practically strangers to me a week ago. Now I'd almost kissed one and another wanted me to come over to his apartment.

If anyone told me this would happen, I would have laughed in their faces. I didn't date my customers. Period. It was not only good business sense, but stating my rule firmly and clearly usually got the man in question to back down. Usually. But again, Rock, Julian, and Slater weren't the ones who'd pressed the issue. Hell, they'd never even brought it up.

And did those three even count as customers anymore? Rock had beaten the crap out of two assholes who'd tried to rob me. I'd helped dress Julian's wounds. And Slater... well, I hadn't had much direct contact with him, but he'd been there on that crazy night out in North Haven.

I sat down on my loveseat and pulled my knees up to my chest. The small couch reminded me of how ridiculously large Rock had looked on the sofa at Zoey's place.

It had scared the hell out of me when I saw that shard of glass in his neck. Partly because I was a bit squeamish, but also because I didn't want him to be hurt. He's seemed unstoppable when he beat up those two bastards who pulled guns on me. It was sobering to see a powerful man like him hurt.

If a guy like that could be injured, then so could I. When I'd pulled out a shotgun at the bar, it was because I thought I had to. My whole life, I've had to take care of myself. Sure, my mom tried her best, but as a single parent, she'd worked very long hours. Mostly, I fended for myself.

What would've happened if Rock hadn't been there? Or if he'd chosen to do nothing like the people at the other table?

It was a scary thought, and I hugged my knees to my chest. I'd always taken pride in being able to take care of myself, but the truth was, I was a small woman and there were some very bad people in the world.

If Rock hadn't stepped in, I could've been seriously hurt—or worse.

This shouldn't have been news to me, but somehow it was. Probably I'd pushed that knowledge away during the aftermath. And then the very next night the three guys had appeared on my friend's doorstep, all bloody and injured. That had wiped the thought right out of my head.

Maybe.

Over the years, I'd become adept at brushing aside troubling ideas. There simply hadn't been time to deal with them. I'd worked a job since I was fifteen, and during my few semesters of college, I'd studied my ass off while working then, too. So there hadn't been time to focus on unpleasant things.

Plus sometimes I flat out didn't want to. Like the night my mom had told me about her cancer.

A tear rolled down my face as I thought about how those guys could've killed me. I owed Rocco. Even though Piper had stitched him up the other night, that didn't make up for what I owed him.

I stood up, already moving toward the bathroom. I didn't know why Rocco wanted to see me, but I knew I wasn't going to show up at his place in sweats and with messy hair, which was sort of my uniform for my days off.

Before I hopped in the shower, I sent Rocco a one-word text.

Sure.

Rock's apartment building was not what I'd call fancy, though it was a lot nicer than mine. The brick exterior only had a few spots where the red blocks had crumbled. The entryway smelled musty, and there was an "out of order" sign on the elevator. But my building didn't even have an elevator.

I paused outside of his door feeling nervous. I straightened my skirt in case it had gotten crumbled up while I was climbing the stairs. Then I checked the buttons on my silk blouse. Three were undone, which seemed like a good compromise to me between "nun-like" and "slutty."

Taking a deep breath, I rapped my knuckles on his door. He opened the door, and I swallowed hard as I looked up at him. He practically filled the entire doorway. I was used to looking at him from behind the bar. Up close, he seemed even bigger. His biceps bulged and stretched the sleeves of his dark gray t-shirt. It was easy to see how he'd been able to wipe the floor with those guys who'd tried to hold up the bar without breaking a sweat.

Though pretty much every part of him was large, his stomach was flat under his t-shirt. And his black jeans were tight enough to make my thighs clench.

He had a slight smirk on his face, and I realized that I hadn't been very subtle about checking him out. Oops.

"Hey, Maggie. Thanks for coming."

"H-hi." I resisted the urge to roll my eyes at the weakness of my voice. I needed to pull myself together.

My ears picked up a funny sound coming from within his place. I couldn't put my finger on it, but it sounded like a low rumble.

"You look nice," Rock said, making me feel like I was on a date. But if this were a date, I was fairly sure he'd be picking me up from my place, not the other way around. He seemed like he'd be an old-fashioned guy in that regard.

"Thanks."

He stepped back. "Come on in."

I stepped forward, noting the huge leather sofa before locating the source of the rumbling noise. To the right, a young boy was kneeling on the floor, his forearms on a coffee table. There had to be about twenty different dinosaur figures spread out in front of him. He was holding one in each hand. They appeared to be fighting.

"Tommy." I had never heard that kind of gentleness in Rocco's voice. Most of the time, it was deep and raspy. "This is Maggie."

Tommy looked up curiously as he set down his dinosaurs.

"Hi, Tommy," I said. He looked to be about six or seven.

Rocco crouched down next to the child. "Maggie's our guest tonight. What do you say to her?"

"Hi. Nice to meet you." He ended his polite greeting with a shy grin. Two of his front teeth were missing, making his smile more adorable than words could say.

"Nice to meet you too, Tommy." The boy looked unbelievably tiny next to the huge man, but still, the dark eyes were the same. The tan skin. The Italian heritage.

Tommy was Rocco's son.

Rock spoke to his son as I reeled from that information. It had never entered my mind that Rocco might be a dad.

"Maggie's going to stay with you. I'll be back in a few hours."

Tommy nodded, but that was news to me. I was here to babysit?

"Will you be back before I go to sleep?" Tommy asked.

Regret crossed the big man's face. "No. But I'm sure Maggie knows how to tuck kids in."

Did I? I'd done some babysitting in my teens. I'd done whatever I could to earn money, but it had been a while.

"We'll be fine," I said to both of them, though I couldn't quite remember the part where I'd agreed to babysit. But I owed Rocco, and Tommy was adorable. He seemed well-behaved, too. Of course, maybe any kid would be well-behaved with a giant man right next to him.

But no, that wasn't it. There was genuine affection between these two. That much had become clear in just the few minutes I'd been here.

Rocco straightened up, and once again, I was struck by how big he was. Would I ever get over that reaction? "Be a good boy for me, champ. I'll see you tomorrow morning." He jerked his head toward the entryway to the kitchen, and I followed him in there.

"I'll be as quick as I can," he said in a low voice.

I nodded, knowing better than to ask what he would be doing.

Rocco studied my face, as if trying to read my unspoken thoughts. "Thanks for doing this. The girl I use canceled at the last minute because she had a date." He scoffed. "A date! She's only sixteen."

A laugh bubbled up in my throat. If I'd had any

doubts that he was a parent, that line would've removed them. He'd sounded like a disapproving father.

I glanced back at the living room to make sure Tommy hadn't appeared in the doorway. "And his mother—?" I didn't want to be nosy, but that was something I needed to know. What if she showed up and saw some strange woman watching her son?

"His mother decided a long time ago that she had no interest in being a mother." Rocco's tone was gruff but not bitter. It sounded like something he'd resigned himself to a long time ago. "A lady next door watches him after school along with her grandson. It's not easy, but I make it work. But tonight, I needed help."

I smiled at him. "Just like I did when those two guys pulled their guns on me at the bar."

Rock's expression darkened. "That was a freebie—you don't have to help me tonight because of that. In fact, I can pay—"

"I know that," I said quickly. "And tonight is a freebie, too."

"Thank you." A corner of his mouth tilted up. "It wasn't exactly a hard thing, bashing those idiots' heads together."

I bit back a grin. "If I hadn't known better, I would've almost thought you were having fun."

"We play to our strengths." He cocked an eyebrow at

me. "I still can't believe you didn't run into the kitchen or duck behind the bar."

I shrugged. "I'm tougher than I look."

"I'm beginning to realize that. But good luck getting Tommy to actually go to bed. Aim for eight-thirty but expect a lot of diversionary tactics."

"Will do." My voice was hopefully more confident than I thought.

Rock was staring at my face. Self-consciously, I pushed a strand back from my ear. It kind of felt strange to have it flowing free around him. Usually, at the bar, I kept it up and out of the way.

His hand replaced mine, his long finger brushing over my hair and then trailing down my cheek. "Thank you for this tonight, Maggie."

I froze and wasn't able to even nod until he'd taken a step back. Then I followed him to the door and locked it behind him.

Then I went over to find out what was going on in the dinosaur world.

When the key turned in the lock, it was almost midnight. I dropped my phone and swung my feet down from the sofa, searching frantically for my shoes, but as Rocco was already striding toward me, I stood up in my bare feet.

"He asleep?" he demanded.

"Yeah."

"How'd it go?"

"Fine. We—"

"Anything I should know about?"

Rocco seemed like he might fire an endless array of questions my way, so I decided to change up my answers. "I now know that some dinosaurs were smaller than chickens."

The big man blinked as he raised an eyebrow.

"And some ate plants. And a pterodactyl isn't really a dinosaur at all."

Rock's face broke into a crooked grin. "I should've known he'd like you."

"I think he did," I said honestly. "He told me twice that my hair was pretty."

"That's because it is." Rocco reached out, but this time, he stilled his hand before it touched my hair. "You're even shorter in your bare feet."

He was too close. Too close, and just too big, powerful, and masculine.

"Yeah, um, that's how it works."

He broke the intense eye contact. "Want something to drink?"

I pulled myself together and gave him a small smile. "Isn't that supposed to be my line?"

"Not tonight. Have a seat, I'll bring it out."

Settling back onto the sofa, I tried to figure out what was wrong with me. Eighty percent of my customers at the Rusty Bucket were guys. Why did I keep reacting so strongly to him and his men?

Rocco's intense looks and his touch didn't mean anything, I told myself firmly. He'd needed a favor tonight and I'd helped him. It was as simple as that.

Still, I couldn't help wondering what we'd talk about when he came back. It was nice, getting the chance to find out more about him.

While I waited, I spotted one of my shoes under the coffee table. It had a plastic stegosaurus in it, so I decided to leave it where it was.

Rocco returned with an open bottle of Chianti Classico and two glasses.

"Nice," I commented as he poured red wine for both of us. I'd never seen him drink wine at the bar, which made me wonder if he'd gotten it for me.

He handed me a glass and then sat down in the middle of the couch, his powerful body making the whole thing shift. I slid toward him an inch or two and was reminded of how I'd slid into Julian's lap the other day.

Which brought me up short. If I'd almost kissed Julian—and I'd wanted to—why was I feeling this way about Rocco? But it had gotten to me, finding out that this big, tough man was a single father who clearly loved his son.

"Cheers—er, salute," I said, clicking my glass against his.

Rock smiled at my attempt at Italian. "Salute," he said back. "Or, cin cin. That's less formal." He glanced at my bare legs and grinned. "Since you've got your shoes off, maybe less formal is the way to go."

"I'll drink to that." I took a sip, and it was delicious.

Rocco noted my reaction. "Italian wine is the best. Don't let the French tell you otherwise."

"I won't," I said, taking another sip. "Were you born in Italy?"

A shadow darkened his face. "No. Right here in Brooklyn." He drained half his glass. "I'm trying to teach Tommy about Italian culture, but truth is, I don't know a ton about it myself. No one ever tried to teach me when I was a kid."

A memory surfaced. "Julian said you three met in foster care."

"Right." He set his glass down, and automatically, I poured him more. Apparently, you could take the woman out of the bar, but not the bartender out of the woman... or something like that. "We finally ran away from the group home and survived on our own for a while. Then we met a man named Emilio Roselli, and he took us under his wing. He was the first one to teach me about my Italian heritage. The only one."

His words, and the obvious emotion behind them,

touched me. Whoever this Emilio was, he meant a lot to Rock. "I'm glad he did."

He looked a little embarrassed by his heartfelt words, and I spoke again to try to cover it. "*Rocco.* I like the sound of that."

"It's probably the only thing I can thank my own deadbeat dad for." He drank more wine and leaned back against the leather sofa. "I wanted to name Tommy something Italian, but his mother was set on Tommy. If I'd known she was going to take off, I wouldn't have listened to her."

"I'm sorry."

He looked over at me, his dark eyes intense. "*Maggie.*" He said my name speculatively, like I'd just said his. "Maybe I should call you Margherita."

I frowned, confused. "Like the drink?"

He smiled. "Like the Italian version of Margaret."

Oh. That made more sense. But there was just one problem. "That's pretty, but Maggie isn't short for Margaret."

"It's not? What's it short for, then?"

"I don't think I should tell you."

His eyes narrowed. "You don't trust me?"

Honestly? No. He was too powerful. Too dangerous. But that wasn't why I didn't want to tell him. "It's just... it's embarrassing."

His eyes gleamed as he leaned in. "Now I *have* to know."

His voice was low and seductive. Still dangerous, but sexy as hell. When he'd returned home, he spoke softly to keep from waking his son. But now his low voice seemed more about intimacy.

"Magnolia," I whispered. It wasn't something I often shared.

A handful of expressions crossed his face, surprise among them, but then I blinked, and his expression was neutral again. "That's pretty."

My head shook on its own accord. "It's ridiculous, but my mom liked it."

"Not ridiculous at all." He took my hand in his huge one. "It's a tree—so it's strong, like you. And it's a flower—so it's delicate and beautiful. Like you."

"You don't even know me," I whispered.

"I want to," he said. "And I've watched you at the bar."

"Serving drinks."

"Keeping customers happy. Making sure they're safe enough to get home on their own. I pay attention. I notice things. If I didn't, I wouldn't still be alive."

He inched closer. His fingers squeezed mine, and I couldn't help staring at his lips. Those full lips of his that I never thought I'd be this close to—but now I couldn't look away.

His looks had played a role. I couldn't deny that. Every time Rocco walked into the bar, he turned most women's heads. But the flare of desire I felt for him went beyond his looks. Beyond lust. It was his struggle. His iron will to raise that boy all by himself. Coupled with the hidden sensitivity he'd displayed tonight.

Rocco moved in slowly, giving me a choice. And when I made it, I leaned forward to meet him.

His lips were warm as they pressed against mine, and his hand immediately went to my head. He fisted my hair as he positioned me to accept his kiss. It was a possessive move, and I got the impression that he'd been wanting to do that for a long time.

I melted back into the couch as he pressed against me. He was everywhere, his broad chest and massive biceps creating a wall in front of me. I couldn't have wiggled free if I wanted to—but I didn't want to. My lips parted and his tongue darted in, teasingly at first. But then he took over, guiding me, dominating me.

I was lost in a sea of emotions, my blood pumping stronger, and delicious shivers playing across my skin.

Then he put his hand on my thigh.

That was all he did—just placed it there, but I gasped against his mouth. The heat from his large hand radiated up my leg and sparks of anticipation traveled down my spine. Every time his thumb brushed against the fabric of my skirt, I felt a flutter in my stomach. The sensations were overwhelming—it wasn't just the physical touch but the intensity of the moment, the connection between us that seemed to grow stronger with every heartbeat.

His kiss was slow and deliberate—as if he'd been waiting a long time for this and was determined to do it right. It contrasted with the promise of his large hand grasping my thigh, so near to where I ached to be touched.

As his mouth moved over mine, his hand began to slowly, tentatively move up my thigh, sliding under my skirt. His fingers felt as hot as an iron, but I wasn't afraid of getting burned.

I gasped, pulling away from the kiss for a moment, resting my forehead against his. The sensation of his hand, combined with the warmth from his body covering mine was intoxicating.

"Rocco," I whispered, my voice barely audible.

He looked deep into my eyes, the hunger apparent in his gaze. "Maggie," he murmured, voice husky and heated, "you have no idea how much I've wanted this."

I grasped his shoulders and pulled him toward me. His body pinned mine against the couch, and he overwhelmed all my senses. And still, his hand gripped my thigh tightly.

And then I shifted my legs. It was subtle—I only

spread them a little—but the gleam in his eyes told me he knew what I wanted.

His hand slid up my thigh, inch by agonizing inch, and my breathing grew louder. I pressed my lips against his, wanting him to devour my mouth again, and he obliged.

I couldn't move, I couldn't think, I could barely breathe—and it was the most erotic thing I'd ever felt. This powerful man had taken control of my body and my senses, and I loved it.

He curled his hand down, now more between my thighs than on top, and then the tip of his finger grazed across my panties. I jolted as if electrocuted, and he chuckled against my mouth. It was such a warm, sexy sound. I liked a man who knew the effect he had on me.

Rock took my mouth harder as his fingers explored. My legs parted further, and he wasted no time in pressing my damp panties against my slit—and hitting my clit.

I moaned and he pushed my panties aside, cupping me. "Your skin is so damn hot," he rasped against my mouth.

My body was so damn hot—hot for him.

I wrapped my hands around his neck, only barely remembering not to hit the spot where he'd been injured, but he seemed not to care about that. He positioned himself over me for better access, and his lips traveled to my throat as his fingers glided up and down my slit.

Oh. My. God.

His fingers pushed inside me at the same time his tongue did, and I felt claimed. He was in control and that turned me on more than I'd ever dreamed.

He had two fingers inside me when this thumb stroked past my clit. I cried out, and his mouth clamped down on me, stifling the cry. Some distant part of my brain reminded me that I couldn't get too loud, but Rocco wasn't making that easy.

My hips lifted and pressed against his fingers as I clung to him. My head lolled back as his talented mouth nibbled and licked. His fingers pumped in and out as he worked my clit. Tension built inside me, and I wasn't sure what was going to happen when it boiled over.

I gasped, fighting for breath as he pushed me to the point of no return. He pushed his fingers deep inside me, spreading my walls and that was all it took. My back arched and met the unmoving wall of his chest as waves rocked through me. I clamped down on the scream that wanted to escape and buried my face in the crook of his thick neck.

He didn't let up, working me harder as my entire body trembled. I felt like I was on an out-of-control roller coaster—the ride wasn't going to come to an end until he let it.

He groaned as I thrashed in his arms. At wringing out the last ounce of pleasure from me, he finally eased his fingers back and I gasped for air. No one had ever made me come that hard. No one had ever taken over my body and robbed me of my senses like that.

Rocco lifted me up and pulled me onto his lap. His arms went around me as I slumped against his chest, still out of breath. "That was so fucking hot," he said. He raised his fingers to his mouth and licked them, one by one. "You taste better than the wine."

Warmth flushed through me as he held me. When was the last time I'd felt this cherished? Rocco made me feel like there was nothing he'd rather do than to hold me.

He held me for a long time.

7

ROCCO

"Time for a boys' night out," Slater had said.

Just what I needed. One night, we almost got blown up. Another night, Maggie blew my fucking mind. She was so damn responsive to my touch. The way she'd moaned. The way she'd gasped and writhed on the sofa. It was all I could think about. So what the fuck was I doing in a strip club?

But we hit this place a few times a month. It was what guys like us did. One incredible evening with a beautiful barmaid didn't change that, which was probably a good thing. A sweet girl like her didn't belong in my world. She belonged with someone else. In a nice place in the suburbs, with a caring husband, a bunch of kids, and a dog. She deserved a man who could make her his number one priority.

I couldn't do that. Not for Maggie. Not for anyone else. Nobody forbade me to date. It was perfectly fine for guys like me, Slater, and Julian to go out with women. But I had no illusions. As soon as someone decided to take me out, anyone I cared for would have a target painted on their back. They would be killed, because that's how life in the organization was.

Kill or be killed.

Beat your enemy, before they get a chance to beat you. And don't give that enemy anyone he can hurt you through, like a woman.

Of course, one could say that I already had a certain someone. A weakness enemies would try to exploit.

Tommy.

Still, he was my son. My flesh and blood. Giving him up might make him safer, but it would mean foster care. I couldn't stand the thought of my boy going through the same shit we did.

The three of us had bounced around from one foster family to the next. Few of them kept us long enough for us to unpack. But that had been okay with us. When we arrived back at the group home, we had each other's backs. We learned there was no one else we could count on.

"Yeah, baby!" Slater yelled at the woman on stage. Sometimes I envied him for the way it seemed he could turn his brain off and just enjoy the moment. My brain never shut off—not even when a gorgeous, dark-eyed beauty rode my fingers as she came for what felt like forever.

Sometime soon, I needed to talk with her. To set her straight on anything she might have thought I could offer her. But not now. Tonight, I'd be with my buddies and forget about the pretty bartender.

That was what I needed.

So why the fuck did every single woman in this joint look dull compared to her?

Julian kicked me under the table. "What the fuck is with you tonight?"

I shook my head, not wanting to get into it. Instead, I focused on the very nimble young woman who was riding the pole for all she was worth.

And failed to stop thinking about Maggie.

Another pitcher of beer arrived, compliments of the owner. We always had the best seats in the house. That was one of the perks of the jobs. Enforcers like us were vital in the organization. Wise guys had to keep them happy.

Julian turned back to the stage where Whitesnake's "Here I Go Again," was playing from the speakers, red and green spotlights pointed at the stage. It was a spunky redhead's turn now, and she was swirling around the pole, her feet hanging just inches over the floor.

"Shit, she has a nice ass," Slater said. He had a fifty-dollar bill in his hand and looked eager to deliver the tip.

A waitress, who was barely wearing more than the woman on the stage, checked in on us.

"Jack. And a bucket of rocks." Beer just wasn't going to do it tonight.

"Thanks for suggesting this place, man," Julian said to Slater. "I needed a distraction. I can't forget the shit that went down in North Haven."

Slater grinned. "For a while, I thought Rock was going to have a Frankenstein-style bolt in his neck.

Julian winced, not appearing to find that funny. "We've got to find Baxter," he said.

Tension returned, and even Slater took his eyes off the acrobatic pole-dancer.

"And figure out how he knew we'd be there," I grunted.

I made no accusation, but Julian heard one anyway. "I swear, no one followed us."

"Maybe they didn't need to. Maybe they already knew where we were going."

"How?" Slater asked, and Julian pounced.

"You were so damn drunk the night before you didn't even know your name. Someone probably overheard you."

Rage filled Slater's face, and the scars on his

forearms looked more prominent against his white skin. "The fuck they did."

I held up my hands. "We just need to find out what the fuck happened, not place blame." Roselli would be more than happy to place blame whether it was deserved or not.

Slater was still pissed. "Once we find Baxter, I don't give a shit what Roselli says. He's not a made man. We don't need anyone's permission to whack him, not even Gambini's."

"I couldn't agree more," Julian shared his opinion. "He had his chance to kill us. He blew it. We won't."

"We're not going to whack him," I said firmly. "We're going to beat the shit out of him and find out who sent him."

"And then beat the shit out of him some more," Julian said. He got it. Slate shook his head. "Why bother? I mean, I'm all for the beatdown, but I think we know who sent him."

It was pretty clear who he meant. "Gambini. That old fart knows how good we are. He also knows he can't steal us from Roselli." Even though I had no respect for Nick Roselli whatsoever, I was bound to him. We all were unless we could somehow make a grand escape.

Julian shook his head, looking at the nearest stripper without appearing to really see her. "Which sucks. Gambini is a much better Don than Nick will ever be. He's more like Emilio was."

I bristled at that. No one had been like Emilio. But it was true that Gambini was a better man than Roselli. It wouldn't take much.

"He pays better," Slater said.

"And shows his people some fucking respect," Julian added.

"I can't believe this crap." I spoke in a gruff voice, unable to hide my annoyance at the irony. "We'd actually be happy if Gambini were to find a way to steal us from that motherfucker—but since he can't, he tried to take us out."

"We don't know that for sure," Julian pointed out.

His comment was met by silence, and we stared at the woman on stage for a while. Her bottle-blonde hair looked far too light compared to Maggie's glossy black hair. Everything about the stripper looked wrong. She looked fake. Maggie looked real. And she sure as fuck had *felt* real. My hands ached to touch her again.

But that wasn't what she needed. Disgusted with myself, I glanced over toward the bar. My gaze was drawn to a short, thin figure. His back to me, he was talking to some old guy with gray hair. The man in question had bleached hair. Spiky bleached hair.

Sean Baxter.

Holy shit.

I cleared my throat. "One o'clock."

"Shit..." Slater hissed through gritted teeth. "It's him. I was sure he'd lay low for a while."

Julian said nothing, staring at the back of his spiky head. I rose from my seat slowly. Anything too sudden could draw unwelcome attention to me. Baxter left the bar, walking down the hall, probably to take a piss. I rounded one side of the table, Julian and Slater on the other. I sidestepped a waitress and pushed my way through the crowd of sweat, horny customers, Slater following right behind me.

When we were ten feet behind the little prick, he glanced over his shoulder.

Fuck.

He took off, plowing down some poor waitress in the process. Her tray crashed to the ground and slowed him up for a second or two. I barreled after him, my hand on my gun.

I jumped over the broken glasses, Julian flanking me. Baxter lunged towards the back exit, his head bouncing off the hard door. He probably hoped his weight would be enough to open it. What a moron.

The door opened a crack and the guard outside glanced in. "Unfinished business," I grunted as I grabbed Baxter by the collar.

It felt good to manhandle him out into the night air.

The guard pointedly stepped inside, leaving the three of us alone in the alley with Baxter.

Blood pounded in my temples at the sight of the scrawny man in front of me, but I knew I needed to keep a cool head until we got the information we needed.

I dragged Baxter into the alley, passing by parked cars on my right. Next to me, Slater was all but bouncing on his heels. He was ready to kick some ass. Julian was, too, but that kind of violence didn't get him riled up the way it did Slater.

Then a sound stopped me in my tracks. A car was coming down the alley. Fast.

I reacted instinctively, shoving Baxter down as I dropped to the ground. Julian crouched behind a dumpster and Slater was on the ground next to me. Both of them had their guns drawn.

Headlights went on, blinding us. As I blinked against the light, I made out an SUV racing toward us. I flinched, prepared to abandon Baxter and roll out of the way, but then it spun around and screeched to a halt.

The back window was open, and there was only one reason for that.

Shit.

I dove behind a row of trash cans as bullets crackled over me. Slater rolled out of sight. Julian, the only one of us who'd found some decent cover, took aim and fired back. Slugs lodged in the metal trash cans with a deafening clatter, and I soldier-crawled my way over to Julian. Another loud sound nearby told me that Slater was getting some shots in.

As I got to my feet, I looked for Baxter, but he was long gone. Clearly, the little prick had some powerful backers. I trained my sights on the SUV, determined to make those motherfuckers pay.

The windshield of the SUV blew inward and someone inside the car cried out. More bullets flew, but then the SUV backed out away. They'd done what they'd came to do—Baxter had escaped.

"Shit," Slater panted, joining us once the coast was clear. "Now I really want to kill that SOB."

"You guys okay?" Julian asked.

I was covered in filth, but unharmed. Slater had a cut in his arm from a piece of metal that had been dislodged in the gun battle. It would probably form yet another scar.

"Cowardly little shit," Slater fumed. "Had to have a whole crew just to keep him safe."

"He had to have known we'd be looking for him," I grunted.

"If he had any brains, he'd be in a safe house, not a strip club," Julian commented, but we all knew Sean Baxter was dumb as shit.

"Looks like Baxter's more valuable to Gambini than we thought," I said, putting the pieces together.

"Yep," Julian said curtly. "We need to get out of here. This place is going to be crawling with cops soon."

I nodded even though I wanted to punch and kick everything and everyone around me. I'd had that little piece of shit. I was just about to bust him up, but he managed to slip away.

And now we had bigger problems. Roselli would hear about this. Maybe it wouldn't be tomorrow. Maybe it wouldn't be the day after, but he would definitely know about it. He wouldn't like our little stunt one bit. His orders had been clear. Baxter was off limits. We had to find a very good explanation for going after him, or there would be hell to pay.

8

JULIAN

I LOST count of all the "fucks" the three of us said before parting ways.

We were in deep shit.

The guy who'd tried to blow us to hell was still breathing. Worse than that, Roselli would be pissed. We knew we were valuable to him, but we couldn't lie to ourselves. Going against a Don's will was perhaps the worst mistake one could make. A mistake that could cost us our lives.

With Rocco and Slater preferring to lie low for a couple of days, I sensed that doing something was up to me. That was how it worked sometimes. Rock and Slater took over when hotter heads were needed. I was the one they counted on when a more subtle strategy was needed.

Not that that was ever a satisfying route. If it were up to me, I'd go over and shoot Nick Roselli in his fat head. He wasn't even a tenth of the man his father had been. But if I did that, every single family in New York would soon go after me. I'd be dead in a matter of days, if not hours. Nick Roselli was a made man. To whack someone like him, one had to get permission from another Don first. They had to have a serious reason to grant that permission, otherwise, whoever asked for it would get a bullet to the head instead. Those were the rules.

On the other hand, Sean Baxter wasn't a made man. Only Sicilians could have that honor. Guys like Slater and me would never be made. Of the three of us, the organization could only make Rocco, due to his Sicilian blood. And that wouldn't happen if he was dead.

I just *had* to find Baxter.

The Gambini family owned several buildings in all five burrows, but their favorite hangout was in Brooklyn. It was called Pietro's, an Italian restaurant on Jamison Avenue. Named after Michael Gambini's grandfather as a tribute to him, it was almost always packed with members of his crew. My plan was simple.

Getting there and keeping my eyes open for my target.

There was just one issue—I was between cars at the moment. Luckily, I found a Honda to borrow. Of course, the owner didn't know I borrowed it, but I'd return it before morning. If this one didn't blow up, that was.

Long rows of parked cars on either side of Pietro's confirmed what I already knew. That restaurant would be full of burly men in fifty-dollar suits. I could even see some of them near the glass façade, laughing and teasing each other. An outsider would think this was one big, happy family. To me, that was a joke. There was no such thing in my world. One bad mistake was enough for someone to never see the light of day again. It was amazing that those assholes in there didn't seem to know that.

I caught a break, just after nine-thirty. Sean Baxter walked right out of that restaurant with one of his buddies, all smiles and happy. Seriously, this guy didn't have an ounce of self-preservation. Guess he thought that being associated with the Gambini family would protect him. And it would—up to a point.

He got into a white BMW and drove off. For all my desire to beat his head into a spiky blond pulp, I hadn't actually decided what to do with him yet. So much for being the one who planned. But Baxter was just a lapdog. He was Gambini's errand boy. He was too low on the food chain to have decided to go after me and my boys. If Don Gambini really had decided the three of us needed to go, I wanted to know why.

I followed him through the narrow streets of

Brooklyn, making sure to stay well away from him. He wasn't completely dumb, and looking for a tail was second nature to guys like us. About fifteen minutes later, I realized I was on familiar grounds. I could see old, small houses around me. Down the street, I noticed the incomplete frame of a building. I had seen that scaffolding so many times that I could remember which parts of it were rusty and which ones weren't. The Rusty Bucket was just a block away from that unfinished building.

For a moment, I thought about dropping my pursuit and heading in for a beer. Maggie was probably working, and it would be good to see her. I still remembered what it had felt like to hold her narrow hips. To feel her sweet ass on my lap.

But I had to find out what the fuck Baxter was up to now.

I pulled over behind a blue van, watching the taillights in Baxter's BMW flash red. Baxter parked his Beemer seven cars ahead, right under a light pole. He was only about thirty feet from the Rusty Bucket. He got out, crossing the street toward the bar.

I slid out of my borrowed car, moving through the darkness after him. I ached to grab him and force some answers out of him, but there were too many people around.

Baxter slipped behind a Jaguar and stepped onto

the sidewalk. There was an empty lot right next to the Rusty Bucket, and I made my move. I lunged over the hood of the Jaguar like a fucking stuntman. The force of my attack knocked Baxter off balance. He fell to the sidewalk, cursing on his way down. A small box fell out of the inner pocket of his coat, as I gripped him by the shoulders. I rolled us over, dragging him into the empty lot and away from the streetlights.

Flipping him over, I sat on his scrawny chest. My blood was boiling as I punched him. There'd be time to ask questions later. But by the time he was moaning in pain, clutching his face, I reined myself in.

"That's for North Haven, you piece of shit." My fingers locked around his thin throat. "Who the fuck sent you?" Baxter just groaned, his fingers groping at the sidewalk.

I slammed his head into the hard ground. "Answer me."

Instead, a weird grin settled on his bleeding mouth. He held his hand up, and at first, I thought he was trying to take a swing at me. But then I saw it. He had a little black bundle in his hand.

Shit.

"Another bomb?" I snarled, as I wrested it out of his hand. "Is that all you know how to do?"

Baxter grunted, and I smashed my fist into his nose

as I tried to work through this turn of events. "Gambini paid you to blow up the Rusty Bucket?"

"I'm not telling you shit," the prick said, his voice weak but triumphant. "I'm a dead man if I do."

"You're a dead man if you don't," I warned, but at this point, Baxter didn't seem to think he had anything to lose.

So I needed to change that.

"Your boss is just going to shoot you in the head," I argued, my arm jerked back. "I'm debating between beating you to death and gutting you." I pulled out a knife and held it against his neck. "Why the fuck would Gambini have you blow up that bar?"

My knife dug into his neck and blood flowed onto the dirt below us. This bastard deserved to die in this empty lot. I twisted the knife, noting that I was cutting him in almost the same place that the shard of glass had hit Rock.

Baxter squealed. "Okay," he gasped, trying to wiggle away from the knife, but I had him pinned.

"Tell me why Gambini wants us dead."

"He doesn't," Baxter gasped, and I decreased the pressure on his neck by a fraction.

"Not Gambini," he choked out, blood dribbling all the way down to his jaw. "Roselli."

I rolled my eyes. Baxter would say anything to save his own skin. "Bullshit."

"It's true. Roselli was pissed that you thought you could rob the bank without asking him first. So he hired me and told me where you'd be."

How the fuck had he known that? If this prick was telling the truth.

"You expect me to believe that our own boss tried to kill us?"

"It was meant to scare you off. Think, man. If Roselli wanted you dead, he'd have had me put that bomb in your car."

"So why blow up the Rusty Bucket?"

Baxter shrugged. "More punishment. He knows you three like that place."

Maggie's face flashed through my mind. "There are innocent people in there, you bastard."

"You should've thought of that before you tried to screw over your own Don."

I smashed my fist into his nose, and he screamed. "Get the fuck up." I picked up the bomb as he rose shakily to his feet. Then I marched him to his Beamer, slamming him against the side of the car. While he tried to catch his breath, I reached in his pocket, pulling out a ring of keys. There were two fobs on there, one for the Beamer, and one for something else.

I opened the driver's door and Baxter all but fell in. Weakly, he tried to pull the door shut behind him, but I stood in the way keeping it open.

He looked up at me. "It wasn't personal."

Maybe I could believe that about North Haven. But this, tonight? Planting a bomb in a bar full of hard-working men? Not to mention Maggie. I saw red again and punched Baxter's fat head, knocking him out.

I threw the bomb into his car and slammed the door. I looked around as I jogged back to my car. No one was around. No one had seen. No one was in harm's way.

I started up my car and pulled out, making a U-turn. With one last glance in the rearview mirror, I pressed the button on the other fob on Baxter's keychain. For the second time in a week, I felt an explosion. Heard the car alarms go off. And knew that Baxter was no more.

I tossed his keys on the seat next to me and drove away.

9

SLATER

THE NOISE of my cell phone buzzing on the nightstand pried me from my deep sleep. I reached over, my eyelids refusing to open. By feel, I brought it to my ear.

The only acceptable interruption to my sleep would be if it was the stripper I'd slipped my number to earlier before the shit hit the fan.

But it wasn't.

"It's me," a familiar voice said.

"Julian?" I croaked and sat up. "What the fuck? You okay?"

"Remember Baxter?"

"Yeah."

"That's all he is. A memory."

"Holy shit. Seriously?" I shook my head and

lowered the cell phone enough for me to see it, as if I couldn't believe I was hearing this. "Is this a joke?"

"No." His voice was grim. Julian did what needed to be done, but he didn't like it. "I found him outside of The Rusty Bucket. He was going to blow up the joint."

"What? Why? They have the best sliders."

"Yeah, well, I changed his plans for him. Let's just say that his Beamer has a pretty big sunroof in it now," Julian said. "Anyway, I need a favor."

Instantly, alertness filled me. If one of my buddies needed something, then by god I was going to do it. "I'm listening."

"I want you to go down there and check if anybody saw me."

"You let someone see you?" My voice rose two octaves up.

"No, but you never know. Just pass by and check things out for me. Can you do that?"

"Yeah," I breathed out. Part of me still wondered if Julian was serious. "You really took care of that little twerp?"

"Yes. Are you heading out?"

"Yeah."

Questions tumbled around my head as I pulled on some jeans. Somehow, Julian had just stumbled into Baxter? Who, for some reason, was going to bomb

Maggie's bar? That shit made no sense. But at least the story had a happy ending.

Gambini's little bitch had caused us a major headache. We'd been trying to get our hands on him, but we hadn't had any luck.

So yeah, I'd go check it out. Make sure my buddy had done the job cleanly.

And I hoped like hell I'd see a big crater in the street.

10

MAGGIE

"There was an arm on the street. An arm! Right there in the middle of the street!" Burt, the retiree, wouldn't stop saying that. To anyone and everyone in the Rusty Bucket who would listen.

When the car bomb went off, smoke and debris had filled the street. I'd practically had to wrestle Burt away from the door. He had as much sense as a tree trunk.

Minutes after that explosion, five patrol cars showed up on the scene. Cops in uniform wanted to interview everybody in that bar, while forensics collected evidence and what remained of the unfortunate guy in that car. Predictably, I had to close down the bar and wait for my turn to talk to the police.

Newsflash: revved up customers who'd just

witnessed a crime were lousy tippers. Not that anyone who came in this place had a lot of discretionary cash.

Well, except Rock, Julian, and Slater. It wasn't like they were rich, but they seemed to get by okay.

I frowned as I wiped down the counter of the bar. Hopefully those guys were nowhere near here tonight. The odds of them being the poor bastard in the car were very low, but still, I worried.

It took cops two hours to get to talk to me. The whole thing lasted ten minutes or so. After that, they said I was free to go.

Frustrated and angry with those idiots, I locked up and headed out.

Thankfully, my apartment was not far from my workplace. When I'd had no more money for college, I'd had to look for a job and a place to live nearby. One of the cooks had to take three busses to get here.

I walked briskly down the street, trying to ignore the wreckage in the street. Even though I walked this route every night after work, strain filled me. It felt as if one crime, the car bomb, had made it fair game for other crimes to take place.

A man was crossing the street, and my head swung round before I consciously recognized him. For a moment, I thought it was Rocco. Though, I hadn't heard from him since the night I went over to his place, I would've liked nothing more than to fall into his embrace. It had been one hell of a night.

But it wasn't Rocco, it was Slater.

"Hey," I said, pausing and raising my hand. Somehow, I knew better than to call his name out loud.

He was startled for a moment and then jogged over.

"Maggie," he said, stepping onto the sidewalk. "You all right?" He had brown hair that was in need of a cut. His short beard was neatly trimmed, however. He looked as if he needed sleep.

"Yeah. I was inside when it happened."

"Good."

"The cops said that nobody got hurt, apart from the driver of that car. He's dead."

"That's too bad," Slater said evenly. Then he flashed me a sexy smile. "Before I saw that the bar was closed, I was going to drop by and have a word with you."

"Really?" That surprised me.

"Yeah. I heard you went over to Rock's place the other night. How did it go?"

I stared up at him, my mind going blank. What the hell was I supposed to say to that? That his friend sure knew how to finger a woman? And in the back of my mind, I was pissed off at Rock for being so indiscreet.

"He can be a real handful," Slater said, when I didn't respond. "Did he give you a hard time about going to bed?"

"No, he didn't even suggest that," I said, half a second before I scrunched up my face in confusion. "What?"

"He's a good kid, but he can be a handful at bedtime."

Oh my god. He was talking about babysitting Tommy, not what Rocco and I had done. I regrouped as quickly as I could. "He wasn't so bad. I know a lot more about dinosaurs now."

Slater grinned. "Me, too." He down and frowned. There was something dark on the ground of the weedy lot next to us. Slater kicked at it, sending packed dirt flying.

A car came by, and in the illumination from its headlights, I could see Slater flinch. His voice was steady, though. "How about I walk you home? You must be shaky after what happened."

My mouth opened to tell him that it was okay. That I didn't need him to do that. That I could take care of myself. But instead, I said, "Yeah, that would be great."

Where the hell had that come from?

"Lead the way."

Slater walked next to me on the sidewalk, his lanky body between me and the road. A memory surfaced. My mom once told me that my father did that, in order to protect her. Was that what Slater was doing? He didn't seem the type. Then again, neither had my father. He walked out when I was barely four.

We reached my building, and I paused under the weak overhead light. Slater's eyes were warm when I looked up. Strangely, I felt hesitant to go inside and leave him. Which was stupid. I lived alone. I took care of myself. Or at least, I usually did.

"You sure you're okay?" he asked, gazing at me with concern.

"Of course," I said automatically.

"Then you're nuts." His voice was so casual that it took me a moment to process what he'd said.

"What?"

He grinned. "Well, it seems like you'd have to be crazy to not be affected by two assholes pulling guns on you. Then three assholes showing up bloody and bleeding at your friend's house. And then the bomb tonight."

Oh. When he put it that way, yeah, that was all a pretty good reason to feel a bit disoriented. Plus, I could add my encounter with Rocco to the list. Julian, too.

Bad stuff seemed to happen when these three were around, but there was no doubt they had an effect on me. I just couldn't quite decide if it was a good effect or a bad one.

Almost reluctantly, I fished my keys out of my purse.

I didn't really want to be alone, but I couldn't just stand out here in front of my building all night.

Slater looked around. "Do you know of any place I can get a drink around here? I'm pretty thirsty, and my favorite bar has police tape over it."

Automatically, I glanced down the street. "Sure. There's a place around the corner that—" I stopped when I looked back at his face. It dawned on me that he wasn't asking for a recommendation for another bar.

"I've got something upstairs," I said quietly, and grinned.

As I opened the front door, I wondered if I was crazy. Of the three of them, Slater was the one I knew the least.

But Rocco knew him. Julian did, too. Hell, even Tommy did, if Slater was being truthful about the boy teaching him dinosaur facts, too.

Maybe it was wrong. Maybe it was foolish, but I felt like I could trust him. Not because I knew him, but because they did.

He held the door open for me and I led him down the hall and up the stairs. When he was standing in the entryway of my tiny apartment, I took a step back. "Vodka on the rocks? Do I remember that right?" I knew he liked Tequila more, but I didn't have any, plus, he'd been known to overindulge on it.

"Sounds good." While I fixed it, he sat down on my couch, his long legs sprawled out in front of him.

"So, what the hell happened back there, Maggie? It must have been pretty scary."

"Give me a chance to pour the drinks, would ya?" I said without thinking.

He laughed. "Fair enough. But no tip for you."

I had to grin at that. It had been a weird night and I wasn't feeling my usual self.

I went back to the living room, holding a tray with two glasses and a bottle of vodka on it. My space wasn't large enough to have a coffee table, so I kicked the round ottoman over to the couch and set the tray down on that.

"Thanks," he said, picking up the glass. Without uttering a word, he downed more than half of his drink. He patted the sofa next to him, and obediently, I sat down. Jeesh, what was up with me tonight? But Slater was right. It had been one hell of a week.

"To get back to your question..." I paused enough to take a sip of vodka. "I was in the kitchen when we heard the explosion. The windows rattled and I thought it was an earthquake at first. But then someone said there was a car on fire. The cops were there within minutes."

"That's unusual."

I gave a quick laugh. "Which part?"

"All of it," he admitted. "But especially the part

about the cops. They usually don't show up that quickly."

"If they even show up at all," I agreed.

Slater crossed his leg, resting his ankle on his opposite knee. "When I saw how close the car was to your bar, I worried about you."

His words—plus the vodka—warmed me. "I worried about you, too. You and Julian and Rocco."

His gaze sharpened. "Really? Why?"

"Because you guys always seem to be around when trouble happens."

He leaned forward to pour himself more vodka. "I can't deny that."

"I wish it weren't like that," I said with a sigh.

Slater rested his long arm on the back of the couch, just inches from my shoulder. "Yeah, you probably should stay away from us."

"I mean, I wish it weren't like that for you guys."

He looked away for a long moment before speaking. "This is just what life's like for us."

I reached up and touched his arm, getting his attention. "But don't you wish it could be different?"

I thought he was going to deny it, to stick with his fatalistic viewpoint. But to my surprise, he said, "Yeah, I do."

"Me, too."

His gaze was curious. "What would you change about your life?"

I gave a small laugh, gesturing around my tiny apartment. The paint on the walls was peeling. You could walk from the bed to the stove in under ten seconds. And it didn't even have a real closet. "Everything."

"Come on, give me some details."

Several answers flicked through my thoughts before I settled on one. "I wanted to go to law school."

"Really?" He cocked an eye at me. "I don't see you as the cutthroat type, though Rock told me you know how to handle a shotgun."

"Lawyers can help people, too, you know."

He gave a rueful shake of his head. "That hasn't been my experience."

Yeah, probably not. I still didn't know much about him—or any of them—but it was clear they hadn't had an easy life.

"My mom and I used to watch legal dramas on TV. I know they weren't very realistic, but, well, that's what I wanted to be."

Slater studied me. "You've got the brains for it."

For some reason, a denial rose to my lips. "You don't know that."

"Yes, I do. So what happened?"

"No money. I took a few semesters of college and then I had to drop out."

"Some people don't even get that much," Slater said, but he didn't mean it meanly. He and his buddies hadn't even had that much of an opportunity.

"I know. But my mom—she was so proud when she told me about the money she'd saved up. No matter how bad things got, she took a little out of each paycheck and stashed it away."

"Sounds like a good mom. Is she still—?"

"No. Cancer."

He squeezed my shoulder. "I'm sorry."

I nodded, but my mind was on a tangent. "I'm just glad she never knew."

"Knew what?"

"That the money wasn't enough. That I'd be tending bar. That my life would be like this."

Slater scooted closer. "Maybe she'd be happy to know that you're a good person. A strong woman. And you mix one hell of a good drink."

"All I did was pour vodka over ice."

He grinned. "I meant some of your other drinks at the bar. You make people happy there. You listen to them. Even the jerks."

That almost made me laugh. "Are you in that category?"

"Sometimes."

I nodded, sensing it wouldn't offend him. "But not tonight."

"Nope, not tonight." His eyes were on me. "Come here." He patted the couch next to him even though we were practically right next to him.

I eyed him, trying to gauge his expression. Did he want to kiss me? For some reason, there seemed to be a lot of that going around. And what's more, I kept letting it happen. "Slater, I don't think that's a good idea."

He gave me a cocky smile. "Since you don't even know what my idea is, I don't think you're in the best position to judge that."

I stared at him suspiciously. "What's your idea?"

"Come here and find out."

It was a challenge. And the smirk on his face was irritating. But I didn't back down from challenges, and I didn't let cocky men win.

I scooted over.

His eyes gleamed and he spread his legs apart, pointing at the floor. "Sit down there."

My eyes narrowed and I glared at him. "If you think I'm going to blow you just because—"

He held up his hands in surrender. "Sit down there facing *away* from me," he emphasized. "Though, now I'm really curious about how you were going to finish that sentence."

"Oh," I said meekly. Now that I had some idea

where this was going, I settled down on the floor, my back against the sofa. His long legs were on either side of me.

I felt the couch shift as he leaned forward, and then his hands were on my shoulders. "Oh god," I moaned as he began rubbing.

He chuckled in appreciation of the sound. "I figured you might be tense tonight."

"Go figure," I said, but it felt too good to be sarcastic. His fingers were long and very strong. Delicious shivers radiated from everywhere he touched.

He worked my shoulders until I was completely relaxed and content. Then he tugged on the end of my ponytail. "Can you undo that?"

"Sure." I possibly would've answered the same way if he'd asked me to take off all my clothes. His touch felt so damn good.

When my hair was free, he plunged his hands into it, kneading my scalp. I leaned my head back, my eyes closed. "That feels amazing."

"The way you're moaning sounds pretty amazing," he said. "And if I weren't such a professional, it might have an effect on me."

I giggled, a sound I didn't usually make. "A substantial effect?"

"*Very* substantial."

I could almost imagine his erection. It had to be just

inches from my head, I contemplated turning around and doing the very thing I'd thought he'd wanted from me before, but his fingertips were gliding along my hairline, and I was too content to move.

As his hands worked their magic, I almost fell into a trance. This was exactly what I needed after such a stressful week. It made me grateful that I'd happened to run into him tonight. He'd always seemed the most lighthearted of the three. A bit nuts sometimes, but better natured than Rocco, who could be so grumpy, and Julian, who could be so serious.

Yeah, I was glad he just happened to be on the street when I left tonight. I sighed in bliss as he pushed my head gently forward and began kneading my upper back.

That had been a real piece of luck.

But somewhere, deep in the back of my mind, a little voice emerged through the feel-good hormones.

Had it been luck that he'd just been outside when I left the bar?

11

SLATER

Fuck.

I exited Maggie's building with a raging hard-on. Not so easy to walk with my cock ready to burst right out of my pants. Luckily, there were few people around to be offended. Besides, if they'd met Maggie—and ran their fingers through her silky hair—they'd understand.

Blue balls were apparently my reward for being a nice guy tonight. For giving Maggie what she needed after her stressful night. I doubted she knew how much I wanted to pick her up and take her to bed. To satisfy my cravings and hers. To lick her creamy body from top to bottom and devour her. And then, feed all eight inches inside her, to give her a night she'd never fucking forget.

But no.

That couldn't happen.

I couldn't have her. The last thing she needed was to get more involved with the shadowy world we inhabited. She was already on the fringe just by living around here. I'd been reckless with women's hearts in the past—I knew that, and that was on me. But with Maggie, it wasn't just her heart that might be on the line. She's already been exposed to violence a couple of times in the last few weeks because of us.

The trouble was, I wasn't sure she understood that. I'd seen the hunger in her eyes—for me, and a few times, for Rocco and Julian. The question was why. I never did well in school, but even I could understand a little of the mindset. We represented danger. The unknown. Maybe a wholesome girl like her secretly craved something more than the safe men she'd dated?

Or maybe I was full of shit and fooling myself about the way she'd responded to my touch.

Either way, she needed protection—from us. WE weren't saints, but we tried to leave the people in the neighborhood out of it unless they wronged us or our bosses. Maggie hadn't done either. She was a good, hard-working girl and she deserved better.

So I put her out of my mind—or tried to—and two days later, I received word from Rocco. He'd talked to Roselli. Not the kind of conversation I would've had though. With me, it would've been more like, "Why the fuck did you try to blow us up and then our favorite bar?" And I would've let my 45 do most of the talking.

That was why Rocco was in charge, not me. It still killed me, though. That my friend had to speak civility to the weasel who'd tried to have us killed. To pretend everything was fine. To give that bastard respect he didn't deserve.

Rocco's news was that Don Gambini was throwing a party over at his mansion. Roselli was invited, and as his enforcers, we were going as part of his fucking entourage. Yeah, because that's what you did when someone tried to kill you... you escorted him to a party.

I sighed. In this fucked up world, that was what you did. Sometimes. Until you eventually snapped.

When I reached that point, Rocco or Julian were usually there to rein me in.

Usually.

So that was fucking great. I was going to a party. One where there would be good food, good music, and, possibly, bloodshed. There was always a chance of another crew attacking us—that was why we were coming along. The idea was simple. You take out a Don's men, he's defenseless and summarily whacked. His businesses are up for grabs. Vultures would take over them without any regret. And by "vultures," I mean other Dons.

Still, the odds of that were slim. Roselli had a knack

for pissing us off, but, as far as we knew, he wasn't doing that to a fellow boss. He'd been keeping his house in order. He hadn't trespassed into anyone else's turf and had been following the rules in general. The odds of anyone attempting anything besides getting drunk and harassing the waitresses were low.

But not zero.

On the other hand, this sort of party was a Don's wet dream. For one night, he would show off his wealth and power—so Gambini wouldn't hold back. He was big shit in this city, and he knew it.

Nick would eat that shit up. He felt he was an up-and-coming mob boss, even though everything he had was something his father had built. Not him. But he'd still show up, and act like the big man.

Which pretty much guaranteed that we'd have a miserable time.

Still—free booze. And the good stuff, too.

The night of the party, I had to hand it to Gambini. His mansion in Sands Point was a thing of beauty. It was huge, but that was expected of him. The pathway in the estate made me feel I was in some expensive Miami hotel: Two hundred yards, lined with palm trees. The sea breeze hitting my face was the icing on the topping. Right behind me and my boys, Gambini's security made sure to let his guests in and keep any outsiders out.

Three of his goons were manning the gate, facing a rather long queue of cars.

"Don't you guys wish you owned this place even for a day?" I asked, strolling down the pathway between Rocco and Julian.

"A summer's day? Yeah." Rocco paused as a group of old people, including an elderly Don, passed by. "A winter's day? Hell, no. It's too cold around here."

"What would I do with a house this size?" Julian said. "Give me Gambini's money for a day. I'll buy Roselli's house and his whole fucking block, just for the hell of it."

I chuckled. "I like your thinking, man."

"Winslow!" I heard someone calling out my name behind me. It was a prissy voice I didn't hear often, but I recognized it, and my hackles rose as Brad Connors, Don Roselli's consigliere, came into view. "Don Roselli and Don Gambini wish to speak with you. They're waiting for you inside."

Great.

"He'll be right there." Rocco answered for me as Julian pulled me aside.

"You know what this is about," he said in a low voice.

"Baxter. Gambini's still butthurt about the death of that waste of space." And as the hot head of the trio, he was eyeing me for it.

"He'll want to know if we had anything to do with it. You..."

"I know what to say," I snapped. "I wasn't born yesterday." I loved Julian like a brother, but sometimes, he also annoyed me. Like he was the straight A golden child in the family, and I was the black sheep who was failing all of his classes—which, I had to admit, had generally been the case when we were kids.

At least, when we actually showed up for school.

I strode over to the consigliere, believing this was just a formality. For all our expendability, Dons didn't like to lose their men. It wasn't a matter of love. It was more of a matter of loyalty and experience. Their replacements just didn't have the experience. They had to learn things from scratch. Dons also had no idea whether the new guys would stay loyal to them or not.

I found Roselli and Gambini in a living room the size of a fucking ballroom. They were smoking Cuban cigars as well as whiskey. Gambini turned to me, giving me a nod. I couldn't say I loved the guy, but he was a damn sight better than my boss, who was ogling a passing waitress like the fucking loser he was.

"Mr. Winslow, nice of you to join us," Gambini was polite to me. "It's been a while. How have you been?"

"Can't complain, Don Gambini," I addressed him in a steady tone. "What about you?"

"Not bad, but I've been concerned lately," he

confessed. "You see, one of my men was killed. Violently killed. And much to my surprise, it happened not far from your place."

"I heard that," I said calmly. "That blast woke me up, Don Gambini. I went down to check it out, but I had to stay away because of the cops. I only found out it was Baxter the next morning."

The expression on his aging face tightening, he furrowed his brow. "So, you're telling me you had nothing to do with it? What about your buddies?"

"It wasn't them, either. They were at home," I lied. I had to, or else none of us would see the light of day again.

"And are there witnesses to that?"

"I don't know, sir." My tone was as sincere as I could make it, but I wasn't sure Gambini was buying it. Honestly, I had no idea if the guys had been alone. Rocco would've been home because of Tommy, but there was no fucking way I'd bring that up. Rocco kept his son as far off the radar of men like these as he could.

"So, if I check your phone records, I won't find any calls between you at the time of that blast," Gambini continued. Roselli said nothing, but he was paying attention to my responses. "Correct?"

"Julian called me," I said, keeping eye contact with him. "He wanted to see if I'd heard the blast. He read online that it had happened near my building. Plus, he knows I have a sweet spot for the Rusty Bucket."

"Slater," Roselli began, taking a couple of steps toward me in what was probably supposed to be a menacing way. "If I find out you were behind that bombing, I'm going to the fucking zoo and feeding you to the lions. Probably even they know not to insult Don Gambini like that."

"He said he didn't do it, Nick." Gambini put his hand on my boss' shoulder. Then he turned to me. "That will be all, Mr. Winslow. Thank you."

Fucking prick. Roselli, not Gambini. I couldn't tell if Gambini believed me or not, but in the absence of hard evidence, he'd maintained the peace. Unlike Roselli. I would have loved to throw that asshole through the glass that lined the entire room and provided a spectacular view of the water. We'd served his fucking father for years, yet the son still treated us like shit.

I plucked three bottles of imported beer off a tray as I strode out of the mansion. Roselli was a prick, but I couldn't lay a hand on him, unless I had a death wish.

Finding myself back out on Gambini's lawn, I scanned the area. There was no sign of Rocco or Julian. There were just groups of men in cheap suits like me, surrounding their bosses like the fucking secret service. As I looked for my buddies, I kept an eye on the front gate. It was the closest means of escape unless we wanted to go for a swim.

A silver Mercedes was idling there, and from the way the men had snapped to attention, the guy inside was a VIP.

Except it wasn't a guy, it was a girl. A super fucking hot girl.

The woman left her car to a valet and walked along the path toward the house. She had on a red, ankle-length dress, but the slit that went almost up to her waist showed almost the entirety of a very shapely leg every time she took a step. Gambini's men were certainly paying attention as she strode away, but she never looked back.

Her hair, a strawberry blonde, cascaded down her shoulders, her silver purse glimmering in the lush moonlight. As she came closer, though, my heart jumped in my throat. It took me a few seconds to recognize her, but, once I did, I cursed.

What were the fucking odds of this happening?

She'd noticed me, and zeroed in. "Slater Winslow?"

"Yes?" I said cautiously. I knew where I'd recognized her from—the pictures in Maggie's apartment. But how the fuck did she know who I was? "Who wants to know?"

"Me," she said, making me feel like the dumbest student in the class again. "When I find out that three bloody men show up on my doorstep, I make it a point to find out who they are."

Oh shit. "You're the one who owns the house Maggie and that nurse were staying at?"

"Yes."

"My compliments on what you've done with the place." It was a crappy thing to say, but couldn't she at least have torn down that ridiculous wallpaper?

She glared at me, but I saw a small crack in her façade. My guess was that she didn't like living in a place that looked like a cross between a nursing home and a Hallmark store any more than I would. "I've been on tour. I haven't had much time to do anything with it."

More pieces fell into place. She was a singer. Now that I thought about it, I'd heard a thing or two about her. She sang at restaurants, local festivals, and sometimes, events like tonight. "It's Chloe, right?"

"Zoey." She stepped off the path, leading me toward the trees, and I was amazed that her five-inch stiletto heels didn't sink into the ground. "We have a friend in common. I don't think I have to say her name, do I?"

No, since I'd done nothing except think about Maggie the last few days, she certainly didn't. "No."

Zoey studied me in the low light. "She mentioned you, you know. Before all this. She mentioned the three hot guys who came to her bar and kept to themselves."

. . .

I tried not to react to the fact that Maggie had mentioned us to her friend. "So?"

"So, now she's mentioning you three more. A lot more. I don't know everything that's been going on, but I know how things work with guys like you."

"Guys like me?"

"Don't play dumb. "I've been singing at parties like this for years. They're full of mobsters and their henchmen. You don't strike me as a mafia boss." Zoey's green eyes seemed intent on tearing a hole through me. "So stay away from Maggie. She doesn't know much about this world."

"She's a big girl," I said, as if I hadn't spent days telling myself to stay away from Maggie.

"She is, but she doesn't know this world. She doesn't know what you and your buddies are and what you're capable of. See that it stays that way."

I bristled. "Is that a threat?"

The look she gave me was very steady. "It is."

"Just checking," I said in a casual voice designed to piss her off. "Because usually the people who threaten me don't look as good as you do." I deliberately let my eyes travel down her body and back up again, and let me tell you, it was quite the trip.

But Zoey didn't take the bait, and I could respect that. She was doing her best to look out for her friend.

So I went against my principles and told the truth. "I know I'm no good for her."

"And your friends?"

I sighed. "They know, too."

She nodded crisply. "If any of you forget that, I'm telling Maggie everything I know. That you're criminals, that you're killers, and that you all have super tiny dicks."

Zoey strode off, and I stepped aside, watching her storm away. She was determined to look out for her friend, and I'd place my money on her talking to Maggie whether we behaved ourselves or not.

I downed a beer before resuming looking for my Rock and Julian. Two things were certain. The singer knew how to make an exit—and she wasn't above delivering one hell of a low blow.

12

MAGGIE

THE ANNOYING BUZZER shook me out of a deep sleep. Blearily, I fished around until I located my phone on the bed next to me. It was barely ten. Who the hell was here this early in the morning?

Bartenders were asleep at this time of the day—everyone knew that. And my friends sure as hell did. So whoever was here could just stay out front, except the buzzer just kept going.

What the actual fuck?

"All right, all right," I said to myself as I swung my legs out of bed. They felt like lead, and my mouth was dry. That weird thing about working at a bar is that you could feel almost hungover the next day even if you only served drinks, not partake in them.

I threw on my robe and headed out of my bedroom,

wondering who in the world it could have been this early. I pressed the button on the panel, my eyes still blurry. "Who is it?"

"Zoey. Can I come up? It's an emergency."

Her words chilled me. "Are you okay? Is Piper?"

"As far as I know. Come on, let me in."

I sighed and pressed the button to open the door downstairs, praying that it actually worked for a change. Apparently, it did, because the buzzing didn't return, thank god.

I hadn't known that Zoey was back in New York, let alone that she'd show up here at such an ungodly hour. Still, she was my friend, so I put on a pot of coffee. While I waited, I redid my ponytail, tucking in the loose strands. There wasn't anything I could do about the dark bags that were no doubt under my eyes, though.

At the knock, I opened the door, frowning slightly. As a singer, she kept the same kind of hours as a bartender, yet she looked alert and refreshed. It was annoying.

"Why didn't you call first?" I said after I released her from a hug.

"I knew you wouldn't answer." She stepped into my place like it was a second home. "The buzzer's more annoying."

"You've got that right." I went to check on the coffee as we spoke. "So what's the big emergency?"

"I had a gig last night," she began. "And I ran into one of your buddies."

"I have lots of buddies," I said stiffly, though I already had an inkling of who she might mean. Or, at least, I'd narrowed it down to three choices. But where would she have run into those guys? "Who was it?"

"Slater Winslow."

I frowned as I poured coffee into two mugs. It was absurd, but my first reaction was a flash of jealousy. Zoey had a sultry voice and looked to die for. I didn't like the thought of Slater being anywhere near her when she was in sex-kitten singer mode. "Where was that?"

"It doesn't matter," she said hastily, taking a mug from me. She sat down on the loveseat and I joined her. "But his buddies were there, too. Rock and Julian."

Okay, now, that pissed me off further. "I mentioned those guys to you, and you acted like you didn't know them."

"I never said that," Zoey said, but she didn't meet my eyes.

"You certainly never let on that you did." The coffee was heating up my mind and my temper.

"That's because it didn't matter. I thought they were just customers, and Maggie, you never date customers."

"I'm not dating anyone," I said, though several recent intimate scenes flashed through my head.

"That's not what I've heard," Zoey said. "Admit it—you've fallen for one of them, haven't you?"

One. That was the word I was stuck on.

"I get it," Zoey continued. "They're hot. But they're bad news. All three of them."

At the word *three*, coffee slipped the wrong way down my throat, and I started coughing.

Piper would have sprung into action, slapping me on the back, but Zoey didn't even seem to notice my sputtering. "Oh god, you're falling for all three of them."

I shook my head violently, which didn't help with my coughing spell. Finally, I managed to say no in the weakest voice possible.

"Honey, they're bad news." She shook her head sadly. "I sang at a party hosted by the head of a powerful mafia family last night, and they were there. They work for a Don called Roselli. They're his lapdogs, sweetheart. They do all his dirty bidding."

Shockwaves ripped throughout my system as I stared at my friend in utter disbelief. She had to be wrong. I mean, sure, I knew the guys were involved in some kind of less-than-legal activities. Most people around here who weren't dirt poor were. But the mafia? Henchmen? It didn't seem possible.

And yet... "What was that name you said? The name of the Don you think they work for?"

"Roselli."

My heart sank. Rocco had mentioned a man named Roselli. Rock had made it sound like he was a kindly older man who'd taught him about his Italian heritage. What had the first name been? Oh yeah. "One of them mentioned Emilio Roselli."

Zoey frowned. "This guy's name is Nicolo. And honey, he's a very bad, very dangerous man. And that's who your friends work for."

I set down my coffee and cradled my head in my hands. This was the answer to all the mystery around those three.

The answer to all the riddles.

The *horrifying* answer.

All this time, they had been hiding it.

And I had fooled around with two out of the three of them. Hell, I'd have let Julian kiss me that night they showed up at Zoey's house.

I *had* been falling for them... and I hadn't even known who or what they were.

Zoey patted my back. "Look, you couldn't have known."

"Because you didn't tell me," I retorted.

"I did as soon as I heard you've been seeing more of them. But... if it makes you feel any better, I think they know they're bad for you. Or at least the one I spoke to did."

My head swung around. "You talked to one of them? Who?"

"Slater. He looked so hot in his suit last night. I definitely get the attraction. But he said he'd stay away from you, that they all would."

Slater. That ass. He'd sat right here on this very sofa, rubbing my shoulders and my scalp. Making me moan. Making me think about things I shouldn't have. And that was his idea of staying away from me? He'd been the one who'd invited himself up here—or tricked me into doing it.

Damn him.

After Zoey left, I couldn't get him out of my head. None of them had been truthful with me, but Slater was the one who told my friend that he'd leave me alone, just days after he'd all but invited himself up to my place.

And I'd let him in.

Anger fueled me to make some phone calls.

Thirty minutes later, I was the one showing up unannounced at someone's apartment. Slater's hair was a mess, and he was wearing only faded blue jeans when he finally opened the door. Clearly, he'd been asleep just like I had when Zoey appeared.

Well, then, he could just wake the fuck up.

"We need to talk," I said, and I marched past him into his apartment.

13

SLATER

One minute, I was naked in bed, dreaming about Maggie. The next minute, she was storming into my place, looking pissed as hell. Judging by the steam coming from her ears, the dream version of her was in a better mood.

God, the things the dream version of her had done.

I ran my fingers through my hair as I looked down at her. "What's going on?"

"You're a liar," she said, and she raised her arm, her hand flying toward my face.

I was so shocked that I barely caught her wrist in time. That seemed to infuriate her more. "I know who you are," she said.

"That's good. I'd hate to think you went around trying to smack perfect strangers." The way she glowered at me was kind of hot. Hot, but irritating. "I think I need coffee for this conversation. Did you bring any?"

Maggie's eyes never left mine as she made a pretense of patting her pockets. "Sorry, I didn't bring any. Guess I was distracted by finding out that you and your friends are mafia enforcers."

I sighed. "Your friend, the singer, has a big mouth." Then I chuckled a little. Singers were probably supposed to have big mouths.

"This isn't funny."

God, she was a little spitfire. And utterly pissed off. "Why are you taking shots at me? Were Rock's and Julian's apartments too far away?"

"Because you're the one who told Zoey that you knew you were bad for me. Yet you invited yourself up to my place the other night."

It took me a minute to get the chronology straight. "That was before I told her that."

Maggie scoffed. "Oh, so you're saying that when you came up to my place, you'd temporarily forgotten your job? Or who your boss is? You're saying you thought at that time that you were *good* for me?"

"No," I admitted. "But I was a gentleman, at least." I leaned against the edge of my couch, wishing again for coffee. Maggie had told me she'd wanted to be a lawyer, and for the first time, I could see it. She might look pretty and delicate, but there was steel and resolve underneath that.

"A gentleman? You had your hands all over me."

"All over your back, shoulders, and head," I elaborated. "That hardly makes me pervert of the year."

Maggie pursed her lips, her head cocked to the side like she was preparing her next argument. "You made me moan."

"That sounds like your problem."

Her lip rose and she all but growled at me. I felt like a pit bull being attacked by a chihuahua.

Time to go on the offensive. "I was good that night—I didn't have to be, you know."

"What would you have done, forced me?" Her eyes shot daggers at me.

"No," I said simply, refusing to take her bait. "But I could've seduced you."

She scoffed. "You could have tried."

"Yep." I nodded. "And I would've succeeded."

Maggie folded her arms across her chest. "I'm not that easy."

I got up, circling her. She didn't flinch, not even when I stopped directly behind her, whispering in her ear. "I could've gotten you to seduce me."

"Not likely." Her voice sounded firm, but I sensed a slight tremor.

My hands landed on her shoulders, kneading

gently, a little reminder of how much she'd liked my touch before.

Her muscles were tense under my fingers—at first. Gradually, some of the stiffness left her shoulders, though I could tell she was fighting it.

Then I slid my fingers into her silky hair. Her quick intake of breath might've been hiding a soft moan, and it made my cock stir. "Lean your head back," I whispered.

As expected, my words made her hold her head more rigidly upright. But as I massaged her scalp and occasionally tugged on those soft strands, she grew more relaxed.

Eventually, she did let her head loll backwards. Her hair on my bare chest felt amazing. When I looked down, I could see her face now. Her eyes were closed, and she was biting her lip.

I smoothed her hair away from her ear on one side. Cupping the back of her head with one hand, I supported her while I dipped my head. She moaned softly when I bit her earlobe. "Still think I couldn't get you to seduce me?"

That got her riled up again. She jumped away from me, whirling around. "You're a bastard, Slater."

"Never claimed I wasn't."

"And in the fucking mob."

I didn't deny that either.

"And a liar," she concluded.

That was where we differed. "No, I'm not."

Her eyes flashed. "You told Zoey you'd stay away from me."

"I did. You're the one who showed up on my doorstep today, not the other way around. Are you here to arrest me?"

"I would if I could," she said defiantly as I took a step closer.

"Do you really think that someone like me should be locked up?" I reached out and encircled her right wrist with my fingers.

"Y-yes." Her voice faltered as I folded her hand behind her back, my fingers still around her wrist.

"Toss me in jail and throw away the key?"

As she nodded, I caught her other wrist and pinned it behind her back, too. The position made her chest stick out—a fact that I wasn't going to complain about.

I moved forward, forcing her to back up. She looked up at me when she felt the back of the couch behind her.

"Did you want to go to law school so that you could become a prosecutor, Maggie? Because you seem ready to convict me."

"Prosecutors don't hand out convictions," she protested, trying to free her hands—but it didn't seem like she was trying very hard.

I moved even closer to her gorgeous body. "So you're against crime, you must be pro-punishment, correct?"

"Yes," she whispered, standing her ground. "In most cases."

"How about now?" I let go of her wrists, spinning her around so that she was facing the back of the sofa. Then I captured her wrists again before she could wiggle away.

"I haven't committed any crime," she said, her breath unsteady.

"I disagree, counselor." I pressed my body against hers, grinding my erection into her ass. "You barged into my place. Called me a liar. Tried to assault me."

"No, I didn't—"

"And you're lying right now." I squeezed her wrist tighter. "I think you've earned yourself some punishment."

"No, I... I..." Her protest dissolved into a moan as I ground against her once again. Holding her wrists with one hand, I placed the other on her upper back, bending her forward.

To my surprise, she moved with me, not struggling.

Holy shit. Leaning over the back of the sofa made her rise to her toes, with her ass up in the air. It was a position with a lot of potential. A hell of a lot.

Lightly, I glided my hand over her ass. Just like when I'd rubbed her shoulders, she stiffed at first. But as I kneaded her soft backside her tension seemed to melt away. After a minute or two, she was practically purring like a contented cat.

I had her exactly where I wanted her, but it wasn't enough. I wanted her to want me.

"Crime and punishment, counselor," I whispered. "Your crime was accusing me of being a liar. Your punishment is a dozen smacks on that sweet ass."

"No," she said, but it sounded more like a moan than a protest.

I squeezed her juicy cheek. "Unless you appeal the sentence, that is."

I paused, my hand digging into her sweet flesh.

She didn't say anything.

"I guess the prosecution rests." I wasn't sure if that was something they said in courtrooms, but at this point, I didn't fucking care. I didn't think Maggie did, either.

With my free hand, I tugged up her skirt, each inch revealing more of her creamy thighs. When I saw the first glimpse of her silky blue panties, I grinned. There was a wet spot.

Maggie gasped, aware of the eyeful I was getting. She squirmed for a second but likely realized that made the view even more enticing, so she stopped.

"Good girl," I soothed. "Take your punishment like a good girl."

I had to use both hands to get her skirt up over her hips. While I did that, her wrists stayed clasped behind her back, I noted with satisfaction.

I trailed my fingers along the edge of her panties, and she shivered. Fuck, she was gorgeous. Her skin was soft and flawless. Well, at least until it had my handprint on it.

My thumbs dipped under her waistband, and I eased her panties down, her perfect ass revealed before me.

Holy fucking shit. Where had this goddess been all my life?

I couldn't help squeezing her cheeks with both hands. I'd always considered myself more of a breast man than an ass man, but Maggie was making me change my mind.

But... I had a job to do. There was a prisoner who needed to be punished, and I suspected she'd be pretty damn disappointed if I didn't do my duty.

Moving to the side, I took her wrists in my hand again, pulling my other one back. "Are you ready?" I asked.

"Yes," she answered quietly.

I took one last second to savor the sight of her unblemished skin and then brought my hand down. She yelped and my cock twitched in my pants. The feeling of my palm connecting with her sweet ass was almost indescribable. "That's one," I breathed.

By four, she was writhing on the couch, her reddened cheeks bouncing up and down.

By six, there was a trail of moisture along the inside of her thighs.

By eight, she was panting and moaning.

By twelve, she seemed nearly about to come. I was sure close.

"Good girl," I whispered, running my fingers lightly over her red skin. "Punishment's over, sweetheart."

She didn't move, and I couldn't stop myself. I knelt down, pressing my lips against her heated cheeks. She moaned as I nibbled and licked, and I grinned when her thighs inched apart.

Placing my hand on either one, I spread them further, revealing her pretty pussy. Her lips were red, and plump, and from the way she was squirming, I knew she was dying to be touched there.

Who was I to disappoint her? I pushed her legs apart even more, and I felt her brace her hands against the cushions of the sofa. I pushed my nose against her slit, breathing in deeply.

She was utter perfection and I wanted to feel her come on my face.

My tongue dipped out, lapping at the moisture as I gripped her thighs harder, holding her still. After several long licks the length of her slit, I let my tongue dip into her folds, tasting more of her arousal.

I curled my fingers around her ass cheeks spreading her open to get better access, and she groaned in anticipation.

When I brushed my tongue past her pleasure center, she cried out, the heaving of her chest making the whole sofa shake. "Oh god," she moaned.

That's what I wanted... to make her moan and never let her stop. I pressed my tongue against her opening, swirling it around. She froze in anticipation with my tongue poised to plunge in.

Except it didn't. Instead, I returned to her clit and slid two fingers into her tight channel. She gasped as I pumped them in and out, working her into a frenzy. There was no going back now—I was determined to push her to the brink and then right over it.

"Oh god," she panted as I pumped my fingers in and out of her. I worked her clit with my tongue, no more hesitant little licks. I sucked on it. I nibbled on it. I owned it, as I claimed her pussy with my fingers.

"God, please," she cried out as her legs trembled on either side of my head. "Please."

I didn't know what the fuck she was begging for, but I was determined to give it to her anyway. I pushed my fingers deep inside her and spread her at the same time I sucked hard on her clit. She screamed and thrashed around on the couch, her legs kicking out.

But she wasn't going anywhere—not until I milked her orgasm for everything it was worth.

Her throaty little cries filled the room as her limbs flailed around. And still I didn't let up. I flicked my tongue over her lips. I filled her pussy with my fingers again and again and again. At last, her legs stilled as her body went limp. Were it not for the harshness of her breathing, I might've thought she'd passed out.

My tongue stilled and I eased my fingers out of her soaked channel. I stood up, very aware of my throbbing erection, but this wasn't about me. It was about establishing some trust with her again.

I pulled her panties up and worked her skirt back into place, but she still didn't move. When I gathered her up, she was as limp as a ragdoll. Her eyes were glazed, and her breathing was still a little faster than usual.

Lifting her to my chest, I walked around the sofa, sitting down where her head had been seconds ago. She rested her head against my chest, and I cradled her in my arms for a very long time.

One thing was for certain. Touching her for real was even better than it had been in my dreams.

14

JULIAN

None of it added up. Roselli had nearly blown us up in North Haven as either a warning or punishment for going rogue with a bank job. And then he'd sent Baxter to blow up the Rusty Bucket as further punishment?

Neither Rocco nor Slater bought it.

I didn't buy it, either.

A real punishment would have been for Roselli to have his goons beat the shit out of us. To break our jaws and some ribs. This would have been a proper lesson. It would serve as a reminder for us to never do anything without asking him first. Remembering our pain would prevent us from considering robbing banks or stealing from his friends.

He didn't do that.

The question was why.

Didn't he think his goons would have been able to give us a real beating? Maybe. He had six of those. They were big bastards, but they didn't have what we did.

A ton of experience.

We'd been on the street since his new guys were in high school. Before that, we had to survive in foster families. This meant a lot of fighting, mainly for Rocco. He was our protector, until Slater and I were strong enough to fend for ourselves. So, in case Roselli used those goons to beat us up, they'd probably end up in hospital. He wasn't a fool. I was sure he knew that.

Rocco's opinion was rather different. Roselli could have hired more goons, if his real purpose had been to teach us a lesson. I didn't agree with that. Nick had always been a cheap motherfucker. Spending money actually hurt him. The dollar was the love of his life. He would have hated to pay a bunch of strangers money, just to rough us up.

In any case, I had another theory.

There had to have been something special about The Rusty Bucket. Something that led Roselli to hire Baxter to blow it up. And there was just one person who knew that place inside out: Maggie Owens. She had spent more time in there than Rocco, Slater and I combined. If anyone knew its secrets, that would definitely be her.

So that's why I headed over there around noon, after

a morning spent making the rounds, doing my job. Busting some heads when needed, but all in all, it had been a fairly quiet morning. Which gave me more time to think.

I pulled up outside The Rusty Bucket on a silver Harley. It had been languishing in the corner of the parking garage at my building for some time now, but after my car got totaled in the blast, I'd spent a little time fixing it up.

Easing off my helmet, I took in the little bar. The last time I was here, I beat the crap out of Baxter and stuffed him with a bomb in his car.

Hopefully this time would be less eventful.

I squinted as I crossed the seat. It looked like a few of the windows in front had been replaced. They looked about a thousand years newer than the other ones. It took a minute for my eyes to adjust to the dim lighting in the bar, but then I spotted Maggie setting glass beer steins into rows behind the bar.

"Hey," I said, approaching the counter. "I see you got the place fixed."

"Once the police let us back in here." She sounded bitter, which was understandable. She'd probably lost at least a day or two of wages. "It sucks working at a crime scene." She gave me a very direct look that I couldn't quite interpret.

"I'm sure it does. But at least the place is open now. That Beamer was across the street, not right outside."

"How did you know?" she whispered.

I frowned, but I knew I was on solid ground. "I saw the crater in the street."

Maggie's dark pupils were huge as she stared up at me. "How did you know that it was a BMW?"

"I heard it in the news."

"No, you didn't. They didn't say the make of the car."

Shit. "Sure they did. They always do."

"No, there was a police officer; he kept coming in here to talk to me, and he told me they weren't releasing that information."

"He came back here to talk to you?" I knew I was focusing on the wrong information, but a sudden spike of jealousy flashed through me. Not hard to imagine a rookie cop drooling after Maggie and telling her tidbits to impress her.

She ignored that. "He said it might be a way to find out who planted the bomb. Looks like he was right." She tossed a dish towel on the counter and walked away, heading down a dark hallway.

"Maggie..." I caught up with her. "Maggie, listen—"

"Save it." She whirled around to face me. "It shouldn't come as a surprise. I know what you guys do. And you should leave. I've got a lot of work to do."

Shit, fuck, damn. "I'll leave after you hear me out."

"I've heard enough," she said stubbornly.

"No, you haven't." I grabbed her arm and pulled her down to the end of the hall. The noise from the bar seemed distant here. "You want to know who blew up that car and why?"

"I'm not sure I do. Like I said, you should—"

"It was me," I said, out of options. She clearly thought we were just a gang of mindless thugs, bent on maximum destruction. The truth was a lot more complicated. "The driver had the bomb, and he was outside. Heading here. If I hadn't stopped him, this place would've had a lot more damage than a few broken windows. People would've gotten hurt—maybe killed."

"What?" Her mouth gaped open, and she seemed at a loss for words. "He wanted to bomb the bar?"

Shock turned her face white, and I regretted that she had to hear this. But we still didn't know Baxter and Roselli's real motive—which meant they might not be finished.

"I *had* to do it," I said quietly. "Or else you might not be here right now."

Her tongue darted out over those full, red lips. It took her two tries to speak. "Why didn't you just call the cops?"

My eyes narrowed. "Like the one who kept coming back here to pant over you?"

"He didn't—" Her response was automatic, but then she stopped. Maggie wasn't a fool. She was a beautiful woman who worked in a bar. She had to know when someone wanted a shot with her.

Like me.

"If you say you know about us, then you know that calling the police isn't the answer." There was a lot more I could've said on that topic, but I wanted her to stay away from the underworld, not take a course on it.

"This is a lot to take in," she said finally.

"I bet. Look, I can't tell you much, but the order came from a mafia boss. You can believe anything you want about them, but they don't do jack shit without a reason. Is anyone in this place involved in something they shouldn't be?"

"Probably," she said, which wasn't much of a surprise. "But I don't know of anything specific."

"What about the owner? Does he have a problem with drugs? Prostitutes? Gambling?"

She leaned against the wall, lost in thought. "Not that I know of. I don't see him much, just the manager. She seems okay."

"Someone here is hiding something," I said, feeling frustrated. On the one hand, I was glad that Maggie didn't seem to know much about the dark world I inhabited. On the other, it was annoying how naïve she sounded. "I'm going to find out what it is."

"And if you do, you won't tell me."

I put a finger under her chin, lifting her head to make her meet my eyes. "No, I won't. You already know too much."

Her eyes widened. "Is that a threat?"

"No," I said simply. "It's a regret."

The flash of alarm faded from her face, and I realized that she wasn't scared. Not of me, anyway. Even though she'd just heard that I blew up a man right outside of her bar.

She was naïve, that was for sure. But there were other words for that. Like innocent and pure. And when you found those qualities in a person, you knew they were a person worth protecting.

"I'm sorry you had to find this out."

She shook her head. "It doesn't do me any good to be in the dark."

"It does. About some things," I countered.

She blinked rapidly, and I thought I saw a line of moisture on lashes. "My mom kept me in the dark. About her cancer. She didn't tell me for a long time."

Fuck. How could someone look so sad and so beautiful at the same time? "I'm sorry."

"It's better to know," she said quietly. "Even if it's something bad."

She looked so damn upset. It made me want to do something—anything—to wipe that look off her face.

And so I did.

I reached out and ran my fingers through her glossy black hair. Then I fisted it, tilting her head upwards. Her eyes closed, her dark lashes brushing against her damp cheeks, as I leaned in.

Her lips were warm and plump. As if they'd been waiting for mine. And maybe they had. She sighed as I pressed my mouth against hers. Slowly, her hands slid up my chest, linking behind my neck.

That was more like it. I explored her mouth slowly and patiently. As far as I was concerned, I had all the time in the world. A world that we were rapidly leaving behind. It was like no one else existed except for me and this gorgeous woman.

As I deepened the kiss, I put my hands around her slim waist and lifted her up. Her legs wrapped around my waist as I pressed her against the wall. Now our heads were almost level, and I continued to slowly devour her mouth.

She moaned, a sound that went straight to my hard cock. God, the way she kissed... the way she clung to me... it was hard to believe that this amazing woman was in my arms. Especially not after what she'd just learned about me.

My hands ached to undo her pants. To pull them off and bury myself between her legs. But then someone called her name, someone from out in the bar. Possibly another waitress. I hoped I never found out who, because right now, I could've easily decked them.

Maggie groaned as she swung her legs down. I didn't let go of her until she was steady on her feet. She stared up at me, her lips swollen in a way that made me want to repeat the kiss all over again.

"I've been wanting to do that since the night we showed up on your friend's doorstep," I said quietly.

Maggie stared at me for a moment longer, wiping her mouth with the back of her hand. Then she turned to go, her movements a bit dazed. When she was several feet away, I heard her speak.

"Me, too."

15

MAGGIE

Something had to have been wrong with me.

I couldn't put my finger on it yet, but, deep down, I believed that.

Ever since Rocco beat the daylights out of those two thugs, my life had changed. He, Julian, and Slater had messed me up, but each for different reasons.

Rocco was a single father. Tough on the outside, but tender with his little boy. He was a bit rough around the edges, but he'd had it rough so far. He had been carrying responsibilities that he should have shared with the mother of his child. And both Julian and Slater mentioned how he'd always looked out for them.

Julian was more of a mystery to me. I didn't quite know what made me tick, but he kept his cool. Usually. There had been nothing cool about the kiss he'd given me in the hallway at the bar. That had been all heat. I still didn't quite get how I could desire him right after finding out that he'd killed a man. Of course, that man had been on his way to possibly kill me and my customers. It was something I could barely wrap my head around.

Slater was also hard to define. Easygoing one moment, and hotheaded the next. And somehow sexy as hell throughout. Of course, this was the case with his friends, too. Nevertheless, his raw sexual magnetism was palpable. It took me just moments to get tangled in it.

All this had been swirling in my head for the past three days. Struggling to swim in a sea of indecision and frustration, I realized I needed help. There were two people I knew who might be able to help me figure this out—if they'd put their judgment aside and actually listen. Sure, Zoey had come down hard on Slater and the others when she told me about their involvement with the mafia. And once the adrenaline had worn off, Piper had been shocked at everything that went down at Zoey's place that night out in North Haven.

Still, they were my best friends, and lord knew that I needed some friends to talk to right now.

. . .

Piper had to work the night shift, which meant we were all more or less on the same schedule. It was nice to have friends who lived the same night-owl lifestyle I did. We met for a late lunch at a place Zoey knew. It had a decent assortment of sandwiches and salads, and it wasn't even that crowded in the late afternoon.

"Hey, Zoey," I smiled. "Thanks for this. It means a lot to me."

Her expression was somehow resigned. "I'm not sure exactly what you need to talk to us about, but something tells me that you didn't heed my warning."

I shrugged noncommittally, but she saw right through that.

Piper was waiting just inside the door, and we exchanged hugs before ordering at the counter and getting a table.

Once we were all settled, my friends both looked at me. "Spill," Zoey ordered. Somehow, I didn't think she was talking about the drink I was sipping.

I took a deep breath. "There's a man I can't stop thinking about."

Zoey's eyebrow arched. "Just one?"

Piper laughed. "Of course, just one." Then she looked at my face. "There is just one, right?" Realization hit her. "Oh no. Is it those three men who were hurt?"

"Yes." My voice was small.

"All three of them?" she said in disbelief.

I frowned. "It's not like we're having orgies or something. I just... I've kind of had a moment with each of them, and... I like them."

Piper apparently couldn't wrap her head around that. "Well, obviously, you have to choose one of them."

"No, she doesn't." Zoey set her fork down next to her salad. "There's no rule that says a woman can only like one man at a time."

"Thank you," I said.

"There kind of is," Piper insisted. "That's how most relationships work. You really think it's okay for her to like three men?"

"Yes," Zoey said. "There's nothing wrong with it." She turned to look me in the eye. "Just not *those* three men."

"I'm confused," Piper said.

"So is Maggie." Zoey plucked a cherry tomato out of her salad but then put it down before eating it. "I told you what they do. They're bad men, hon. You need to leave them alone."

That made sense. Perfect sense. Except... "I can't."

"Then why are we here, if you've already made up your mind?" Zoey asked. "Is it advice you're after? Or approval for your actions?"

"Advice." My response was quick. "What would you do if you were in my shoes?"

"We'll get to that," Zoey stated, assuming a more

serious tone. "You said those three were friends. How is it that none of them knows what you've been up to with the others?"

"Up to?" Piper asked weakly.

"Just, you know, some kissing," I said hastily. And, um, a little bit more in some cases, but I didn't say that. "I guess they don't like to share that kind of stuff."

"Then you should," Piper said.

"No, she shouldn't. She's not dating anyone officially. No one's talked about being exclusive. She's done nothing wrong," Zoey insisted. "Except to fall for criminals."

"Criminals?" Piper squeaked.

"Jesus, keep your voice down," Zoey said, looking around.

"Here's my advice," Piper interjected, her voice stronger than before. "Run. Forget about anything you may have done with them. Don't try to get involved with one of those guys, Maggie. Do you really want to get into a relationship with a criminal?"

"Criminals," Zoey corrected, accentuating the plural. "For once, I'm going to have to agree with Ms. Tight-Ass here. Those guys are bad news, and not just because they're criminals."

"This is the part where you elaborate," I told her, her statement adding to my curiosity.

"They're not independent," Zoey went on. "Their

bosses pretty much own them. I've heard this from a Don himself. It doesn't matter when a Don comes calling. His henchman *must* answer, otherwise that henchman is in deep trouble. So, even if you decided to choose one—or more—of those guys, you'd have to bear in mind that you won't be dating just him. It's like you'd be dating his boss, too."

Piper looked scandalized. "So now she's dating four men?"

I rolled my eyes and focused on Zoey. "Let me see if I get this straight. You think I should forget about those three and pretend like nothing ever happened?"

"Not quite," she wagged her index finger. "You mentioned some serious sexual tension between you and that Slater guy, and good god, that man is fine-looking. Why not just have fun with him?"

"Zoey!" Good thing Piper was a nurse—she looked like she was about to have to resuscitate herself.

"No dating," Zoey interrupted Piper. "No romantic involvement whatsoever. Just some good old-fashioned fantastic sex. That's all I'm saying."

"I don't do that," I said.

"Have good sex?" Zoey quipped?

"No, I meant—well, okay, it's been a really long time." My dry spell was well over a year old. "But I don't like to do that sort of thing outside of a relationship."

"So find a nice guy," Piper urged. "Just one. Maybe a teacher or an accountant."

"Sounds like Slater could teach her a thing or two," Zoey said. "Or any of them, really."

"Or none of them," Piper added. "That's still an option. Maybe you could do something else. Like take a language class or something."

Silence ruled for a moment and then we were all laughing. "I may be a bit rusty, but I do know that congregating verbs isn't as much fun."

"I'd go for it." Zoey slugged her iced tea as if it were alcohol. "Just something casual—no strings attached."

"Or not," Piper countered. "Learning a language is something you could put on your resume."

Zoey laughed. "And anything you do with those guys will decidedly *not* be suitable for your resume."

"I love you guys," I said, glancing at Piper first and then Zoey. "Do you know that? And I owe each of you a Halloween costume."

Zoey gave a short laugh. "Why?"

"Because you're the little devil on my shoulder, and Piper is the little angel on my other shoulder. So you should look the part."

That got us laughing again, and eventually, as the conversation moved onto lighter topics, we managed to actually eat.

But I couldn't stop thinking about my situation, and

what they'd said. They had both made some quite compelling arguments. The smartest thing would be to stay away from all of them. But if I didn't—or couldn't—I knew one thing quite clearly. I didn't want to choose just one of them. They were a package deal. I felt that instinctively. They were a unit. A family, even. They loved each other like brothers. I'd never want to come between them or even choose between them. But whether to move forward or stay the hell away—that, I had no clue about. But maybe I didn't have to decide right away. I thought I had some time until one of those three or even all of them came back to my bar.

16

ROCCO

"Where's the pretty lady, Daddy? Why won't she come play dinosaurs with me again?"

Tommy had been repeating those two questions more often by the day.

I could tell Maggie had made an impression on him. In his young mind, she was an ideal playmate. Naturally, my boy had his reasons. He'd told me over and over how fun it was to play with Maggie. How she voiced the various dinosaurs. How she colored with him. How they'd read a book together before bedtime.

My son hadn't had much experience with a woman doing those kinds of things with him. The sixteen-year-old who sometimes babysat was on her phone a lot, Tommy had told me. And after school, when he stayed with the neighbor, he mostly played with her grandchild while she prepared dinner. And he barely remembered his mother.

So yeah, he'd enjoyed having Maggie here to play with him and read to him. And, well, he was his father's son. I suspected he liked the way she looked, in an age-appropriate way.

Couldn't fault him for that. Especially not since I liked the way she looked, too, though in a somewhat less-than appropriate way.

She'd somehow gotten under my skin, which was ironic since it had been me who'd had my hand under her skirt. But god, the way she'd writhed and moaned. Before that, I liked her, yes. Admired her, even. I'm not used to meeting a woman who can catch my eye and yield a shotgun. But since that night I'd made her come, my thoughts had gotten a lot more carnal.

She deserved better than that, but I couldn't help it.

With all the craziness of late, I hadn't been to The Rusty Bucket. Truth be told, going out for a drink had become a luxury I just couldn't afford. Not because of the money it would cost me, or finding a sitter, but because of the weird situation I was in.

Had Gambini bought Slater's story?

Had Roselli?

I didn't know for sure.

What I did know was that I'd be vulnerable out there. I couldn't do much about that during the day—I had work to do. Collecting, talking to Roselli's customers and roughing them up, among other things. But, at night, I would go home and pray that nobody knocked on my door while my son was here.

Not that I thought that was likely. Even mobsters had a code. We weren't animals. Nobody would shoot a little boy's father right in front of him. At least, I *thought* they wouldn't.

All this meant that it was more important than ever to make nice with Roselli, and not let on that we knew what he'd been up to. We had a meeting with him two nights from now, and I didn't feel like leaving my son with a teen who'd be texting her boyfriend the whole time.

So, I made a phone call.

"*Hello?*"

"Hey, Maggie. Rocco here. How's it going?"

"You know, the phone actually tells me who's calling." She sounded amused, and then answered my question. "I'm okay. How about you?"

"Fine. Listen, I've got something to do Thursday night. Tommy's been asking to see you. Can you watch him for me?"

Tommy looked up from his coloring book, excitement in his eyes. I put my index finger to my lips to pre-empt him. I wanted Maggie to come, but it would be a low blow to let my son guilt trip her into it.

Except... she wasn't saying anything. And if that disappointed me, it was going to crush Tommy. I should've gone into my room to make this call. "Never mind. I'll find someone else." It shouldn't be a surprise that she didn't want to come over to my house now that she knew more about what we did for a living. Julian and Slater had filled me in on that.

I sighed and pulled the phone away from my ear.

"Wait!"

"Yeah?" It was stupid, the hope that hit me.

"*What time should I be there?*"

"Seven. Thanks a lot."

"Yes!" Tommy cheered, holding his small fists up in the air. We high-fived each other, exchanging a grin. To celebrate, I got Tommy some chocolate milk, even though sugar at this time of the evening was going to make bedtime even harder.

Later, when he went to his room to change into his pajamas, I thought about Maggie's long silence before answering. She had every reason to stay away from us. According to my pals, she herself realized that.

So what made her say yes? Was it the idea of seeing Tommy again? I had to admit, he was a pretty great kid.

Or was it something more?

Things might be awkward between us. They *should* be, after the way she'd come riding my hand. Sooner or later, we might have to talk about that. I mean, it's not like I fucked her, but it was something that casual acquaintances usually didn't do.

To me, sex and anything around it were a matter of right timing. You couldn't plan it. You couldn't predict when it would happen. You just had to relax and pick the right moment.

Which was why I wasn't expecting to get any action on Thursday night after I got home. After all, I couldn't go wild with Maggie—not with a kid here. I didn't think she'd be so crazy about that scenario, either. Still, I wouldn't mind messing around with her some more. Kissing her. Teasing her. Hearing her moan again. Hell, I would have had to be a fucking idiot not to want to touch someone so goddamn sexy again.

And I was many things, but I was definitely not a fucking idiot.

17

MAGGIE

W*HAT THE HELL am I doing back here?*

I asked myself that question while standing in front of the sturdy door of Rocco's apartment. There were the same bumps and scratches I had spotted the first time I was there. There was even the same, sweet voice from inside. This time, little Tommy sounded thrilled.

At least one person would be happy tonight.

As for me? I didn't think so.

I liked the fact that I would get to see Rocco again. He'd saved me when the bar was held up. I would never forget his power and his strength. Nonetheless, he was the leader of the three, that much was clear. If Julian had killed at least one man in the last week, what had Rocco done?

I'd always dreamed of being a lawyer. Laws were

there for a reason, and I respected them. Rocco and his friends didn't. They had to have broken the law about a thousand times already.

Tommy was probably in the clear, though. I listened to the little boy and smiled as I knocked.

"Welcome back," Rocco said, as he held the door wide for me.

He offered me a warm smile and showed me in. Tommy ran down the hall. Unlike his dad, the boy's hair was getting a bit long, sort of like his Uncle Slater's. That thought gave me pause. Was Tommy close to Julian and Slater? Something told me that he was.

I bent my knees and held out my arms, receiving a huge hug.

"How are you, Tommy?" I asked, closing my arms around his back.

"Maggie!" His voice was like music to my ears, although he was practically screaming in them. "Can we go play now?"

"He likes you a lot," Rocco said, standing over me as he straightened up. "He's been looking forward to this."

"Aren't you sweet?" I patted the top of Tommy's head. "Can you go to your room and find us some cool toys to play with? I'll be with you in a minute, okay?"

"Sure!"

I waited for him to reach his bedroom, feeling Rocco's gaze on me.

"Thanks again," he said.

"I was a little torn when you called me," I admitted, his huge figure towering over me, even though I was standing now. "I, uh, recently learned some things about you and your friends."

He put his hands on his hips, a frown on his face. "What things?"

"Cut the act, Rocco." I found it hard to believe that neither Slater nor Julian had said anything to him since I'd talked to Zoey.

He nodded gruffly but gestured for me to go on.

"Let's say they're not flattering."

Rocco's expression told me nothing. "Will they affect the way you take care of my son?"

"They might," I said, and his expression darkened. "I have to ask you something."

"Go ahead." His face still gave away nothing.

"Is there a gun in here?"

In answer, he patted his hip. I gulped and stepped back. I hadn't realized he was armed.

"Is that a problem?" His voice was tight. "I seem to recall seeing you with a shotgun in your hands at the bar."

I gestured at his midsection. "That's not a problem for me as long as you come back in one piece."

Mentally, I added that I hoped everyone else he encountered tonight would be okay, too. "But I meant here in the apartment after you leave. Are there guns here?"

Rocco's stiff posture relaxed, and his expression softened. "You want to know because of Tommy."

"Yes."

"I have a gun safe. And trigger locks. I wouldn't leave an unsecured gun around a child."

A breath of relief escaped me.

"Tommy knows not to mess around with guns, though I have taken him shooting."

"Shooting?"

Rocco shrugged. "Just, you know, rats and stuff. And a few of those punks who hang out down by the bus station."

I took a step back, my hand flying to my mouth.

Rocco grinned. "I'm kidding, Maggie. I've taken him to the gun range."

"Oh." Color flooded my face.

"I like that," he said, eyeing me.

"Like what?"

"That blush on your cheeks. Sometimes olive skin tones don't turn red, but yours does."

"My skin's not olive." I said it automatically, mostly to cover my embarrassment.

"It's paler, yes. But you have that dark hair—I

thought you could be Italian the first time I saw you at the bar."

The way he was looking at me made me squirm. "I'm not, though." My mother had some French and German ancestry. And she'd told me that my dad's people came from Ireland a long time ago.

Rocco grinned. "Nobody's perfect." He slung on a jacket and took a final look around. "You've got my number. Call if you need anything."

"Will do."

Rocco left, and I tried to regroup my thoughts. Then I headed toward the younger DeLuca, the one who was far less complicated to talk to. Even if the conversations were mostly about prehistoric reptiles.

Tommy's enthusiasm lasted for hours. It made me worry that the child was starved for attention, but that wasn't quite it. He told me about the boy next door he played with after school. And at one point, he mentioned an Uncle Julian, so I was right that he considered his father's best friends as part of the family.

So maybe what he was missing was a woman who paid attention to him. That made me feel a bit strange. I wasn't really the maternal type. Most female bartenders weren't. But still, it was fun hanging out with the boy. Tiring, but fun. The only arguments we had were over his bedtime, and since I'd anticipated that, it didn't catch me off guard this time.

Tommy's steady flow of words—and dinosaur facts—had kept my mind off bombs, police interviews and enforcer confessions. Most of all, they kept away the memories I had from being with Rocco in his living room last time.

But once I finally got him to stay in bed, the preoccupation with my current situation returned.

The biggest question was what might happen once the mafia enforcer returned.

What would I do with him later?

Ask him about his job? No. That felt pointless, and possibly even dangerous. Everyone was responsible for their choices. Rocco had made his own. Though they weren't the choices I would've made, there was no way I would lecture him on how dangerous his line of work was. I was sure he knew that much better than I did.

Fool around with him? God, that sounded so tempting... Having those big hands on my body. Have them touch all my sensitive spots. Staring at him while he rubbed my clit. Seeing the desire in his eyes, just like the other night.

A knock at the door interrupted my thoughts and gave me cause for concern at the same time. I went over to the front door and stood on my tiptoes to look through the peephole. Fortunately, the man outside wasn't from a rival mafia family, ready to gun us down.

It was Julian.

I unlocked the deadbolt and undid the chain.

"Hey," he whispered, looking over me. "Rocco got detained. He sent me back here so you could leave."

"Like arrested?" I said, louder than I meant to.

"No." Julian stepped inside, closing the door behind him. "As in held up."

I relaxed, even though "held up" could have more than one meaning. Julian's relaxed demeanor convinced me that nothing bad had happened to his friend.

"Thanks for coming," I told him, keeping my voice down. "I'll just get my things."

Julian followed me into the living room. The overhead light revealed something on his left cheekbone. It was a small cut, in the middle of a nasty bruise. "What happened to you?" I asked, raising my hand up to his wound. His short beard tickled my palm.

He reached up and cupped his hand against mine. "Maggie." He whispered my name, his nose brushing my forehead. Our gazes locking, I felt sparks of electricity running down my spine. "I keep thinking about that kiss."

"Me, too," I admitted, as his gaze dropped to my mouth.

But this was wrong. A few minutes ago, I'd been thinking about sharing some kind of intimacy with Rocco. But Julian was just so damn tempting—and that was even before I knew he'd taken out the guy who'd been heading for my bar with a bomb.

In an instant, he threw his long arms around my waist. Before I knew it, he was picking me up off the floor with ease. Our mouths smashed together in a passionate kiss, and I hooked my legs around his hips. He spun us around, my back hitting the wall next to the door with force. I snaked my arms around his neck. We were in roughly the same position we'd been at the bar the other day, but everything about this kiss was different.

He'd been thorough and methodical when he kissed me before. Unrushed.

That wasn't the case tonight.

He nipped at my bottom lip, his right hand traveling down past my hip. He cupped my thigh and squeezed, the feel of his muscled body against mine igniting my desire. My skirt rose up a few inches, and he ground his erection into me.

"You taste like peaches and cream," he said huskily. I tilted my head back. He took the hint, his lips landing on my chin. His fingers stroked my thigh as wave after wave of desire rolled through me. His erection was hard to miss, and it seemed to be growing larger with every passing moment.

Our bodies swayed apart before he smashed up against me again, pinning me to the wall once more. My legs spread further apart, and Julian eased his hand between us, his longer fingers hovering at my core. When he palmed my mound, I took one hand off it and used it to cover my mouth. The last thing I wanted to do was to wake the little boy sleeping in the other room.

Shit.

There was a little boy sleeping in the other room.

Sure, his door was closed, but this was wrong. We were in Rocco's apartment. I was here at Rocco's invitation.

So what the hell was I doing with Julian?

Unlike me, Julian knew exactly what he was doing. Literally. His fingers glided over my heated slit, and I moaned in spite of myself. His thumb nudged my clit, he positioned a finger at my entrance.

"You're going to come." He said it as a fact, and I believed him. I wanted to. I was close. But... the damn voice in my head wouldn't let up. The one that said this wasn't right, no matter how good it felt.

He rubbed my clit up and down, making me bite down on the heel of my palm to keep from crying out. He bucked forward, giving me a preview of what I might someday experience. If he was stiff a minute ago, he was rock hard now. His finger sliding through my folds, I threw my head back. The rocking of the wall behind me filled my ears, acting like a call back to reality.

"Stop," I gasped.

"Come for me," he ordered.

"No." This time I meant it. "We can't." I let go of his neck and leaned back, putting a little space between our chests. "Please, stop."

He sighed and pulled back, releasing me from his hold. "Fuck." His voice held more resignation than anger.

"We can't. Not here." Maybe not anywhere, but definitely not here. I tugged my skirt down, trying to ignore the hormones that were still making my body tingle. "I hope you understand."

"I do." He took a shaky step back, and I made sure not to look at the bulge in his pants. "You're right—not here."

I waited, half expecting him to suggest some place else, but maybe he was thinking about how we'd let ourselves go too far in his buddy's home, too.

There was a smudge of my lipstick on his lips. I reached up and brushed it off with my thumb. "Goodnight, Julian."

I waited a moment for him to leave, but then remembered that he'd come here to take over babysitting duties from me. I gathered my things and went to the door where he waited for me.

"Goodnight," he said simply.

As the door closed behind me, I leaned my back

against it, my hand over my chest while I tried to calm my breath. Though my mind had finally decided what we were doing was wrong, my body hadn't gotten the message. My cheeks were flushed. My heart had not stopped racing. To make matters worse, the ache between my legs was killing me.

My libido was telling me to go back inside, but I knew I'd done the right thing.

18

SLATER

A COLLECTION GONE WRONG.

Those four words neatly summarized the shit that had gone down yesterday.

Roselli's customers hated to pay the huge fees he charged for "protection." Most did it anyway, but a few had the guts to stand up to us when we came to collect. That was when things got ugly.

Yesterday was a classic case in point. Phil Thomson, a bar owner in Manhattan, didn't like it at all when Julian said he still owed twelve grand. He believed the amount was closer to six. When we cornered him, Julian was closest to him, and the bar owner sucker punched my friend when he tried to escape.

Of course, when we caught up to him, we made him regret trying to play tough. Three broken fingers, two black eyes and a ruined pride was the price he had to pay for his stubbornness. It wasn't a task we enjoyed, but it was what we did. Roselli made the rules, and we enforced them.

Roselli was quite happy with us when we delivered the money. Typical Nick. I half believed that he had a hard-on for money. The more he got, the bigger the boner. To be honest, if anyone brought me a bag of three hundred-and-twenty thousand dollars, there was a good chance I'd have an erection, too. He demanded to meet with us again tonight, in order to tell us about "something big."

I didn't bother with what that was. More often than not, my definition of "big" was different from his. To Roselli, any deal that would make him more than ten grand was considered big. Most mob bosses would laugh if they heard about that. It was amazing to think that this guy was, in fact, a Don. He just didn't function as one. Every time I heard him blabber on about fifteen or twenty thousand bucks, I missed his father. If Emilio had been still around, he would have slapped some sense into his asshole son and passed along his title to someone worth carrying it.

Rocco, Julian, and I met up outside Roselli's mansion, under the cover of darkness. From his driveway, I could hear girly screams and giggles, along with the occasional splash of water. I groaned. It wasn't that difficult to anticipate the scene we were walking in on. Roselli was in the water with three beauties. There was a lot of splashing and groping going on, and no swimming suits as far as I could tell.

That was good in the case of the woman, and really, really bad in the case of Roselli.

"Think anyone would notice if we shot his tiny dick off?" Julian muttered.

"Shut up," Rocco ordered, stepping ahead of us.

Roselli looked up when we approached, his weasel-like face showing mild interest. "Girls, the party's over," he announced, heading for the stairs out of the pool. "Get the fuck out." He had such a way with the ladies.

His housekeeper hurried toward him, a thick white robe in her hands. She handed it over and went back inside as the three of us gathered around him.

"I'm still getting heat from Gambini about Baxter," Roselli remarked. "Anything new about him?"

"Not really," I spoke first. "We've been asking around on the street. No one's heard anything."

"Keep me posted," he added, toweling water off his face. "Gambini's been busting my balls about him." An asshole like Baxter wasn't much of a loss, but Don Gambini didn't get to where he was today by letting something like this go.

"I'm curious about that big thing you mentioned

last night, boss," Rocco said, deftly changing the subject. "Is there a big shipment coming in?"

"Not for about three weeks," Roselli answered. "It's something else. That barmaid at The Rusty Bucket."

"What about her?" Rocco's eyes narrowed.

"I want you to take care of her."

For the first time in at least a decade, I jumped at the benign meaning of that phrase. Maybe because I'd been thinking of Maggie a lot lately, along with exactly the kind of care I'd like to apply to her body.

But then his meaning hit me. It was like someone stabbed me in the gut and twisted the blade in the wound. None of us said anything, but out of the corner of my eye, I could see my buddies freeze in shock.

Roselli wanted Maggie out of the picture? No mafia boss would ever use the actual words "kill him" or "kill her." They preferred more subtle phrases like the one Roselli had used.

"Why her, Don Roselli?" Rocco saved me from the trouble to pose that question myself, plus, he managed to keep his voice neutral. "We've been going to her bar for months, and she seems pretty decent."

"You mean you think she's hot."

Rocco shrugged, not denying it.

"Does she represent a threat of some kind?" Julian asked. I was glad they were here, keeping things calm, not escalating the situation and making it worse.

Which is exactly what I wanted to do. I wanted to pull my knife and sink it deep into Roselli's stomach.

"You're not here to question my decisions," Rocco grunted. "You're here to carry out my orders."

"Does she owe you money?" I broke my silence.

Roselli turned his anger on me. "What part of *that's an order* didn't you get?"

Rocco stepped in. "It's just that you usually tell us why we're doing things. I'm confused, too. If she's a threat, let us know what kind so that we can do the job right."

Rock's words were measured and respectful, but they just seemed to rile Roselli up more.

"Shut the fuck up," he growled, his squeaky voice and his angry expression tempting me to throw that son of a bitch in the pool. "I told you to take care of her! Stop second-guessing me and fucking do it already! Get out of here and don't forget to collect from Myers Saturday."

Fuck this shit.

It was hard to turn away from the man who'd just ordered a hit on Maggie. I had half a mind to go back there and gut him, like my first instinct had been. Julian put his hand on my arm, urging me forward.

Shit.

The only thing that helped me keep my anger in check was confusion.

For Roselli to be dodging our questions was strange to say the least. For him to not provide a reason for us doing something this permanent was even more unusual.

We strode away from him in silence, the gloom in our faces saying everything we couldn't in his presence. Reaching the driveway, I threw a glance back over my shoulder. The pool was empty. There was no sitting at the gazebo beside it, either.

"Fuck that," I snapped, and took a deep breath. "What the fuck do we do now?"

"I'm not touching a hair on her head," Rocco stated, and Julian nodded his agreement.

"There's the fact that Maggie's never hurt a fly. And Tommy likes her." He hesitated. "Me, too."

"We all like her," Julian added.

Rocco shook his head. "I mean, I really like her. The, uh, first time she was at my apartment, things got pretty hot between us."

The shock of his confession hit me like a bucket full of ice cubes. "How hot?"

"Things got a little out of hand," Rocco said. "Like my hand. Under her skirt."

Shit.

"I've had an encounter with her, too," Julian said as Rocco stared at him, and my shock intensified. He looked at me. "I suspect we all have."

I nodded, not willing to confess the exact nature of my experience with Maggie. "So she's three-timing us?" That wasn't a pleasant thought, but it certainly wasn't a reason to take her out.

Julian shook his head as we gathered next to Rocco's SUV. "I don't think that's it."

"Then what is it?" Rocco grunted.

Julian looked off in the distance, seeming to gather her thoughts. "I think maybe she likes each of us, in spite of herself. In spite of what she knows about us. When I relieved her from babysitting the other night, things got a little hot and heavy, but then she stopped. Out of respect for you, Rock."

"Maybe she doesn't really know what she wants," I said.

Julian nodded. "We've each spent some time with her during some intense situations. She's not part of this world, so it's probably been a lot for her."

"Doesn't mean she has to make out with three guys, though," Rock said.

"Yeah, but it doesn't *not* mean that, either. Who are we to question her coping methods?"

"You really think she likes each of us?" My question made me sound like a shy middle-school boy, but I wanted to know.

"Yeah, I think so," Julian answered. Then we both looked at Rock. Eventually, he nodded.

"All right, this is definitely something we need to think about, but there are bigger issues," Rocco said. "Can either of you think of any reason Roselli wants us to take out Maggie?"

"Beats me," I said, at the same time Julian said, "No clue."

"We need to find out," Rocco concluded. "I bet Conners knows."

I nodded in agreement. As Roselli's consigliere, he would definitely know more. "But what if he doesn't want to give up Roselli's secret? Let's face it. If Connors betrays the Don, he's as good as dead. Roselli will have him taken out by midnight."

"And he'll probably have one of us do it," Julian added.

"One problem at a time, boys," Rocco attempted a deeper tone, his gaze darting back to me. "*Of course* Roselli will want us to put a bullet in Connors' head. That doesn't mean we're going to do it. When that day comes, we just won't be able to find him. Catch my drift?"

"That could buy us a little time," I admitted. "We can't take any chances, though. If anybody sees the consigliere somewhere in New York, Roselli will have us hunt him down 'til he's dead. We'll have to put that fool on a plane."

"To where?" Julian's question irritated me. He was

supposed to be the ideas man—where the fuck were his ideas?

I scowled, eyeing him with frustration. "Who cares? He just has to leave the city. Where he chooses to go is his own problem."

"We pay a visit to Connors. Tonight," Rocco said, his expression tight. "Now, let's talk about Maggie." He sucked in a long breath. "I can't say that it wasn't a shock, hearing that she's done something with each of us, but that doesn't mean I want her dead. We can't let that happen. No way I'm unloading my gun in her just because that fucker said I should."

"We won't let that happen either." I was glad that Julian had said 'we.' Sometimes, these guys acted like I was a loose cannon with no morals, and that just wasn't true. Usually.

"Obviously, Roselli's expecting us to finish the job," I pointed out. "I don't think it's likely he's told anyone else."

Julian nodded. "He knows we like her bar. He asked us because she knows us and trusts us."

"And because it's our job," Rocco grunted.

"I'm with you, but, again, we shouldn't take any chances," I advised, lowering my tone. "One of us will have to watch over her, while the other two pay a visit to Connors. And whoever tails her has to promise he won't go near her. That kind of distraction could get her killed."

To my surprise, neither Rocco nor Julian would make that promise.

"Seriously? I'm the voice of fucking reason here?" I let out a long exhale. "All right. Since you two can't trust yourself to keep your dicks in your pants, I'll do it. I promise you, I won't touch her."

Not touching Maggie was a fucking shame. But losing Maggie altogether was downright tragic.

"Sounds like a plan." Rocco unlocked his car. "I'll call you after we've had a chat with Connors."

"Okay."

Heading back to my car, I was half tempted to go back and switch with one of them. Beating information out of Connors sounded like a lot more fun than watching over Maggie without her knowing. That meant spending endless hours in my car, drinking about half a gallon of coffee to stay awake.

Still, it had to be done. It was the only way to make sure Maggie was safe.

For now, that was. Long term, I had a feeling that was going to be a difficult job.

19

JULIAN

"I don't like having to do this," Rocco said. We were drawing closer to Connors' place and hadn't spoken much up until now.

The thing was, I knew what Rock meant. We knew Connors. He'd been on the family's payroll since before we were even born. Getting information from him would be tough as hell. On the other hand, we'd get that information from a reliable source. If there was one person in this world who knew Roselli's secrets, it would have to be Brad Connors.

But just because I didn't like it didn't mean it wasn't necessary. "You said it yourself. Connors will know why Roselli put out a hit on Maggie. What else can we do? Ask his housekeeper? Or break into his fucking house and look for clues?"

"Emilio used to love Connors, man," Rocco reminded me of the relationship between those two. "The first money I ever made in the family? Connors gave it to me. It was Emilio's of course, but it was the first time anyone ever told me they were proud of me."

Family. Rocco didn't use that word lightly, because we hadn't had any as kids. Except for each other. It sounded dumb to outsiders, but in our world, family was everything. Not the one you were born with, the one you worked for. When Emilio was the Don, we were a true family. With Nick in charge, it was more like a toxic workplace.

"I know it sucks to go after Connors. But we've *got* to do this. Maggie's the innocent here, not him. You know I'm right."

"That's what I hate the most," he confessed, turning into the consigliere's neighborhood. "There's nothing else we can do, other than speak with Connors."

"Show time," I said, as Rock pulled over down the street from the house. The consigliere's home looked nice and cozy, much like every other property around us. Situated in the middle of a plot, a Victorian-style house was surrounded by four oak trees. It featured a rose garden in the front yard and was separated from other properties by a white picket fence. "What's the plan? Where do we break in from?"

"Break in," Rocco scoffed, rolling his eyes at me. "Look at the time—and look fucking around you."

Damn it…

Rocco was right.

It wasn't even nine o'clock yet. There were people around. An older couple having drinks on their porch. A man and his son unloading bags from their trunk in a driveway. It wasn't exactly the right time to be busting in windows.

"We're not animals—we'll knock," Rock said.

Well, sometimes we weren't animals. Other times, I wasn't so sure.

We walked up to Connors' door, my eyes on his living room window to the left. The lights were on, his big-screen TV flashing in the corner.

Rocco rang the bell, with me standing just a foot behind him. Connors' scrawny figure filled my view moments later. The sixty-eight-year-old couldn't have weighed more than a hundred fifty pounds. Several inches shorter than me and Rocco, he looked at us like he'd just seen a ghost.

"DeLuca? Knight?" he said our last names, craning his neck over Rocco. "Do you gentlemen have an appointment?"

"It's urgent," Rocco said, taking a step forward. Connors had no choice but to move backward into his living room. I clicked the door shut behind me.

"I'm going to cut right to the chase, Mr. Connors." Rocco made his intentions crystal-clear. "This morning, Don Roselli put a hit out on a woman who's got no connections with the organization. Her name is Maggie Owens—she's a barmaid at a bar in Brooklyn. What can you tell me about that? Because our boss wouldn't say much when we asked him."

Connors had witnessed too much over the years to show his surprise at Rocco's question. Even though those kinds of questions were highly dangerous in our line of work. "I'm afraid I don't know," Connors said in a steady voice. "I've never heard of that woman. If you gentlemen will excuse me, my show is about to start."

"He's not getting it," I told Rocco, standing on his left flank.

"Let's try this again," Rocco suggested, taking a large step towards the consigliere. "We've got no beef with you, Connors. But we also don't make it a habit to take out innocent young women for no reason. Roselli wants Maggie Owens dead. Why? What did she do to him?"

"I can't tell you," Connors said, his composure slipping the tiniest bit. I noticed he was no longer claiming he didn't know.

Rocco's meaty hand moved to the consigliere's throat. His grip tightened and a line of sweat appeared on the older man's forehead. "I really didn't want to do this," my friend said. It was probably no consolation to Connors that it was true.

Rock lifted the consigliere right off the ground. The older man's feet thrashed, and he clutched at Rocco's hands, but he didn't stand a chance to free himself from that vice-like grip.

"Looks like we've got a bit of a time crunch," Rocco said. "So I'm asking again. Why did Roselli put a hit out on that woman?"

"I don't know!" Connors chocked out. "You have to believe me!"

"Do we?" I wondered, stepping in the gap between him and Rocco. "Do it," I urged my friend. "I told you he wasn't getting it."

I watched as Rocco banged his fist into the old man's jaw, his head jerking in the opposite direction. Rock released his grip and Connor dropped to the floor like a bag of rocks. Rubbing his throat, he attempted to sit up. I made sure he stayed down with a foot to his chest.

"Where the fuck do you think you're going?" I asked, bending down over him. "You think we're done with you?"

"I'm still waiting," Rocco reminded him, kneeling beside me. "You can either give us the info, or we're going to beat it out of you. Your choice."

"Roselli will kill me if I tell anyone," Connors croaked.

"And guess who he's going to give that order to?" I stared down at him. "Us!"

"We won't hurt you if you tell us." Rocco's voice was steady while Connors squirmed underneath my boot. "We'll get you out of New York—even out of the country."

"I can't." His small hands closed around my ankle.

"You're really starting to piss me off." I pressed my boot down into his chest. "A little more of this, and I'm going to bust your ribs. Speak!"

Shit. It really did feel like his ribs were about to give way. That was not what I wanted. To my relief, Connors nodded.

"Okay," he said. Rocco and I had done this enough that we recognized a genuine surrender when we saw one.

I eased my foot up and off of him. Rocco offered the older man a hand up.

"There's a will," Connors rasped when he was sitting in his recliner.

"Wait a minute," Rocco interjected, furrowing his brow. "Emilio Roselli left a will?"

"Yes," Connors confirmed, and Rock and I exchanged a puzzled glance. We'd all heard the opposite. "Emilio knew what kind of man his son was. Then again, Emilio was no saint himself."

I'd never heard Connors say anything against our

old boss. Rocco was pissed off, his hand twitching as if he wanted to strike the older man. "Watch what you're saying about him," he growled.

Connor held up his hands defensively. "I don't mean he's like Nick. I just mean... Emilio liked the ladies, especially when he was younger."

"Before he was married?" I asked.

Connor looked me in the eye. "Yes. And after. His wife turned a blind eye—she had to. And he kept it discreet, but sometimes, things happened. Like when he got a housekeeper named Sheila pregnant."

"Go on," Rocco demanded, leaning a bit forward, but I'd already seen where this was going, and my jaw dropped.

"Sheila Owens," Connors elaborated.

"Fuck," Rock hissed, getting it. "Maggie is Emilio's daughter?" He looked as stunned as I was. "But she told me her father left them when she was a girl."

"Then she lied to you, or more likely, her mother lied to her."

Rocco was still stunned. "She's really Emilio's daughter?"

There was a more pressing issue, however. "Which means she's also Nick's half-sister."

"Later in his life, he felt guilty that he'd never been there for Maggie. That he didn't know her. I think the more he learned about his son, the more he wished he had a relationship with his illegitimate daughter," Connor said. "Since he didn't, he tried to rectify that mistake in his will. He left ninety-five percent of his fortune to Maggie. The remaining five percent was supposed to go to Nick."

"This is fucking *insane*," Rocco said, staring past the older man's head. I banged my open palm into my temple, choosing to keep my mouth shut.

"So that bomb that Baxter was taking to the bar, that wasn't meant to punish us, was it? It was meant to kill Maggie." Rocco's tone revealed that he already knew the answer.

"Precisely," Connors affirmed.

"So why'd he hire Baxter instead of sending us?" I asked.

"I don't know. I suppose it's possible he thought you might not take the order well." There was a hint of irony in the older man's voice. Which meant he was recovering from his ordeal.

Rocco helped him up, he kept a tight grip around his wrist. "One last thing. Has Roselli said anything about that hit to other crews?"

Shit, I hadn't thought of that. There could be goons heading her way right this moment. Hopefully Slater was doing his fucking job and keeping her safe.

Connors gave an icy smile. "I thought you were a smart man, DeLuca. This is your real punishment for planning to rob that bank in North Haven without your boss's consent. Don Roselli is well aware of your connection with that girl. Taking her life will shore up his inheritance and it will hurt you. It's a win-win for the Don."

"Shit," Rocco said, and I had to agree. He strode off, but not just to pace. He went to a little bar on the far wall and poured a glass of scotch. "Thanks," he said when he delivered it to Connors.

For a moment, I was struck by how batshit crazy this all was. In what other job did you nearly choke someone to death and then bring him a drink afterwards?

But this was how the game was played. I knew it. Rock knew it. Connors knew it.

We were both lost in thought on the drive home. The implications were enormous. Don Roselli funded his entire operation with the money made by his late father—money that wasn't supposed to be his.

Rock, however, was thinking of Maggie. "She is Italian after all," he said when we were twenty minutes away.

"Huh?"

"I always thought she looked Italian, and she said

she wasn't," Rock said. "Can you imagine not even knowing something so basic about yourself?"

I sighed. "Looks like there was a lot she didn't know. Things that her fucking mother should've told her."

"She might have been trying to keep her safe. Emilio, too. We don't know the whole story.

"I feel like my head is going to fucking explode," I told Rocco.

"We've got bigger fish to fry right now," he responded, rubbing his jaw. "Breaking the news to Maggie. She's not going to believe it. Any of it."

"Can you blame her?" I wondered, throwing a quick sideways glance over at him. "Fuck, man. This is like telling her she won the lottery ten times in a row. What are the odds of that happening?"

Rock snorted. "Yeah, a lottery that also comes with a price on your head. It's a good thing we're the only ones who know about the hit. It means she's safe."

He said it confidently, but I think that deep down, he knew better.

"For now, maybe," I said. "But if we don't carry out the job, Roselli will hire more men."

"I've got a place we can stash her away," he said, making me wonder. When we'd been younger, we'd had a safe house, a place we could go to when shit hit the fan. But now that we were part of the Don's organization, it wasn't necessary. Usually.

I didn't ask any questions as I stared at the road ahead of us. My mind was still fucking reeling. In a matter of weeks, Maggie had gone from being the cute girl at our favorite bar to someone important to us.

And that could wind up getting us all killed.

20

ROCCO

"Don't speak ill of the dead, child." An old granny at one of my short-lived stays with a foster family had said that. She'd been an ornery old bitch, but she had a point. The dead were somehow blameless. It was the living that caused all the problems. Few of them were decent, and even fewer gave a crap about anyone else.

I'd thought that Emilio was one of the good ones. After we ran away from our final group home, we'd lived on the streets. Begged in the park. Robbed rich kids in their prep school uniforms. Emilio had taken us in. He had put a roof over our heads. The man filled our stomachs with food and gave us purpose. He's saved us. He'd saved me. By teaching me about my heritage. And about the kind of man I wanted to be.

But you know who else had a crappy childhood?

Maggie. And he'd left her and her mother to fend for themselves.

I couldn't get past that part of it.

During our time at Connors' house, it crossed my mind to ask him to show me that will. I just couldn't believe what I'd been hearing. I couldn't wrap my mind around Emilio's selfishness.

In the end, I didn't do it. There was no reason for me to see that piece of paper. Roselli's actions alone had proved its existence.

He was determined to put Maggie in the ground, so he could keep his father's fortune. He had attempted to do that once already. The second time, it was up to me and my boys. And, although we had to have a little chat with her, going after that woman was not an option.

If I hadn't stepped in when Keeler and Portis held up her bar, I wouldn't be in this position. I would've gotten to know her—and she likely wouldn't even be here. That thought stopped me in my tracks for a moment. Roselli sent those assholes to take Maggie out. But it didn't play out, in my opinion. Nick was an idiot and a cheap bastard, but even he knew better than to entrust those morons with an important job.

To my mind, that was just a weird twist of fate that started us down this path. Now she was my friend. My boy liked her. My friends did, too.

Which meant we had one hell of a problem on our hands.

To me, it was important that we stuck to our everyday routine. I didn't want to make Roselli suspicious. For the moment, he had to believe we were actually going to carry out his orders. The following day, this routine included collecting from Bob Myers, owner of Napolitana, a restaurant in Manhattan.

Myers was a typical degenerate gambler. Nine times out of ten, he would lose money. The one time he'd win, he'd brag about it for a week, before gambling some more. He'd been repeating this cycle for the past couple of years. That was when he borrowed money from Roselli for the first time. I liked his restaurant—his chefs could do amazing things with hand-rolled pasta. Whenever I walked into that place, the smells alone were enough to make me want to eat about half its menu. It was too bad Myers was in charge of that otherwise decent restaurant.

Cars speeding down the road behind us, Julian, Slater and I went down the stairs to Napolitana's basement. Being the first to enter, I swept the large area spreading out in front of me. About two dozen people in white uniforms and big hats were standing near the kitchen counters. Using their knives, they were chopping vegetables, fish, and meat. Some waiters were coming in and getting out, with huge trays in their hands. In the upper left corner, smoke was pouring from the rotisserie. Myers was on the far side, talking to one of his cooks.

Our gazes meeting, I read fear in his face. His Mediterranean complexion turning pale, he had a hollow gaze in his gray eyes.

"Hey, Bob." I slowly closing the gap between us. "How's business?"

"Not great," he spoke in a weak voice and folded his arms across his chest. "I've been struggling around here."

"I'm curious," I addressed him in an ironic tone. "If business sucks so bad, what do you pay these people in? Tablecloths? Or is it wine?"

"Look, guys," he requested, his gaze traveling from me to Slater and Julian on either of my flanks. "I know I've missed a payment or two, but I've got a lot of expenses these days. My son's getting married in a couple of weeks; you know how expensive weddings are. Also, my daughter's graduating from…"

"Yeah, yeah…" I interrupted, my imposing stature dwarfing his tiny 5'7" figure. "Come on, Myers. You know the drill. Give us the money, so we can get the fuck out of here."

"I don't have it, I'm afraid," he claimed, the beads of sweat under his hairline betraying his tension.

"Don't make it more complicated than it has to be,

Myers," Slater spoke in a calm but chilling voice—a special talent of his. "You know how this goes. You pay on time? Everybody's happy. You don't? Roselli's pissed and he sends us to collect, one way or another. You said your son's getting married soon. You don't want to miss your boy's wedding, do you?"

At that point, a thud from behind me drew my attention. I whipped my head around, and spotted two men just past the entrance, holding rifles. That stupid prick.

The first bullet crackled through the air. One of them whistled past me and got lodged in the wall in front of me, Myers whirling around to flee. I lunged to the right, not in the mood to take a bullet today.

I landed hard on my chest and rolled across the floor as every chef in the place screamed and ran around like idiots. Slater had a good position behind a stainless-steel refrigerator, but he held his fire, not wanting to hit one of the cooks.

Good. Decent Italian food was really hard to come by.

A spray of bullets hit a counter near me and suddenly, I was covered in bits of carrots and cucumbers. A bullet ricocheted off the edge of a pillar on my left with a deafening bang. I looked over and my heart sank. Julian hadn't been able to find cover, so he was crouched behind that pillar, and it was too small to shield much of him. Fuck.

Bullets rained over his head, ripping off chunks of paint and concrete. His hair was full of plaster. Slater was the only one of us not covered in debris from the shoot-out.

One of the gunmen was sneaking toward me from my right. He stepped in some alfredo sauce and slipped, giving me a chance to take the shot. The man's yelp distracted his accomplice, and Slater fired. A moment later, there was a thud as the man hit the deck.

Julian jumped up, training his gun on the injured man. "Talk, motherfucker," he snarled, kicking him in the side. "Who sent you?"

I strode over, swearing internally. I'd just assumed that these two goons were here to protect Myers. Until Julian's question, I hadn't thought they might be here to target us.

The injured man moaned. "Fuck off!" Pain was written all over his face as he coughed out blood.

Slater, who'd taken care of the other man, appeared, his gun also drawn. "Can I end this motherfucker?" Knowing my friend, it could have been a bluff to get the guy to talk—or it could've been a genuine question.

I was torn. It would be nice to blow his fucking head off. He wasn't an innocent like Maggie. He'd shot at us first. But Julian was right. If there was more to this than met the eye, we needed to know. And the cops already had to be on their way, so we didn't have much time.

Just as I was about to beat the crap out of him, a buzzing sound came from nearby him. Slater shoved him out of the way and searched the mess of pots, pans, and ingredients until he pulled out the killer's phone.

His face darkened as he looked at the lock screen. A preview of the text he'd just received showed there.

A text from Roselli.

It read, "Are they gone?"

Son of a bitch.

Julian looked murderous. "Unlock your phone," he demanded to the guy on the ground.

The asshole looked up at us defiantly.

I pushed aside the rage in my head and spoke in a steady voice. "It's simple. You unlock your phone, and you go to a hospital where they'll fix you up. Some pretty nurse with big tits will bring you your meal. Sounds pretty good, doesn't it?"

Slater delivered the alternative. "Or your family can hold your funeral services on the edge of the river after we dump your body." He delivered another kick to the guy's ribs.

After a moment of deliberation that was clearly for show, the man groaned, holding out his hand for the phone. Slater didn't give it to him but allowed him to use the keypad to unlock it. "Should I just say it's done?"

"Yeah," Julian said, looking grim.

Slater and I turned back to the dumb fuck on the ground. Knowing what had to be done next, I shoved the barrel of my gun into his mouth. His eyes widened, but I didn't allow him to complain.

One more squeeze of the trigger brought the matter to a close. Roselli, that little prick, had double-crossed us. We'd followed his orders. We hadn't liked it, but we'd done it, and he'd had the nerve to pay someone to take us out. That's how grateful he'd been to my boys and me. Two seasoned shooters, armed to the teeth were our reward for more than a decade of service to the Roselli family.

"Myers could have been part of this," Slater commented. "I'll go get him."

"You saw him, Slater," I reminded him. "He was scared shitless when we walked in. Not to mention he wouldn't let his kitchen turn into a fucking warzone."

"Shit!" Julian swore, giving the dead man one more kick.

"Boys, I'd say it's time we lay low." I holstered my gun.

"What about Maggie?" Slater asked instantly.

"Her, too."

"She's not going to like that," Julian said.

"Who says we're giving her a choice?" I grunted.

We were quiet, contemplative, and covered in food as we drove away.

Leaving the city would be like leaving behind the past fifteen years of my life. A small part of me was thrilled. Taking orders from Roselli? Nope. Not anymore. Despite this new revelation about Emilio's past, I still thought he was a hundred times the man his son was.

But this was more than just a professional relationship gone sideways. Roselli hadn't put a hit out on just Maggie. He had put out a hit on all of us. The Don wouldn't leave a stone unturned to find us. My only hope was that we would get to him before he could hurt us.

21

MAGGIE

None of the guys had been to the Rusty Bucket for days. I couldn't help thinking about it as I wiped down the bar, locked the cash drawer, and prepared to leave.

On the surface, that was a good thing. They were dangerous. They were literally killers. If I never saw them again, that should be a win in my book.

So why couldn't I stop thinking about them?

Each night as I worked my shift, I looked up when the door opened, wondering if it would be them.

It wasn't.

Which, again, was a *good* thing. Or at least that's what I tried to tell myself. Because truth be told, each man had gotten under my skin. Rocco with his devotion to his son. Julian with his big plans and his loyalty to his friends. And Slater with his... well, I hadn't quite figured him out, but he was more than just a sexy guy who turned me on. Though that was a factor, too. I never would've thought I was the type of woman who'd liked to be spanked, but let's just say that he proved me wrong.

They all were.

And it's not like I knew what I'd do if and when they did show up again. What I'd say. What they'd say.

But I sure as hell had spent far too much time thinking about it. Mostly, though, tending bar at the Rusty Bucket kept me too busy to get *too* lost in my thoughts. At least until it was time to close up, like now.

That's when the worry hit full force. Walking home at two or three in the morning was never exactly comfortable for a woman on her own, but lately, I'd been getting more apprehensive about it. No matter how late it was, I'd always encounter a few people, but just in the last few days, I'd had the strangest feeling that there were somehow other people out there. People I didn't see.

It was probably paranoia, but a few times, I could have sworn there was someone nearby, but somehow just out of sight. In the daytime, that feeling was annoying, but easy to wave off.

But at night? Not so much.

It was chilly as I walked back home after my late shift. As always, I clutched the small canister of mace on my keyring. I'd had it for ages, but it was only recently that I kept it in my hand, my finger poised to spray it.

Given the hours that I kept, it was kind of amazing that I'd never had to use it, though I had decked a couple of guys at the Rusty Bucket who'd gotten handsy. And I'd pulled that shotgun the night those thugs tried to hold it up, but it turned out I hadn't needed to because Rocco was there.

Still, I was a small woman, walking the empty streets at night. I never let my guard down in situations like that—especially not lately.

I was near my building when I caught sight of a man out of the corner of my eye. He was skulking near a closed coffee shop and wearing a ski mask.

Shit.

Instinct kicked in, and I took off, running toward my place. I glanced back and my adrenaline spiked as I saw him on my heels. That's when I ran smack dab into the broad chest of a second man.

He caught my arms, pinning them at my side. The jolt of running into him had made me almost drop the mace. Now, it was pointed uselessly toward the ground. Even through the panic in my mind, one truth broke through. There was nothing a woman my size could do against one of these brutes, let alone two.

I was trapped.

My lips parted, waves of fear washing over me. I opened my mouth to scream, but no sound came out. It didn't matter, though. A guy came up behind me, his fingers covering my mouth. His accomplice was quick to grab me by the wrists. Yanking them back, he tied my hands over my lower back. In seconds, they were dragging me toward the street.

I thrashed around, trying to get away, but it was useless. In that tight hold, my screams drowned out by that thug's hand.

"Don't fight it, babe," a low, raspy voice said. "We're not going to hurt you."

Yeah, right.

In the dark, I didn't see the curb, so I stumbled at the sudden step down. Strong hands grabbed me just before I slammed into a black sedan. The trunk popped open, and I dug my heels in, trying to keep them from dragging me toward it.

But the two men easily lifted me off the ground. They put me in the trunk on top of an old musty blanket. Beyond that, there was the faint smell of gasoline.

I wiggled around, my arms trapped behind my back as I tried to look up at my captors. "What do you want from me?" I asked, staring at the two masked men.

The only answer I got was the lid of the trunk closing. There was a certain finality about it.

There was nothing I could do as the car began moving. I was trapped. There was no way out. Yet the panic in me wouldn't let me rest. I kicked at the sides of the trunk. I rolled over and managed to get to my knees, trying to push the trunk open with my back. I shouted. I cried.

None of it did any good.

Eventually, my panic and tears receded. I focused on doing what I could to make myself comfortable. It wasn't easy, with my wrists tied behind me, but if I were to have any chance of escape later on, I'd need my muscles to be loose. After a lot of wiggling around, I managed to prop myself up on the, positing the old blanket over the ragged parts of the bottom of the trunk.

My mind was running through scenario after scenario, trying to figure out what the hell was going on, but I had nothing. Had enemies of the guys kidnapped me? Had those two thugs who'd held up the bar come back for revenge? My mind went in circles, and eventually, I drifted off a time or two.

When the car stopped, I was thrown forward like a ragdoll. We made a turn, and it was clear we weren't on a paved road anymore. The noise of tires digging into dirt filled my ears as I bounced around painfully. After ten minutes of that, the car jerked to a halt and the engine shut off.

The sound of doors opening made my pulse spike, and I braced myself for whatever was coming next.

Someone pressing the trunk button from the outside, I blinked, trying to make sense of what I was seeing. Rocco, Slater and Julian were standing over me, a starry sky above them as a cold breeze chilled my skin.

"Th-this..." I stuttered. "This must be a bad dream. I'm going to wake up any minute."

"Not a dream," Slater said, reaching down to stroke my cheek with one of his long fingers as if to prove it.

"Get her out of there," Rocco commanded, his tone stiff.

I still couldn't quite process what I was seeing. "It was you guys?"

Julian gripped my arm, lifting me out of the trunk. Once I was on my feet, he swung me around, cutting the bonds. He immediately began rubbing my sore wrists, but I jerked away from him.

I backed away, my ankle turning on the gravel underneath me, but I glowered at him when he reached out to steady me.

A million thoughts raced through my head. Fear was a big one. Why had they brought me out here? Why had they fucking kidnapped me? Confusion, fatigue, and anger were present, too.

And also... relief? That didn't seem right. These

guys were known killers. And yet somehow, my stupid brain didn't really believe they'd hurt me.

Probably a lot of kidnapping victims had thought that and learned the hard way that they were wrong.

Unable to handle all those emotions at once, I settled for looking at my surroundings.

Right in front of me was a small, cozy cabin. The air was much colder than in New York City. Tall trees surrounded it, but it was too dark to see much beyond that.

"Where are we?" I rasped, my throat dry.

"Where in the world *are* we?" I squinted up at Rocco.

"Near the Catskills," Rocco answered, and he handed me a water bottle. I didn't want to take it from him—I didn't want anything to do with him—but I was really thirsty. "This is my cabin," he said as I unscrewed the cap with shaky fingers. "You're safe."

"Safe?" Anger made me forget about my thirst. "You just fucking kidnapped me!"

Julian answered. "Sorry about that. We didn't have time to explain things back in New York."

"Time?" I sputtered. "How long does it take to say, 'Hi, Maggie. Please get in the car—in the car, not the trunk—and we'll explain on the way.'"

Slater eyed me. "Would you have gotten in?"

"Yes," I said stiffly, though I had to admit that I might not have. Slater looked unconvinced as well.

"It wasn't just that," Julian said with a sigh. "It was also for appearances. If anyone saw us, well, it had to look like we were taking you away against your will."

"Which you did," I pointed out. "But why?"

"Because of our orders," Slater said quietly, but I didn't understand what he meant.

I had a million more questions for them—and a thousand nasty names I wanted to call them, but I focused on what was probably the most pressing point. "So what's the big emergency?"

"Julian, you're up," Rocco stated, gesturing him closer.

Julian turned to me, his arm raised as if he was going to touch me, but then he pulled it back. "There's no easy way to say this, but we were ordered to kill you."

"What?" Shock filled me, but somehow, my reaction was incredulousness instead of running, like a normal person would.

"We're not going to," Slater said. "But our Don ordered us to take you out."

"So that's why you brought me out here," I said in a small voice. It made all the sense in the world, but still —I didn't quite believe it.

"No. That's why we did some research and tried to

figure out why," Rocco said. "You may think we're mindless thugs who just follow commands—and that actually is how it usually works. But we don't go out shooting people anytime we feel like it. Our boss wouldn't say why he wanted you dead, so we took it upon ourselves to find out."

"Long story short, we discovered something about you, Maggie," Julian said, and this time he did place his hand on my arm. "And about your father."

My what? "I haven't seen him since I was four," I said. If these guys thought my deadbeat dad had something to do with this, they were insane.

"Actually, you've never met him," Julian said. "His name was Emilio Roselli."

That wasn't true, but the name caught my attention, and I turned to Rocco. "You mean the man who took you in. The one who taught you about the Italian culture."

Rocco nodded.

"What's that got to do with me?"

"He knew your mother, Maggie. She was a housecleaner, right? He met her, they hooked up, and nine months later, you were born."

"That's impossible," I breathed.

"It's true," Rocco said. "And I'm sorry to say that he left you two on his own. He was married, you see, and I guess he felt he had no choice."

I inhaled sharply. My mom had slept with a married

man? But that was assuming that this was true, which was impossible.

"It's true," Julian said, as if reading my mind. "But we don't know the whole story, and neither of them are around to ask." His words were painful even though I'd never met one of the two people he was referring to.

Suddenly, I laughed. This had to be a joke. These guys must've brought me out here for a weekend tryst, and the kidnapping was probably their idea of some kind of kinky foreplay. After all, I'd gotten very turned on when Slater spanked me.

"Maggie?" Julian asked with a worried look at my expression.

"You guys are joking," I said, relief sweeping through me. "I have to admit, you had me going there for a while."

In the light from the moon, I examined each of them in turn. Slater's unruly hair was even wilder than usual because of the ski mask he'd worn. Rocco looked troubled, but maybe he just had a good poker face. And Julian was still watching me with concern.

I stared them down, waiting for one of them to give away something.

A twitch.

A tiny smile.

Either would have enabled me to realize that this was a classic case of a crappy joke.

Neither came.

Their expressions remained as serious as they had been throughout their narratives.

"This isn't a joke, Maggie," Rock said. But it had to be. It just couldn't be real.

"I know it's rough, hearing that the man you thought was your father isn't," Julian said, but I cut him off angrily.

"That jerk was nothing to me. He abandoned us." When you thought about it, that should've made it easier to accept that he wasn't my real dad, but according to these guys, my real father hadn't ever even laid eyes on me. "Please, just take me back to New York. I don't want to be here."

"Which is why we had to nab you the way that we did," Julian said gently.

"I won't tell anyone," I said, my eyes pleading. "Please let me go."

"This isn't a joke, Maggie," Rock said. "You're in danger."

"Yes," I said, running my hands through my hair. "From you guys."

Slater leaned against the trunk, just a half foot from me. "No. From people worse than us."

"But why?"

Julian explained. "You're the daughter of Emilio

Roselli. His son, Nick, inherited his millions when he died. And apparently, he doesn't want to share."

My breath hitched. "You're saying I have a half-brother?"

"Yeah, but he's a really bad man," Rocco said, his voice gentle. "He put a hit on you because he doesn't want you to get your hands on his money."

"I don't' want his money," I said bitterly. It was blood money.

"It doesn't matter," Julian said. "Apparently, Emilio left a will that names you as the main heir. That's why Nick wants you dead."

Shivers ran down my spine, but I did my best to think logically. I'd always dreamed of being a lawyer, and they needed to think on their feet.

"Why now?"

The men exchange glances. Finally, Slater spoke. "Since you didn't know, you weren't a real threat. But, uh, we did something to piss Roselli off, so he ordered us to kill you as punishment."

That was all kinds of insane. "My death would somehow equal punishment for you three?"

The look on their faces confirmed that it would.

Julian took up the thread. "We also think that Roselli got word that we'd met you and were hanging out with you. I guess he got worried that we'd eventually figure it out."

"Which you did," I said softly. I turned my back to them, trying to think. The crisp night air that filled my lungs was steadying, somehow. I faced them again. "So what happens now?"

"We lay low for a bit," Rocco said. "There's a price on all our heads now."

A new thought hit me. "Where's Tommy?"

"He's safe," Rocco said gruffly, but what did that even mean?

Julian leaned over and whispered in my ear. "Drop it."

My mouth opened, but one look at the pain on Rock's face made me heed Julian's advice.

Slater jumped in to cover the awkwardness. "One thing we can do is to make sure the story is true, about your father. If it's not, then that changes things considerably."

"How do we do that?"

"DNA test," Julian said. "Where does your father live? The man you thought was your father?"

"I have no idea. He abandoned us. I haven't heard from him since I was a kid."

"But you can give us his name and last known location," Slater pointed out.

Yeah... I could. But should I? He was an awful father, but that didn't excuse sending three armed men after him. Then again, I didn't owe him any loyalty. "Seth Harper. Last I heard, he was living in Queens."

"We'll find him," Julian said.

"I want to talk to him." My words surprised both the men and myself.

"That's not necessary."

"I've been pissed off at him for two decades for the way he abandoned us. Now, maybe I'm not even his kid. That would explain a few things."

"He was still married to your mom," Julian said. "He still abandoned her."

"All the more reason to talk to him."

"Well—"

Rock cut off Julian's response. "We'll see. For now, let's get inside." He looked around. The first glimmers of daylight were shattering the dark. "We need some sleep. We've got a long day ahead of us tomorrow."

I wanted to insist again that they return me to Brooklyn, but deep inside, I was starting to accept that that wasn't an option. So I nodded and followed the men to the steps of the cabin. It wasn't like I had a choice. I was miles and miles away from home and absolutely exhausted.

Maybe when I woke up, I'd find that this crazy night had all been a dream.

22

SLATER

"One of us stays here at all times," Rocco had told us. "The other two head back to New York and try to figure out a way out of this shitshow."

I had to admit Rocco's plan was our best hope.

Although this cabin was about three hours from the city, someone had to watch over Maggie. We knew he'd kept this place secret from the family, but the organization was powerful. Someone from the nearby town of Shandaken could give away the location and have Maggie executed in a heartbeat. No one was willing to gamble with her life, and that included staying alert.

The man guarding her had to keep his hands off her.

That was a tall ask, though. We were all three

attracted to her. What red-blooded man wouldn't be? I could still feel how her ass had bounced under my palm. How she'd tasted. How she'd writhed around when she came.

So yeah, that was a big ask.

Seeing her lying in bed, arms splayed out sideways, her bare legs exposed, her big breasts stretching that gray t-shirt of hers...

Wow.

Just wow.

I couldn't stay in the back bedroom for more than thirty seconds or so. The temptation was just too much for me.

"Slater?" I heard her groggy voice behind me, stopping me just two paces from the exit.

"Morning, sunshine." I kept my gaze forward. "Why don't you put some clothes on and meet me in the kitchen? I made coffee."

I didn't wait for her to respond. I headed out and focused on the coffee pot on the counter, trying to slow my heartbeat. Every time I was within fifteen feet of Maggie, my pulse would spike like a fucking war drum.

Sliding a red coffee mug across the table, I saw her shuffling out of the bathroom down the hall. She'd pulled on the black slacks she'd worn for her shift last night.

She yawned, seating herself across from me. "Thanks."

"Julian packed you a suitcase," I told her. "It's right next to the couch if you want to change."

She raised an eyebrow. "You broke into my apartment?"

I couldn't help grinning at the indignation in her voice. "Isn't that the least of our crimes... *counselor*?"

She flushed as I reminded her of our steamy encounter back at my place.

"Don't start that shit again," she muttered, all but burying her face in the mug. "You know you could have explained things to me, instead of kidnapping me."

"And what fun would that have been?" Though things were tense last night, I'd enjoyed tying her hands behind her back. But the glare she gave me now wiped the grin off my face.

"All right, I'll be good. But time was of the essence. Right now, Roselli thinks we're dead. He's an idiot, but it won't take him long to figure out otherwise. When there's a price on your head, you don't hang out and talk things through."

"You could have asked me to get in the car with you."

"And would you have?"

She looked away, probably realizing as well as I did that she still would've put up a fight.

"What if we'd led with: hey, your dad's not your dad and you have a half-brother who wants you dead?"

Maggie still wouldn't look at me. "You've made your point. But I still think you should've handled things differently."

"We're not perfect," I admitted, not that she'd likely thought we were. "We make mistakes—and we don't want to make one with you. Which is why it would be really nice if you didn't do anything stupid like try to run off. We're miles from anywhere."

She nodded, but I doubted she'd heed my words. I'd have to keep an extra close eye on her, which wasn't exactly a hardship.

"Anyway, why don't you get cleaned up and get dressed. We're going to go on a road trip."

She arched an eyebrow. "Will I be in the trunk for this one, too?"

I laughed. "Not unless that's what floats your boat."

Maggie ignored that. "Do I get to know where we're going?"

"Sure." I gave her a cheerful smile. "We're going to pay a visit to dear old fake dad."

"What?" Her skin paled, but I let my answer stand.

There was no doubt in my mind that everything Maggie knew about her father was false. Her only actual blood relative, Nick Roselli, wasn't going to stop. Even if all else failed, he would come after her. The family fortune was just too important to him. Way more important than his own flesh and blood, if he even considered her that way.

The sooner she accepted that, the safer she'd be.

23

MAGGIE

Sitting in the passenger seat as Slater drove, I gave myself a mental talking to. Seth was the last person I wanted to see, but he'd clear things up. He'd confirm that he was my actual dad, and then these three would give it a rest. And then I could go home.

Except it wasn't that simple. Nothing was these days.

That conversation I would have with my father? It would the first in my adult life. I hadn't seen that bastard in eighteen years. Ever since he dumped my mother and me, he pretended we didn't even exist. Even if he wasn't my real father, he'd been married to my mom. That had made me his stepdaughter, kind of. Would it have killed him to stick around?

But to Seth, I was apparently a big, fat zero. Something meaningless. Worthless. A nuisance of some sort. Someone he walked out on when she needed him the most.

During that long drive to Queens, I considered discussing all of this with Slater. He wasn't always in full-on seduction mode. Sometimes he actually seemed to listen and be an understanding guy.

Still, I hadn't forgiven any of them for the kidnapping last night. Plus, I didn't trust them. Okay, so I believed that they wanted to keep me safe, but that wasn't the same as trusting them.

The only one I could count on was myself, so I kept my thoughts to myself. Besides, he's spent almost all of his childhood in group homes and with foster families. He'd likely never known what it was like to be held by an adult who loved you more than life itself. He never saw a parent walk in the door, smiling, happy to see her child after a hard day's work.

At least I'd had my mother growing up. It would have been a lot better to have my father around, too, but Slater hadn't had either parent. Despite his flaws, that hurt my heart, and I was hesitant to talk too much about my childhood when it had clearly been less traumatic than his.

Much later, he pulled up outside of the address he had for Seth. My hands shook so I clasped them in my lap as I looked at the modest, single-family home. A touch made me look down. Slater placed his large hand over mine and squeezed.

The warmth in his gaze offered me a tiny amount of courage. I didn't tell him, but it was somehow what I needed to get my butt out of his car.

At first glance, Seth seemed to have done well for himself. The house wasn't new, but it wasn't in bad shape. There was a blue, pickup truck parked upfront and a white Toyota.

"You've got this," Slater said as we approached the house.

"Jesus..." I whispered, running my fingers through my hair. "I haven't seen him in almost twenty years. I don't even know where to start."

"You had hours to brainstorm that with me on the way over," Slater pointed out, but not meanly. "Why didn't you?"

"Because I knew I'd get emotional," I attempted an explanation. It wasn't a good one, judging by his frown. "I'm sorry."

"It won't be easy, but won't it be better to know where things stand? Be strong, Maggie."

"I'll try," I promised.

That was easier said than done.

I sucked in a deep breath and headed toward the front door, but the sound of running water made me realize I didn't have to knock. A man emerged from the side of the house carrying a hose.

Slater stepped in front of me like a bodyguard. "Seth Harper?"

The man flinched slightly while I stared at him, looking for something I remembered.

"Yes?" he said. Well into his sixties, he was actually in pretty decent shape. He had a pair of faded jeans on and a black t-shirt, white hair gracing his head. Beyond him, a sprinkler was watering a rather narrow patch of lawn.

I moved to Slater's side. "Hi, Seth." My voice shook.

"Morning, miss." He let the water from the hose pour onto the ground as he looked at me. "May I help you?"

"Take a good, hard look at me," I demanded, coming to halt just five feet from me. "Then, you'll understand if you can help me or not."

"I'm sorry, I—" He stared at me, his face turning white. "Maggie?"

I nodded.

"Jesus, you look like your mother. Not the coloring, but your face, your eyes... Jesus. What are you doing here?"

"Surprised to see me?" I asked. "Clearly you didn't think that would happen when you ran off."

"You were a child," he said, color rising in his cheeks. "You have no idea what was going on."

"I know you left," I said.

"With good reason," he said, still angry. "Look, Maggie, I know you were just a kid, but you had no fucking clue—"

Slater took a menacing step forward. "Don't talk to her like that."

"Who the fuck are you?" Seth asked.

"A friend," I said quickly, placing my hand on Slater's chest to stop him. "Let me handle this," I pleaded.

Then I turned back to the man I was increasingly sure wasn't my actual father. "What do you have to say for yourself?"

"He's one of them," he spat out, eyeing Slater.

"One of who?"

"You know what I mean." Seth's attention returned to me. "I may not know who he works for, but I know the attitude. I've seen this shit before. Did you bring him here to scare me or beat me up?"

"I'd be glad to do either," Slater said, anger darkening his gaze. "So, I suggest you start talking before I lose my temper."

"What do you mean, you know the attitude?" I asked, hoping Slater would behave himself.

"The whole wise guy attitude," he emphasized,

bringing his gaze back to me. "I thought I'd never see it again, but here you are. Your mom wanted you to stay away from guys like him. I'm very disappointed in you, Maggie."

"Disappointment from the man who abandoned us," I said in a voice full of sarcasm, but his words had hurt. From the tension in Slater's body, he knew it, too.

"I didn't abandon you." He shook his head. "They made me leave. When I met your mother, she was working at a restaurant in lower Manhattan. She was already pregnant with you. I didn't mind—I was too infatuated with her, I guess. We got married, and you were born. Things were normal for a while. We didn't have a lot, but we were happy enough for four years. Then one night, some mafioso and his henchmen dropped by the shoe store I managed. He said he was the father of Sheila's child. I didn't buy it—she'd fed me some bull about how the man who'd impregnated her had been killed in a car accident. But then he showed me pictures. She was in a maid's uniform at his house—he was there in the background. And I... I believed him."

Slater nodded. "So then what happened?"

"He told me to leave Sheila alone. That I'd be in a world of pain if I didn't. And then he let some of his men prove it to me." Unconsciously, he touched an old scar on his cheek.

"Why didn't my mother tell me any of this?" Slater put his arm around me.

"She didn't know why I left. I'm not proud of it, but I just told her it wasn't working out and took off."

"Just like that?" There was an edge to Slater's voice.

Seth looked down at the grass. "As I said, I'm not proud of it."

"She could've told me you weren't my biological father, though. That might have made it a little easier." Possibly. But it still would have been crushing. And possibly more than a four-year-old could face. But she'd had decades after that to tell me the truth.

"She was probably just trying to protect you," Slater said.

Seth took a step closer, but one look from Slater had him backing off. "So you took off and a woman and her young child all alone," he snapped.

"A woman who whose child was from another man," Seth said quietly. Then he sighed. "Those guys scared me, okay? I'd never encountered anyone like them. I told myself that it wasn't worth my life."

The tears flowed harder. Would Seth have stayed, if my real father hadn't threatened him? It would've made all the difference in the world to my mother. To have someone help with the childcare after those first few years. To have two incomes. To have some support.

"I'm sorry, Maggie," Seth said.

Slater squeezed my shoulders, steadying me. "Let's get out of here, sweetheart."

I looked at Seth, but I couldn't think of what to say. In a way, he'd been a victim, too. A victim of the awful world that Rocco, Julian, Slater, and apparently my biological father had inhabited. But the pain was too much. I was dealing with too many of my own feelings to focus on Seth's.

The best I could give him was a nod. He gave me a small smile in return. Then I let out a sniffle and walked away. As much as I wished I could say more to him, the person I really wanted to speak to was my mother.

She'd lied to me, and she'd lied to him—or at least she never warned him about the dangerous world my biological father inhabited. And she had to have known. She cleaned his house after all. A shiver ran through me. Had she ever washed blood—his or someone else's—out of his clothes?

Seth had left us, just like she said. But now I knew that he had a reason. He'd done it in order to protect himself. Apparently, he hadn't cared who would protect us.

I couldn't stop crying once I was back in the car. Not even Slater's hand, reassuringly patting my leg, helped.

24

MAGGIE

I ROLLED OVER, opened my eyes, and stared at an unfamiliar ceiling.

It didn't have the usual cracks like the ceiling in my tiny apartment. It wasn't even the same color.

Then it came back in waves. The kidnapping. The cabin in the woods. That was enough to make my head ache, but then a nagging voice in the back of my mind was telling me that there was more.

Oh god. I'd talked to Seth. I'd found out that my mother had lied to me. About everything. And that my biological father had run off a man who might have potentially stood by our side.

"Maggie?"

Though the low voice was gentle, I bolted up right

in bed, clutching the sheets around me. Rocco was sitting in a chair at the foot of the bed, watching me.

I stared at him for a long moment and let my head fall back on the pillow. There was no way I was ready to face all of this.

"More sleep is not going to make all your problems go away."

Propping my head up on my elbow, I glared at him. "Stop that."

"Stop what?" He was wearing a light blue t-shirt and black jeans. Both were tight enough to showcase his impressive muscles.

"Reading my mind."

He chuckled. "I'll do my best."

I sighed. "Is it your day to babysit me?" From the light coming in from the blinds, I figured it was morning. I'd slept at least twelve hours since Slater and I got back, but I didn't feel rested.

"Yep."

"You could have done that from out there." I gestured toward the main room of the cabin. "There's no way for me to escape from here."

I thought he might laugh again, but he didn't. "I just figured you maybe needed someone to watch over you," he said. "If that seems creepy, then—"

"It doesn't," I interrupted in a low voice. It actually sounded kind of nice.

"Do you want to talk about yesterday?" It was clear from his question that Slater had filled him in on what happened.

"No." I sighed. "Yes."

"Let me know when you decide."

Stretching out flat on the bed, I stared at the ceiling. "I kind of think maybe I need to—even if I don't want to."

"I can understand that." There was a creak from his chair and then footsteps. His face appeared above me.

Without prior thought, I scooted to the side, patting the bed next to me. Looking surprised, he sat on the edge, but that wasn't what I wanted.

Shoving a pillow at him, I slid over some more, giving him room. "I can't talk about it while you're looking at me."

He grunted, kicking off his shoes. Then he stretched out next to me, making the whole bed shake. "Never thought you'd invite me into your bed."

If Slater had said those words, maybe Julian, too, they would've been a come-on. But I didn't get the sense that Rock was in that kind of mood today. He'd had a shock, too. Just like I'd learned some new and disturbing things about my mom, he'd learned some things about Emilio.

"What was he like?" I asked.

"Who?"

"My... your... Emilio. What was he like?"

Rocco sighed. "I'm not sure I know anymore."

"I feel that way about my mom. But tell me a good time you remember."

There was silence, and I could practically hear the big man next to me sorting through his thoughts. "He taught me to play football."

That surprised me. "American football? Or soccer?"

Rock rolled onto his side to watch me, then he caught himself. "Sorry, you said you couldn't talk if I looked at him."

"It's okay," I said. "Tell me about the football."

"He liked soccer best—most Italians do. But when he moved here, he got into American football. Went to the games. Learned how to throw the ball. And he taught me."

"Did you ever play on a team?" With his size, he probably would've been good at it.

"No. I'd dropped out of school by that point, but sometimes we'd get a game going in the park. It sounds dumb, but it was the first time anyone had done anything... fatherly with me. I mean, how many movies have a scene where the father plays catch with the son?"

"*Field of Dreams*." It was the first thing that came to mind, but then I couldn't think of any more. There were probably lots, though.

"I never had that in foster care. Either the fathers of

the family weren't around, or they just didn't care. Or they were scared of me," he added bitterly.

My hand snaked out, reaching for his. "It was their loss."

"And mine," he said plainly. "Neither one of us had the childhood we deserved, did we? That's why I'm trying so hard to make sure Tommy has a good one."

The anguish on his face tore at me. "Where is Tommy?"

Rock looked away. "He's safe."

"Tell me." My instincts told me that this was something Rock needed to talk about more than his old father figure.

"I dropped him off at his grandparents' house." Rock's voice was barely a whisper, and the tone suggested he was confessing to something horrible.

"He has grandparents?" That didn't make any sense given that Rocco had been raised in foster care.

"His mom's parents. She doesn't want anything to do with him, but they've kept in touch. They send him gifts for his birthday and Christmas."

"Had he met them before?"

"A few times."

His face was so anguished that I reached up to stroke it. The stubble along his jawline scratched my fingertip. "He'll be safe there, won't he?"

"Yes." He took my hand again, holding it in his.

"They're rich. Got a big old mansion in Rhode Island. Gated and all. He'll be safe."

My heart went out to him, even though I didn't quite see the issue. "He'll be okay there, right? I mean, it's not forever." Even as I said this, I realized I didn't know the endgame here. Surely we wouldn't have to stay on the run forever?

"He will." Rock's voice was barely a whisper. Then he looked me in the eyes. "But what if they want to keep him?"

Understanding hit me and I moved closer, my leg touching his. "He's your son. They can't do that."

He shook his head. "If they sought custody—what judge would ever look at them and look at me and not rule against me?"

"A judge who's seen how good you are with him."

The look in his eyes made him seem older than he was. "Look at my lifestyle, Maggie. It's no good for a child. If I really loved Tommy, I would have sent him to live with them years ago."

A tear slipped down my cheeks. His pain was just so raw. "You've made a good life together. You've done the best you could."

He shook his head again. "Sometimes that's not good enough."

"Yes, it is." I closed the distance between us, and his arm went around me. Desperate to stop the sad words pouring from his mouth, I pressed my lips against his. He was unmoving at first, but finally, he pulled me closer and kissed me back. He needed comfort, not blame and shame, right now.

Reaching out, I rubbed his massive bicep as I burrowed against him. I needed comfort just as much as he did. He cradled me against his chest as his mouth moved on mine. There was something so damn enticing being held by him. He made me feel tiny, and I was a fairly petite woman to begin with.

But it was more than that. He made me feel safe—as if nothing could ever harm me while I was in his arms. It was an amazing feeling.

Rock nudged me forward, and I rolled onto my back while he leaned over me. His hand rested lightly on my stomach as he continued to claim my mouth with his own. His palm was so large, his fingers played. Warmth radiated from his skin.

And suddenly, I wanted to feel his skin on mine. I reached between us and tugged my t-shirt up. Desire filled me as his hand rested on the bare skin of my stomach. He groaned, his calloused thumb rubbing along my smooth skin.

Then his hand slid upward. I moaned when his fingertips brushed the underside of my breasts. Then he cupped my entire breast in his hand, the sudden warmth making me gasp.

I arched my back, pressing against his hand.

"You like that?" Rock whispered against my mouth.

"God, yes."

He tugged at my shirt, and I pulled it up over my head, baring myself to him.

"You are so fucking gorgeous," he said as he stared at me. Then his fingers captured my nipple and I groaned.

The nipple he wasn't rubbing felt cold, but he remedied that pretty quickly. He dipped his head and lapped at it, his big tongue engulfing it.

It felt amazing. So damn good. And it wasn't just the sensations, either. It was him. I wanted him. So badly.

But then there was that damn nagging voice in the back of my head. And no matter how the things Rock was doing felt, that voice just wouldn't shut up.

"Rock, wait..." It all felt so good that calling a halt to the action was the last thing I wanted, but I had to. "Please, just listen for a moment."

He didn't let up, teasing my nipples with my talented tongue and fingers.

It was the last thing I wanted to do, but I slid my hand down and captured his chin, forcing him to look up at me. "I care about you," I began. "A lot. But you should know... I also have feelings for Julian and Slater."

"I know," he said.

"I didn't mean to—wait, what do you mean, you know?"

"I know you have feelings for all of us."

"You do? And you're not mad?"

His eyebrows arched. "It's not like I can blame you for liking two guys I think are pretty damn great. They're like brothers to me."

"But—"

He pinched my nipple, making sure he had my complete attention. "Do you want me to have a problem with it?"

"No, but—"

"Because I don't. Do you?"

Even though every cell in my body craved his touch, I forced myself to think about the question. "Well... I've never felt this way about more than one man before."

He smiled. "There's a first time for everything."

Apparently considering the matter closed, he latched onto my nipple again, his teeth grazing my sensitive skin. I stared at the top of his head for another moment, confused. But he was a big boy—a very big boy. If he said it wasn't a problem, then maybe it really wasn't.

Rather than dwell on it any longer at the moment, I let my head fall back on the pillow, enjoying the sensual sensations. I squeezed my thighs together, enjoying the friction as he sucked on first one nipple and then the other.

And then it wasn't enough. I ran my fingers through his short hair. "I need you inside me," I whispered.

He paused and then looked me in the eye. "Are you sure?"

"Yes," I said, still rubbing his head. "I want this. I *need* this. And... I think you do, too."

He nodded. "I do."

I slid my fingers down to the waistband of my sweatpants. Raising my hips, I started to tug my pants down, but he took over. His large hands pulled my sweats off in record time, and suddenly, I was naked.

His eyes raked over my body, and one hand plunged into my hair. "So goddamn beautiful," he said, almost reverently.

But there was only one way I wanted him to worship me. I fumbled at his clothes, wanting him to take them off, and he obliged, standing up next to the bed. His eyes never left me as he pulled off his clothes, and then he was naked, too.

Holy shit.

It wasn't just his muscles that were big. Not just his overall size. He was big all over. Every single inch of him.

In fact, one part of him was bigger than I'd ever seen. I reached a finger out to stroke his huge erection, marveling at its size. His balls were heavy, and they swung when he moved back onto the bed.

Pressing against his naked body, skin to skin, was so much better. His skin was like fire, and I felt a delicious warmth that I'd never experienced. I parted my legs, bringing my knees up, and he moved in between them, hovering over me. He was so strong that he looked like he could maintain that position all day.

Rocco stared into my eyes. "I'm gonna make you come so hard."

I believed him—and I wanted him, so damn badly. I reached between us and stroked his cock. I could barely fit my fingers around it. There was steel under his flushed skin, and I couldn't wait to feel it spread me open.

Fumbling, I angled his cock toward my slit, but he took over. He gripped his cock, hard, and rubbed the tip against my slit.

The groan I let out was carnal and raw. I couldn't remember ever wanting a man this badly. I squeezed my knees around his hips, trying to draw him into me.

And then he plunged his cock in.

I cried out, a moment of pure shock and bliss. It was like being thrown into the deep end of a pool—all the sensations hit all at once. Rock held himself there, waiting for me to adjust to the stretch, while he stared into my eyes. Then I squeezed my walls around him, barely able to do it because of his girth. He took that as a sign to start moving.

I clutched his arms as he slid in and out of me, each time stretching me further. I'd never felt so full before. I never knew it was possible. His cock was hard and hot, and it made me think that the other times I'd had sex had just been a warm-up.

This was the real deal.

Rocco was all man, and as he pushed into me, he made me feel like the luckiest woman on the planet.

"You're so damn tight," he panted.

I bit my lip as he pushed in again. "You're so damn big."

"Am I hurting you?" he asked, looking down at me.

"It feels amazing." Though I'd probably be aching tomorrow, it was totally worth it. "I like feeling you fill me up."

"Good," he grunted. He drove in again, this time tilting my hips up and off the bed. It made it feel even deeper.

My breasts bounced as he thrust into me, and his dark eyes alternated between watching my face and watching my chest. Then on every fourth or fifth stroke, he leaned down to kiss me.

Then he pulled out, and I moaned at the loss. I felt empty, like something was missing. But all he did was to grab my legs and rest my ankles on his shoulders.

When he drove in again, I cried out. The position let him go deeper than ever.

Leaning to one side, Rock picked up my hand and kissed it, like an old-fashioned gentleman. But then he pushed my hand between our bodies until my fingers were resting on my heated mound. "Touch yourself," he said, withdrawing so that just the tip of his cock was inside me.

I strained my hips, trying to draw him back in, but he just stayed poised there, waiting. Finally, I slid my fingertip inside my slit and brushed past my clit. His smile was hungry as he watched the desire flash across my face. He moved his hips in circles, his cock pressing into my inner walls from different angles. It felt good, very good, but I wanted him seated inside me again.,

"Rub your clit," he urged, and I knew what I had to do to make him fill me up again.

My breathing grew ragged as I looked him in the eye, my finger rubbing my swollen clit. "Please, Rock," I begged.

His grin grew cocky. "You want it?"

"Oh god, yes."

"You want me to take you hard?"

I did. Desperately. But I also recognized that the man who was teasing me and working me into a frenzy was a far cry from the one who'd been so upset before, and I was glad. He needed this. We both did.

And right now, I really, really did. "Please take me," I gasped as I worked my clit with my fingers.

He pushed in and I screamed out. This time there was no hesitation. He drove all the way in, pulled back, and in again. I shrieked as he took me, pounding me, making me feel more alive than I ever had in my entire life.

"Harder," I gasped, though I wasn't sure that was possible. Somehow, he did, his face intent as he worked me harder and harder. "I'm close," I gasped.

"Wait," Rock ordered, but it felt damn near impossible.

My eyes closed as my head rolled from side to side. The tension inside me made my legs tremble, and I could barely keep rubbing my clit—except I had to. It felt like if I didn't come soon, I was going to literally die. "Please, Rocco..."

"Wait," he demanded, speeding up his thrusts.

"Don't stop," I panted. "I'm so close."

"Now," he demanded, pushing his cock all the way inside me and holding it there. It pulsed inside me as my inner walls clamped down hard. I screamed, my upper body rising off the bed. Wave after wave of the most intense orgasm of my life poured through me.

"Fuck!" Rocco roared as he came. I could feel his cock emptying inside me, and another wave of pleasure ripped through me.

I grasped his arms, holding on as I tried to ride out the intensity. He cussed and grunted, and I loved the display of raw, masculine power.

I felt like I was second from passing out when he finally eased back. He removed my feet from his shoulders, and he pulled out. He collapsed next to me on the bed, and I turned to face him, my chest still heaving.

Neither one of us were in any position to speak, but he rested his hand on my hip as he stared into my eyes. An aftershock made my body jolt, and he smiled as he felt me move under his hand.

"Holy shit," I finally said when my breathing had calmed enough for speech.

He grinned and leaned forward, pressing his forehead against mine. "Agreed," he said, his voice raspy. His long fingers rubbed the bare skin of my side. "You were so hot when you came on my cock. You looked like a goddess." He reached for the covers.

"No," I said, stopping him. "I don't want the covers. I just want you holding me."

He smiled. "I can do that."

And then he did… for a very long time.

25

ROCCO

I HATED LEAVING Maggie the next day. I'd already left my son, and that had been hard enough. It killed me all over again to leave Maggie, but Julian would take care of her.

And there were other things I needed to take care of.

We were in a tough spot. Any fool could tell you that.

Roselli had turned against us.

A mob boss with powerful connections was determined to put us in the ground. Our years in the family didn't mean jack shit to him. We had to be removed.

But he had made a mistake. It wasn't surprising, really. Unlike the other Dons I knew, Roselli had never bothered to adhere to tradition, and tradition was everything in our world.

No matter how much they loved the dollar, no matter how much they loved to fuck around with prostitutes and snort cocaine, mob bosses did have to obey certain rules. And those applied to everyone—no exceptions.

The rule Roselli had broken?

Don't try and take out your own blood.

Family ties were considered sacred. A blood tie was the strongest of all. Friendships, marriages, and everything else were not as important as this one. You hunt down your brother? Your sister? One or both your folks? You're dead in the water. There was no forgiving that. You could have ranted on about your motives and how strong they were, but that wouldn't do you any good. In the end, you would get a bullet between the eyes. A disgraceful death you brought upon yourself for disrespecting your flesh and blood.

Unfortunately, men like me and my buddies couldn't make a made man like Roselli obey the rules. Made men were considered untouchable. To go after a Don, one of his fellow bosses had to give you the green light. Without it, you couldn't lay a hand on them. Doing that equaled a death sentence—and even more certain than the one we were under now.

Even talking to another Don about it was a risk.

There was also a good chance you'd get whacked yourself, in case the reason you provided didn't sound good to the Don you requested permission from. Simply put, unless a made man had done something despicable, you'd wind up dead in his stead.

But I couldn't leave this alone.

Not with four lives hanging in the balance.

Slater, Julian and I were used to this shit. This had been part of our lives for a long time. Rival crews had gone after us in the past and we had come out on top. Even if we had ended up with a bullet in our heads, some would have called it "fair." We weren't angels—everybody on the street knew that.

Maggie on the other hand? No. She couldn't have that threat looming over her. She couldn't have wise guys chasing after her, because a mob boss was too greedy to follow his father's last will and testament.

I *had* to reach out to a Don. Amid this insanity, discussing Roselli's antics was perhaps the sanest call.

So, the day after Maggie and I had shared that incredible moment in bed, I reached out to Don Michael Gambini. I respected the man. Unlike my boss, he rewarded loyalty. He knew the rules, and for the most part, he played by them.

"DeLuca. Someone said you were dead." He sounded as if he hadn't believed it, and his next words proved it. "I had a feeling you'd call."

"Hello, Don Gambini. May I ask why?"

"Call it a hunch. What do you want?"

"Could I meet with you, sir? Someplace public. Today if possible."

"A meeting? What for? So you can walk me through what you did to Baxter? It was you, DeLuca. Either you or one of your guys. I know that now."

"This is much bigger than me and my guys. Believe me, Don Gambini. You're going to want to hear what I have to say."

"Elaborate."

"It's about my boss. That's all I can say on the phone."

Gambini sighed. "Enrique's. Times Square, tonight, eight-thirty."

"Thank you, sir. I'll be there."

After the call ended, I couldn't quite identify the Don's tone. Angry? Except he was one of the most level-headed men I knew. Maybe... resigned? That seemed more like it. Dons didn't usually speak ill of each other, but he had to know what kind of man Nick was. And knowing what kind of man Gambini was, I doubted he approved.

That didn't take away the risk of going to speak to him about my boss, but it had to be done. For all our sakes.

. . .

Later that evening, Slater and I crossed Times Square. For once, he was calm and collected. I wasn't. I kept checking my watch as the noise of traffic grew and dropped. The two of us arrived at Enrique's about ten minutes early, but Gambini was already there. To me, that revealed concern on his part.

The older man was sitting at the best table in the back—no surprise there. Four of his men were at tables all around him, while one more was sitting next to him. This was a classic example of a Don's behavior. He had plenty of men watching over him, hiding in plain sight.

"Sit down," he said, gesturing to the two seats in front of him.

"Don Gambini." I tipped my head down to show my respect to him, Slater following suit afterwards.

"Screw the niceties." He leaned forward. "I know one of you offed Baxter. The question is 'who.'"

"No." I shook my head in refusal, maintaining eye contact with him. "With all due respect, the real question is 'why.' We've known each other a long time, Don Gambini. You know Winslow and Knight, too. You really think we'd take out someone just for kicks?"

"DeLuca, I've been a player since before you were born," he remarked, his voice stiff. "I've seen shit you wouldn't even dream was possible. Try again. And you'd better impress me."

"Your man was freelancing the night he was killed," Slater interjected, his voice steady as a rock. "Don Roselli had hired him to blow up The Rusty Bucket as punishment for us casing a bank without telling him. That's what Baxter said anyway. He'd been lied to, though."

"That's right," I confirmed with a firm nod. "Recently, we found out that Emilio Roselli had an illegitimate daughter, named Maggie Owens. Guess what? She's a barmaid at The Rusty Bucket. She was the real target, because as it turns out, Emilio Roselli wanted the bulk of his money to go to her. Not his son."

"Hmm..." Gambini mused, lowering his gaze. "I'd be well within my rights to have my men shoot you dead just for saying all this bullshit. I'm sure you know that."

"Of course we do, sir," Slater spoke, his voice low but intense. "But it gets worse. Just days ago, Don Roselli ordered us to kill that same woman—his half-sister. And when we didn't do that immediately, he sent two gunmen to take us out in Napolitana."

"That's what that was about?" Gambini arched an eyebrow. "It wasn't a bad little restaurant."

"Sir, I don't think you—"

"I understand the implications, young man. You're saying Roselli is way out of line."

"Yeah." I gave a swift nod. "He put out a hit on his

own sister. Don't you think he should be punished for that?"

"That's not for you to decide."

"No," Slater agreed, looking the older man in the eye. "But it is for you to decide. This isn't the way we do things."

"I'll admit, killing a young woman isn't ideal."

"Not just a young woman, Don Gambini," I said. "His kin. His sister. I thought the organization had some principles."

"Let me ask you something," Gambini said, his eyes sharp. "You've been in Roselli's family for what? Fifteen years? When was the last time you heard a Don got whacked for breaking the rules?"

His question had me thinking for several seconds. Slater and I looked at each other, an ugly truth setting in. Judging by my friend's demeanor, he couldn't think of an example any more than I could.

"Never," I murmured, pursing my lips.

"So, you realize the position you're putting me in," Gambini went on, bringing his gaze to Slater first, and then, to me.

"He's dangerous," Slater said. "When he doesn't follow the rules, he puts us all at risk."

"Quit blowing smoke up my ass," Gambini said.

"Are you saying it's not true?" I asked.

"Remember who you're talking to," Gambini warned.

"I don't mean it like that," I said. "I've just always heard that protecting your blood relatives comes before anything else. But you're right, we haven't been involved as long as you have. So I'm asking you."

The Don sidestepped my question. "Think of what you're asking of me," he said instead. "You come here with some crazy story about Roselli's bastard daughter without a shred of proof, you admit you took out Baxter, *and* you want my approval to go after your boss? You boys are either insane or have balls of steel."

"Or both," Slater joked, and I elbowed him hard. Now wasn't the time.

"I realize it's far-fetched, but..."

"Far-fetched?! That's an understatement. But if you get me proof—scientific proof—that she's Roselli's half-sister, I'll consider it. But even if I sanction the hit, have you given any thought to how you'd do it? Because he'll have about two dozen pricks like you guarding him at all times, now that you've gone rogue."

"Gone rogue?" Slater repeated.

Gambini arched an eyebrow. "Well, you're not at Roselli's beck and call, and you're clearly not dead, so what else is he to think?"

"We'll worry about how to do it when the time

comes," I answered. "If I get you the evidence you need, will you give us the go-ahead?"

"Just run that DNA test, DeLuca," Gambini said, his voice low and firm. "I'll think about it."

"Thank you for your time, Don Gambini," I said as we rose. The meeting hadn't gone exactly how I'd expected, but we were walking away unharmed. That was something.

Once we were on the street, I turned to Slater. "Call Julian, catch him up, and have him get a hair from Maggie. Then we'll get something from Roselli so we can do the DNA test."

"How?" Slater asked skeptically.

"Probably another visit to Connors. He can get it. And I want a copy of the will, too."

"He's not going to be very happy to see us," Slater warned. He'd heard all about Juliana and my visit last time.

"I'll make it nice. Besides, he's already told us about Maggie. That's the big one—the rest is small potatoes compared to that."

I kept thinking about the Don's words as I navigated through the Manhattan traffic. Gambini had made very good points. We had screwed with him, we had brought him an insane scenario, just so he could authorize a hit on Don Roselli. Although I could understand his frustration, his wealth, power, and status prevented him from comprehending the position we were in.

An untouchable man like him didn't have to worry about hits. He could target others but couldn't become a target himself. But us? We were desperate men. And desperate men sometimes did desperate things.

26

MAGGIE

"Morning," I said to Julian, when it was his turn to babysit me again. I couldn't put my finger on it, but I felt a little less comfortable around him than I had at first. He'd been the first of the three that I'd felt a connection to, back on that night when the three of them showed up, bloodied and injured, at Zoey's house. Back when Piper had fixed them up.

But then he and I had gotten hot and heavy at Rocco's house, and I'd cut things short. Did Julian resent that?

He might—especially if he had an idea of what Rocco and I had been up to recently.

I sighed as I poured myself some cereal. I still couldn't get that encounter with Rocco out of my head. It had started off as two sad people comforting each other, and it had turned into something amazing. Every time I thought of it, it made my cheeks flush and my clit ache.

But Julian's distant attitude was bringing me down. "How are things back in New York?" I asked.

He just grunted as he looked at his phone screen. Either he wasn't a morning person, or he was pissed about something.

The image of the bar at the Rusty Bucket popped into mind. I missed the hustle and bustle there. I missed my customers. I'd called in to work and claimed I had a family emergency a few days ago. That was true—but the emergency was that I didn't know who my family was. Or at least not my father.

"Thanks for enlightening me," I said, but there wasn't any heat behind my voice. "How about the other project, the DNA. Has the university gotten the results yet?" He'd taken in a strand of my hair and a glass that Roselli—my possible half-brother—had drank out of. I was a little unclear on how Rock and Slater had obtained it.

Julian set his phone down. "I was just checking, and no."

Okay, maybe he wasn't angry. That was good. "Did you eat already?" I wasn't exactly a domestic goddess, but I could fix him some eggs.

"I'm good."

Carrying my bowl, I sat down across the table from him. "So, after we get those results back, what will we do? If they're a match I mean. Do we get them notarized or something?"

Julian stared at me, his eyebrow raised. "This is the underworld, not the DMV."

"Well, I don't know how it works," I said defensively. "Even with a copy of the will, Roselli might dispute the legitimacy of it."

Those mesmerizing blue eyes rolled. "You crack me up sometimes." He wasn't laughing when he said it, however. "Roselli is a cheap, mean motherfucker. He's not going to dispute anything, because he's got a faster way of dealing with this—putting a bullet in your head. We'll try and take him out first, if we get the okay from the organization. If we don't...?"

"Yeah?"

"Use your imagination."

I knew I shouldn't have been shocked or scared. And yet, at his last sentence, I was both. I wasn't used to having my life threatened. I hadn't adjusted to this new reality yet. I suspected it would take a while for me to do that. To make matters worse, I couldn't forget who had put me in this situation. The woman I had looked up to my whole life. My mother.

Julian was staring out the window, presumably at

the beautiful scenery, but when he glanced back at me, he scowled. "Don't cry."

"I'm not." Or at least not much.

"I'm not trying to be harsh, but well, this situation we're in sucks. This isn't a matter that can be resolved in a court of law. To be honest, it's probably not going to end well—for any of us."

His words, and the manner in which he delivered them, chilled me. "Then why bother? Why hide up here? Why not just go back to the city and take our changes?"

He stared at me. "Do you *want* a shorter life?"

"No."

"Then we stay here."

"Fine," I said stiffly. "Good thing I have such pleasant company."

Julian looked away, but not before I caught the corner of his mouth twitching upward. "Glad you think so," he muttered under his breath.

After that, I did the dishes. Then I made the bed. I even cleaned the bathroom. I was completely out of ideas. The guys wouldn't even let me use my phone because they said someone might be able to track it. They got to use theirs, though, which was annoying. They told me theirs were different. Not sure if I believed that, though.

By midmorning, I was bored out of my mind. Julian

had gone out to check the perimeter—which may or may not have been an excuse to get some fresh air. I decided to take advantage of his absence to try to remember some poses I'd learned in a yoga class at the community center ages ago.

Balancing on one foot on the shag rug in front of the sofa, I attempted one pose after another. None of them were super accurate, but the stretching felt good.

At least until Julian strode back into the cabin while I had my head down and my ass up in the air. Stupid downward facing dog. It was the only pose I was sure I'd gotten right.

Julian whistled. "And I thought the view was good out there."

I scowled, dropping onto the carpet and crossing my legs. "Well, what else am I supposed to do?"

He sat down in an armchair across from me. "I'm sure as hell not going to stop you. Proceed."

"Get your cheap thrills elsewhere, pal."

"Those are in short supply lately." He shook his head ruefully. "You're really not going to continue?"

"Of course not."

He cocked his head to the side. "How about if I make lunch?"

"Nope."

"How about if I give you a million dollars?"

"Nope." But then I thought of something. I'd spent

so long worrying about if my supposed half-brother was going to kill me that I hadn't spent much time considering the inheritance itself. It seemed like a real longshot that I'd end up with it, but it would be good to at least know about it. And it was a way to pass the time that didn't involve mooning Julian. "Did Nick really inherit millions?"

Julian sighed, apparently accepting that no more yoga was going to happen. "Yeah. And not just that. He's got a bunch of businesses, too."

"Legal ones?"

"Both kinds." His forehead wrinkled as he thought about it. "On the legal—ish—side are some spas, tanning salons, nail salons, and I think a hardware store or two."

"And those could be... mine?"

"They would've been already, if the will had been followed."

"Weird." It just didn't add up. "Why would Emilio leave those to me when he never even wanted to know me?"

Julian's expression darkened. "Well, he knew his son, so must've known he was an asshole." He sighed. "I can't tell you why he did the things he did, but I found him to be a fair man. A good man, even, which is rare in this business."

I hugged my knees to my chest as I thought about it.

"What if I just renounce my claim to all those things? Would Nick leave me alone?"

"No," Julian said shortly. "He wants you out of his hair permanently."

"Great."

Julian was staring in my direction, but I didn't think he was really seeing me. He seemed lost in thought. But then he abruptly met my eyes. "Want to make lunch together?"

"Sure."

Twenty-four hours later, all three men were in the cabin, making it feel claustrophobic. Rocco had actually given me a kiss on the cheek when he arrived. It made me blush, since it was in front of the other two, but I liked it all the same.

Slater had handed me a shopping bag. Inside were two paperbacks, a handful of magazines, and a bar of chocolate. "Julian said you were going a bit stir-crazy," he said with a wink.

They also brought lunch, some Chinese food they'd gotten along the way. For a while, all concerns left my mind as I enjoyed the tangy chicken and the delicious sticky rice.

Then Julian's phone rang.

We all tensed up and stared at him while he answered.

"Yes, this is he." His eyes settled on me, and I could guess who was calling. Tension filled me and I tapped my fingers nervously on the table.

All Julian was doing was nodding and saying "uh-huh," and the anticipation was killing me. When Slater reached over and stilled my nervous fingers with his, I latched on, squeezing his hand nervously.

Finally, Julian hung up.

"Well?" Rocco demanded when I couldn't find my voice.

Julian turned to me. "You and Nick share DNA. You're half-siblings."

My shoulders slumped as I continued to squeeze Slater's hand. I'd been expecting this, but still... it was somehow still a shock.

"We knew this was the likely outcome," Rocco said gently. "Roselli's put the hit on you for a reason. You're a threat to him."

That was almost laughable. How could I be a threat to anyone? But it wasn't really me, it was my existence. And my parentage.

"Guess it's official," Julian said. "We're at war with the Roselli family."

A tear slipped down my cheek. "Doesn't this mean that I'm part of the Roselli family?"

Slater squeezed my hand once more before pulling his back. "Yes, but a far superior branch of it."

"And that's not what he meant," Rocco said, jerking his head at Julian. "By family, he meant the entire organization."

"Oh, is that all?" I gave a watery little laugh.

"It is daunting. But the next step is to pick up the documentation of the test and take it to Don Gambini," Slater said.

"We will," Rocco said.

As I looked from one man to another, I couldn't hold back the tears.

"What is it?" Rocco asked gently.

"I can't believe my mom kept this from me."

"If you ask me, she wanted to protect you," Rock said. "That name would have been a burden. Your mom probably wanted you to have a normal life. To be an average nobody. Roselli's life ain't what you'd call normal."

"Rocco's downplaying it," Julian commented. "You don't know what you'd be in for, if your name was 'Roselli' instead of 'Owens.' In fact, no one can, until they've seen it for themselves. I could tell you a thousand stories of people who wound up dead, because at some point, they screwed up. *That's* how easy it is for someone to lose their life in the so-called family, Maggie. One mistake is all it takes. So, yeah—I agree. Your mom probably saw what was going down in your dad's life and decided to keep you out of the loop for your own good."

"He wasn't my dad," I said swiftly. But then I thought of Seth. Seth hadn't been my dad, either. "Excuse me. I need to be alone."

The guys exchanged looks but didn't say anything when I retreated to the back bedroom.

To cry.

Again.

That felt like all I'd been doing lately. Crying and sleeping. But then I remembered sleeping with Rocco —or not sleeping, actually—and those sexy memories made me feel a little better.

An hour later, when the knock at the door came, I hoped it was him, but it wasn't. It was Julian.

"Can I come in?"

"Sure."

He ignored the chair with my clothes slung over it and strode right to the bed. I scooted back against the headboard, and he sat on the edge. "You okay?"

"Not really."

"Fair enough," he said. He had on a button-down shirt with the sleeves rolled up. The hairs on his forearm caught the light from the window. "It's a lot to take in." He sighed. "And I know I haven't exactly been helping you through it."

"I thought you were mad at me."

He raked his fingers through his hair. "I've been

trying to keep you alive. We all have. It's not an easy job, especially since we're also trying to keep ourselves alive."

"I realize that."

"I don't know that you do. You've been up here, completely isolated. And yes, bored as hell. But you haven't seen all the precautions we're taking. To make sure no one jumps us when we're in the city. To make sure no one follows us back here. To make sure no one finds you. Organized crime is a huge business, Maggie. Their reach is pretty much endless. They have money and power."

"So you're saying it's hopeless?"

"Of course not. But... maybe instead of thinking of your mother lying to you, it would be easier to focus on that side of things."

"The power?" I couldn't imagine ever having that for myself.

"Yeah, and the money. There's a lot you could do with that kind of money."

"Like be a crime boss?"

He shrugged. "If you wanted to. It's a seductive life—the life the three of us chose." He paused, frowning. "Well, maybe we didn't choose it, but we ended up here. But you could do good with that money."

I frowned. "It's dirty money."

"Then do something clean with it. A girl I knew in

foster care, she now runs a shelter for women on the run from domestic violence. They could always use a cash influx. Or you could fund a no-kill animal shelter. Or buy a hospital wing. Hell, you could go to law school like you always wanted to. Become a lawyer, and rob from the rich to give to the poor."

In spite of myself, I laughed. "That's Robin Hood, not a lawyer."

"Whatever." He waved that away. "I don't know why Emilio wanted you to have his money any more than I know why he never got to know you. But—if we make it out of this, there'll be some perks down the road."

Perks. I nearly snorted. Was that how he referred to millions of dollars? But he was trying to cheer me up, in his own way. His own way just seemed to be grumpier than it used to be.

I opened my mouth to thank him, but something entirely different came out. "When I said before that I thought you were mad at me, you didn't deny it."

He tilted his head to the side, studying me. "It's been a busy time. Everyone's under a lot of stress."

"I get that. But you just did it again. You switched topics."

He shook his head ruefully. "You remind me of a teacher I had in middle school. Mrs. Parker. She never let me get away with non-answers, either." He looked away, exhaling loudly. "I may have been... a bit out of sorts."

"A bit?" I scoffed.

"Maybe a little more than a bit." His blue eyes locked in on my face. "I was jealous."

That was the last thing I expected him to say. "Of the inheritance?"

"Of your relationship with my friends. You seem to be moving forward with Rock and Slater, but going nowhere with me."

I stared at him, not sure what to say.

"You look like a deer caught in headlights," he observed. "I'm not accusing you of anything—just stating facts."

"It's not a fact," I said slowly. "It's just how things worked out."

"Things didn't work out very well for us in Rock's apartment," he said.

"Because it was *Rock's* apartment," I emphasized. "This is all new to me. You think I regularly go around falling for three different men at once? It feels wrong but it also feels right, somehow. I don't even understand it myself, but I know that it only can feel right if there are some boundaries. If no one gets hurt. And getting frisky in Rocco's living room felt wrong."

"Getting frisky?" he mocked, and I smiled a little. It was a rather prissy phrase. Then his expression turned serious. "Do you mean it?"

"About boundaries?"

"About falling for three men at once."

I nodded. "I never expected to—but then again, a hell of a lot of unexpected things have been happening lately."

"That's for damn sure," he said. "You're sure you haven't been trying to freeze me out?"

An impish thought took hold. "If you come closer, I'll prove it to you."

He grinned and immediately slid toward me, his knee lightly touching mine. "Can I kiss you, Maggie?"

I leaned in close, my gaze on his full mouth. "That depends."

"On what?"

"If you'll climb in bed and fool around with me for a while afterwards."

He flashed me a grin. "I thought you'd never ask."

27

SLATER

"We've got Roselli by the balls now."

Rocco couldn't hide his excitement.

Holding that pack of papers, he was in high spirits that morning while he and I were on our way to the meeting with Don Gambini. In his mind, we were one step closer to the approval we desperately needed. One step closer to a simple "go ahead" that would rid us of our joke of a Don and mark the end of his reign.

Most importantly, it would mean getting Maggie out of his crosshairs.

That was, *if* it worked, and I wasn't so sure.

Rocco seemed to be forgetting something basic about mob bosses.

Their crews could shoot at each other to their heart's content. They could have one, two, or a half-dozen casualties at a time, but no mob boss would lose any sleep over that. This was the nature of our job and the perils that came with it. Was any Don going to mourn those losses? Shed tears for a loyal member of his crew?

Hell, no.

Their next move was always this: hiring more men.

Nobody is irreplaceable. Everybody is expendable.

But for the Dons, things were different. They didn't order hits on each other. There was a balance across the city. Everyone knew what they should be doing and where. For instance, Hell's Kitchen was Gambini's turf. He could sell guns and push coke to any interested parties. Most of Brooklyn belonged to Roselli. He could lend money and sell methamphetamine to all the desperate souls out there, and take advantage of junkies' need for a hit.

So, by taking out a Don, that balance would be disrupted. There would be confusion, in which players would stake their claim to the affected areas. For a while at least, there would be a lot of unrest and a lot of shooting.

Public shooting to be exact.

That was the entire organization's worst nightmare.

Bullets flying all over the place in broad daylight, in front of dozens or even hundreds of people. Witnesses could give bosses a headache. None of us could control what they told the cops. Mob dealings should always remain secret. Dons hated the notion of being exposed. Even a simple deal like a gun trade should never be disclosed. If that happened, they had to tie up loose ends by killing everyone involved. They didn't mind that, but they preferred doing things in the shadows. No one could see them in the dark.

Regardless of all that, my attention was split that morning. Part of it was on Maggie.

Part of it was always on Maggie these days.

And that wasn't like me. Don't get me wrong, I liked women. I liked the ones who stripped at the club. I liked the ones who went down on me after I bought them a nice dinner. Hell, I even liked the pudgy worker at the corner bakery who always gave me an extra Danish.

But I *really* liked Maggie. She was gorgeous, smart, and funny. And different. I'd never met a woman like her.

And right now, she was in danger.

Which is why we were walking into Enrique's again.

Don Gambini was even at the same table. It was déjà vu all over again, as the joke went. Gambini seemed to be a creature of habit.

His men were still all around, but that was where the similarities ended. The seat beside him was empty. For some reason, he'd sent his right-hand man away.

"Good morning, Don Gambini." Rocco used his

indoor voice and was on his best behavior as he set a large brown envelope down on the table. "The DNA results."

The elderly Don tore open the envelope and pulled a pair of reading glasses out of his jacket pocket. He squinted at the first page of the packet for quite some time. Then he sighed. "Oh, Nicolo, you stupid, stupid boy."

"It's just as we told you, sir," I reminded him of our words during our previous meeting. "Roselli has an illegitimate sister and he's trying to get her out of the picture. You don't do that with family."

Gambini looked up. "I guess he doesn't consider her family."

"But Emilio did. He cared enough to leave her the vast majority of his fortune."

The Don didn't look convinced, so I tried again. "She's got Emilio's blood, sir. His genes. His DNA. She's his child even more so than Nick is, because she's not an asshole."

That line received a faint grin from the Don, but then it quickly faded. "Your boss is guilty. You know it—I know it. You don't fuck with family. He should have taken it like a man and given his sister her cut, no matter how much it was."

My heart sank. "I sense a 'but' coming."

"You're right, Winslow," he admitted. "What

happens to Roselli's enterprises if you remove him? There's going to be chaos in the streets. Rival crews will want to take advantage of this disorder and step in to claim Roselli's turf."

"That's a problem for another day," Rocco responded. "We'll deal with it. You won't have to worry about chaos. All you need to do is give us the green light. What's right is right, Don Gambini. Roselli must pay."

"Maybe we should resolve this quietly," he suggested, interlocking his fingers. "Maybe I could tell him to step down and retire. He'll just take a few million and disappear in Sicily. He owns a lot of real estate over there."

I jumped in before Rocco could respond. "With any other Don, that would work. It would be the honorable thing to do." Rocco gave me a side glance, trying to judge where I was going with this. "But Roselli isn't honorable. That guy is so cheap that he won't even tip a hobo for wiping dust off his windshield. You really think he'll settle for a couple of million bucks and move to Italy? Because I don't."

"Slater's right," Rocco agreed. "There's no way Roselli will just go away quietly. He won't let anyone else touch what he thinks is his. He'd probably take Maggie out even if there was no chance for him to stay in power."

Something about the way Rocco said her name seemed to have caught Gambini's attention. "You like the girl."

Rocco nodded.

"And you, too, Winslow."

"Yes."

The Don shook his head. "I suppose that's your worry. As for Roselli, I know how cheap that fucker is. But this still isn't an easy call to make. I still don't know how you're going to maintain order in the streets after he's gone."

"With all due respect, we've been doing this for a long time. It's our job," I said carefully, my tone calm. "Once Roselli's gone, we'll gather up every gang leader and explain things to them. If they step out of line, if they try to claim even a block, they're dead. Simple as that."

"I'm going to need more than that," Gambini stated, resolve lining his face. "Your word just isn't enough. I don't care what you have to do. Hire mules; people you trust; people you know won't fuck you over, but keep distribution up and running. After all, I think you'll benefit from this, too. That drug money is going to go straight into your pocket."

Drug money. Just hearing those two words together made my stomach churn with disgust.

I hated drugs. So did Rocco and Julian for that

matter. We'd never touched them—not even a joint. Now, Gambini's terms involved us taking over the drug trade in Roselli's stead. Nothing could change. Every gang in the area had to stay out of this business, because he was too afraid of the repercussions.

Rocco gave me a long look. After all these years together, he could read me, and I could read him. And I knew, as certainly as I knew my name, what he'd tell me if he could. We weren't doing this for us—we were doing it for Maggie. All of this was for her, to keep her alive.

"We'll do it," Rocco told the Don. "We'll start recruiting people tonight. They'll replace Roselli's guys. There won't be a gap in ownership on our turf. You have my word."

As Rocco and Gambini shook hands, I worked to keep my face neutral. This was going to change everything.

Gambini looked satisfied. "You have my permission to take care of Roselli. Dump him off the top of the Empire State Building for all I care."

"Thank you, sir," Rocco said, and I nodded in agreement.

"Just remember, you only get one shot at this, boys," Gambini cautioned. "If you fuck up, Roselli's going to be so pissed that he's going to send every wise guy in New York after you."

And on that note, we took our leave. I'd barely made it to the sidewalk before I gripped Rocco's arm, stopping him in his tracks.

"So now we're dealing drugs? For fucking real? Tell me you were jerking Gambini off."

"Of course I was," Rocco said, furrowing his brow. "I wanted him to believe I gave a fuck about those goddamn drugs. You know I don't—I never will. Plus Maggie would probably never speak to us again."

"But he's right. We have to do something to prevent a power grab."

"We will," Rocco said with a frown. "But I guarantee it's not going to be us pushing drugs."

"So, what are we going to do?"

"Hell if I know. Let's talk to Julian and figure something out."

"Sounds good."

And it also meant we'd be seeing a certain gorgeous young woman again, really soon.

28

MAGGIE

It was a repeat of yesterday. Rocco and Slater were heading back here with lunch. Julian and I were cooped up at the cabin. The only difference was, Julian and I were on much better terms.

Oh, and then there was the little fact that we were on pins and needles about what Rocco and Slater might have found out. I didn't know what I was more worried about—if Don Gambini said that they could take out Roselli or if he said they couldn't.

Both seemed pretty damn dangerous options to me. So much so that I hadn't been able to enjoy my morning with Julian, even though I sure as hell had enjoyed fooling around with him on the bed yesterday.

Then they were there with good news. Gambini had approved the hit. Julian gave a whoop and picked me up, spinning me around. He set me down and before I could even catch my balance, Rocco gathered me up in a bone-crunching hug. Then Slater did, too. It felt weird to be celebrating the possible demise of my half-brother, but if it was a question of him versus the four of us, I voted for the four of us. Besides, from everything everyone had said, Nick sounded like a real jerk.

But then, during lunch, they'd dropped a bombshell.

Slater broke the news. "Gambini had a condition to sanction the hit on Roselli. You know about his meth distribution network, don't you?"

"Yeah," Julian nodded. I, of course, was clueless. "What about it?"

"He wants us to take over it," Slater explained, making me stare at him in disbelief. "When Roselli's gone, we're supposed to use our own mules to move the product. That's what Rocco promised him anyway." Slater glowered at the big man. "He even gave him his word."

"When the fuck did we decide we wanted in on the drug trade?" Julian asked, narrowing his eyes.

"We didn't," Rocco said, his voice dropping in volume and intensity. "Gambini knows it's going to be hell out there if Roselli drops dead. Gangs will swoop in and try to take advantage of the mess to establish their own distribution network. He wants to avoid this shit. I had to make a call, or else he wouldn't have given us the green light to kill Roselli."

"That's a shit call." Julian eyed him with anger. "I've seen what meth does to those junkies. I swore to myself I'd never get anywhere near that shit."

"Well, we can reverse it," Rock said. "I'll just give Roselli a call and invite him up here to take us out. I'm sure he can be here by dinner."

Julian rolled his eyes.

"Do you actually *like* being on the run?" Rocco demanded, the sarcasm gone. "Taking all these precautions? Being vigilant every fucking second of the day? For me, it means not seeing my son, and leaving him with people who might not give him back." Anger filled his voice, which wasn't usual. When Rocco got upset, his voice usually got lower.

I stood up, abandoning my food, and walked over to him. I hugged him from behind, leaning down to talk to him. "You did the only thing you could do," I said. "And we all know that." I shot a look at the other guys. "You had to get Gambini's approval or none of us stood a chance."

"Yeah, but now we have to be able to do what we—what Rock—said we'd do," Julian said. "And I don't know how we'd do that even if we wanted to. We don't have any men who work in distribution. We don't know anything about that side of the business. We don't even know where to start."

"Gambini's all about maintaining some kind of order on the streets," Slater added. "When Roselli's out of the picture, his distributors will lose their jobs. The drug trade business in Brooklyn will be up for grabs. Without a new player in place *immediately*, things are going to get nasty out there. Gambini wants us to be that new player, but we've never been involved in the drug trade. All we ever did was collect from Roselli's mules."

That was sobering. There was so much about this that I didn't understand. But there was one thing I did know. "Blaming Rock's not going to do any good. He's doing all of this for us."

"He's doing all of this for *you*," Julian said, but he didn't sound resentful.

Rocco nodded and then reached back, cupping the back of my head. He pulled me in for a quick kiss.

My heart warmed even as my mind was still in worry-mode. These men were risking everything for me, and there wasn't even anything I could do to help. I didn't know their world, but I did know the real world. And in the real world, money ruled.

That's what it was all about.

That's why the brother I'd never even met wished to

have me killed. So he could spend his millions, without worrying about his late father's illegitimate child.

I chose my words carefully. "The problem isn't really the drug operation, is it? It's the money it represents, right?"

Slater nodded, looking at me thoughtfully. "I guess you could say that."

"Roselli's drugs..." I started, eyeing the guys one at a time. "What does he sell, exactly?"

"Crystal meth," Rocco answered. "He's got a bunch of chemists manufacturing it near Rochester. I've been to that place; it's deep in the woods. The front is perfect. That lab is in the basement of an old sawmill."

"What if, uh..." I paused, thinking of how to phrase my next sentence. "What if something were to happen to that lab? Not the people working in it. Just the lab."

"What are you saying?" Julian asked.

"Destroy it," I heard myself say in a clear, assertive voice. For the first time ever, I wondered if I did have something of my biological father in me after all. "Just hear me out here. The destruction of that lab will put a dent in Roselli's cash flow, but without any lab, there'll be nothing for rival crews to take over."

"Is it just me, or is she starting to sound like a crime boss?" Slater said.

"Roselli knows we're on the run and laying low,"

Julian said, thinking out loud. "He wouldn't expect us to make a move against him."

"He'll figure out it was us," Rocco said glumly.

"What's he going to do, though," Julian said. "Kill us twice?"

"Or twice as painfully," Slater said. Then he caught sight of my face, which I could feel the blood draining out of, and hastily said, "Just kidding."

Yeah, right.

This was a whole new world for me. A disturbing, dark, horrifying world. It wasn't my choice to be in it. It sure as hell hadn't been my mom's choice. She'd wanted to keep me away from it, even if it meant lying to me.

But the simple fact of the matter was that I was in it, and so were these men. We were in it together, in fact. So it was time to stop being a useless accessory. A pleasant distraction for whichever man was in charge of guarding me that day.

We were in this together, and we were in for the fight of our lives. So it was time for me to do my part.

I'd never gone down without a fight, and I wasn't about to start now.

29

MAGGIE

Despite the fact that it was my idea, I was a nervous wreck the day the men set out to destroy the drug lab. There was just so much that could go wrong. They could get hurt. They could be killed. For some reason, I kept having visions of them being trapped behind a locked door somewhere, banging on it frantically while fire and lethal fumes moved closer and closer.

It was an image I couldn't get out of my mind.

But they were ready. They'd spent night after night on research. It was Julian's moment to shine. He understood the technical side of everything better than the others, and he was the planner of the group.

As for me? All I could really do was to give each man a warm send-off before they went. And I did, one by one. I pulled Slater into the bathroom when he passed by in the hallway. His kiss was explosive, and he ran his hands all over me.

I found Julian outside, checking under the hood of their getaway vehicle to make sure everything was in order. His kiss started slowly but grew into an infernal.

And then there was Rocco. He was the one who sought me out, waiting until the other two had gone out front. I moved into his arms, but there was something else he wanted first.

"This is the address and phone number for where Tommy is." He held out a slip of paper. "Memorize it and then destroy it. If I don't make it back, I want you to go and find him. Please."

Tears sprang to my eyes. "Don't say that," I protested, but I took the address and let him gather me into his arms.

"I have to," he said gruffly. "I'm a father. He'll be okay with them, but he's going to need you."

"He needs *you*." This conversation was making me even more upset than I had been. Rock was the strongest, bravest man I knew. I hated that he thought he might not return.

He looked me in the eye. "Hopefully, he'll have me for a long time. But if something happens, I want you to look out for him."

I nodded. Of course I'd do that for Rocco. But I

wasn't sure how much good I'd be to Tommy. "He barely knows me."

Rocco cupped my face in his hands. "But *I* know you. You've got a good heart. My boy needs someone like you in his life. Can you do that?"

"Of course." I looked into his dark eyes. "But come back to me. Please."

"I'll do my best."

His kiss was slow and thorough, but it was tainted by the salty taste of my tears.

While they were gone, I paced. I cleaned. I did whatever I could to pass the time. At least they'd left me with a phone that was safe to use. And a gun—two, actually. Slater had shown me how to use both. Trying to match the level of vigilance the guys always had, I kept one at the ready. Then I watched an online video on how to take apart and clean the other one. I did that a half dozen times until the movements felt familiar.

And then I waited. Worried. And paced some more.

Finally, at nearly four in the morning, headlights flashed across the cabin. I leaped up from the chair I'd dragged over to the window, praying that I'd see three men climb out of the car.

And I did.

Thank god.

"It's done," Rocco said when I raced up to him. His face had soot on it, and his shirt was torn, but he looked okay. Julian and Slater did, too.

Alcohol flowed in abundance after that. My stomach had spent too many hours tied up in knots to partake of much, but the men deserved to celebrate their victory. So I became their bartender, which was actually fun. I'd missed mixing drinks more than I thought.

But eventually, the stress of all the waiting, worrying that one of them might be killed, caught up with me. My eyes started to droop as I sat on the couch, snuggled in between Slater and Julian. One of them picked me up and carried me to the bedroom. I barely mustered the strength to kick off my shoes and strip off my clothes before I collapsed onto the mattress.

It had to be the middle of the afternoon by the time I woke up. Someone had pulled the bedroom curtains shut, but light still slipped through. Cool air did, too—a little too cool. I swung my legs over the side of the bed, my eyes barely open, as I tried to muster up the energy to go close the window.

But then I sensed a presence. Someone had moved to the window, just like I was going to do. I opened my eyes to slits, the buzz in my head reminding me that I'd had a bit too much to drink last night. My eyes widened when I took in the nearly naked form in front of me.

Julian had his back to me as he messed with the window coverings, giving me a chance to take in the powerful muscles of his back and the cute butt that was clad only in black boxers.

"Nice," I said, and he turned, startled, but that didn't stop his eyes from roaming all over my bare skin.

"I didn't mean to wake you," he said softly. "I just thought you might be cold." He ran a hand over his short beard, which looked in need of a trim. "I just woke up, too."

The sight of his bulging chest muscles and those chiseled abs generated a deep longing within me. Plus there was the fact that he was alive, and so were Slater and Rocco.

That made *me* feel alive—and full of longing.

I curled my index finger towards him, my gaze still a bit blurry. He moved around the corner of the bed, maintaining eye contact with me. He looked torn. "Do you want me to get you a robe?" He may have suggested it, but from the bulge in his boxers, I could tell that his cock was just fine with my lack of clothing.

"No."

"Don't tempt me, Maggie." He took a step closer.

"Why not?" I shrugged my shoulders, my gaze dropping down to his crotch. "I know I want this."

He took a sharp breath in as I clutched either side of

his shorts. "Rocco and Slater are in the living room. They're going to hear us."

"I don't care," I murmured, pulling the shorts down his thighs. His stiff cock filled my view. It twitched, like it was seeking my attention. And I was going to give it a lot of that.

I wrapped my fingers around the base of his shaft, breathing softly onto the head. I snaked my tongue out of my mouth, taking a quick swipe. A sigh of anticipation escaping me, I parted my lips and guided him into my mouth. He groaned as I engulfed him. His hands stroked my hair as I began to bob up and down.

"You're crazy, but fuck, that feels really good," Julian uttered in an admiring tone, tilting his head back. I eased back, my lips making a popping sound the moment I released him.

"I know, but you love it," I teased, looking up at him. I moved my fist up and down his shaft, feeling the weight and heat of his erection. My tongue darted out, lapping up a drop of precum. Then I took him into my mouth again.

Julian groaned, and out of the corner of my eye, I glanced toward the door. If Rocco and Slater didn't know what we were up to in here, they soon would.

I ran my free hand up Julian's thigh, scratching and teasing. His legs were so strong and powerful. I liked stroking them, but I knew a place he'd enjoy being touched more.

Cupping his balls, I sucked him in hard, taking as much of his rock-hard cock into my mouth as I could. His hands tightened in my hair as his moans filled the room. I squirmed on the bed, knowing I was making a wet spot. I love the fact that I was getting him so turned on.

With one last gentle tug, I let go of his heavy balls and focused solely on his cock. In, out. Swirl my tongue. Suck. Moan against it so he could feel the vibrations. I hadn't done this in a long time, but I hadn't forgotten how—and I couldn't remember ever enjoying it this much.

His groans got louder as his hips thrust forward. His grip on my hair intensified as his body shook with need. And when he shot his load down my throat, he let out a groan that could have woken the dead.

He sank down on the bed next to me, his cock spent, his arm going around me. We were still like that, minutes later, when there was a knock at the door. Julian pulled the sheet up high enough to cover my breasts before he said, "Come in."

Rocco stood there with Slater behind him. "This a private party?" Rocco asked.

I glanced at Julian, a question in my eye. He cocked

his head to the side, studying me while he thought it over. But I wanted to leave it up to him.

"Yeah, it is," he finally told his buddies. But then he added, "*This* time."

Shivered danced over my bare skin. I clenched my thighs together under the sheet.

Slater saw that and chuckled. "Looks like our girl's looking forward to next time."

I really, really was.

30

SLATER

Asking around, trying to find out a Don's location was a whole lot easier when you didn't have a price on your head. *Much* easier.

Still, there were people who were loyal to us, as long as we assured them that Roselli would never find out. Plus, there were a few idiots who didn't even realize that the three of us and our Don weren't on good terms anymore.

But mostly, the word on the street had spread.

People knew he wanted us gone.

Questions like "why" just didn't matter. Money talks, bullshit walks, as they say.

And speaking of money, it was a joke.

That cheap son of a bitch had only offered ten grand each for us.

To a seasoned professional, this would be laughable. Hired guns were expensive. They cost a lot more than a miserable ten thousand bucks. To the average junkie or pimp, though, this was a lot of money. Which is why the ones Julian and I contacted sounded desperate to meet with us. Once we mentioned we were back in town, they all got excited. They spoke too fast. They suggested meeting places. Surprise of surprises—those places were far too secluded. I heard them talking about underground parking lots, dead-end streets, and crap like that. Maybe those crackheads thought we were born yesterday, but there was no way we weren't going to fall for that bullshit.

And while some of them were eager to get in good with Roselli, most weren't too motivated for that measly amount of money. Of course, if Roselli had known we were behind the destruction of his precious meth lab, the price would've gone up a lot. But Julian's plan had worked. Roselli likely had his suspicions, but no one could prove it wasn't an accident. Labs like that were full of dangerous chemicals. Shit happened.

Especially when the three of us were there to make it happen.

And then after days of fruitless searching, I finally caught a break, in the form of one of the bouncers at a local strip club. He shared some news that I paid handsomely for.

"Gambini and Roselli's crew won't shut up about this fundraiser at the Ritz, man. It's in six days. Everybody will be in the lobby at first. Come midnight, when most people are gone, wise guys will be up on the roof, because they're flying in some ballet troupe, these dancers from Eastern Europe. Twelve of them. Roselli can't wait for that party—those poor girls!"

We'd been searching for a time and a place where Roselli would be all alone. Instead, I'd discovered a venue where he would be surrounded by a bunch of mafia bosses and their lap dogs. Still, this was the only piece of information we had. Something told me Rocco and Julian wouldn't like it. If I was being honest, I hated it, too. But it was the only lead we had.

Back at the cabin, Rocco and Julian had already broken out the whiskey. They were drinking on the couch with Maggie perched between them. From the big smile on her face and her mussed up hair, I assumed my friends had taken good care of her while I was gone.

That had been happening a lot lately, but the freshly fucked look worked for her. It certainly always made my cock come to attention. Except not tonight. There was too much on the line and only a few days to plan.

Maggie poured me a drink, but then she retired to

the back bedroom. Multiple orgasms always made her sleepy.

As we drank, I shared what I'd learned.

As I'd anticipated, Rocco wasn't pleased. "That's not going to work. We'd be walking straight into the arms of every fucking mobster in New York City. There's no way in hell we'd get out of the Ritz alive."

"I don't want to give those fucks the satisfaction, Slater," Julian added. "They want to kill me? Let them hunt me down on the street. I won't get caught like a mouse in a trap."

"I hear you both." I eyed Julian first, then Rocco. "You're right. If we walk into that lobby, we're dead in the water. Everybody knows our faces. But—and this is a big but—this is the only thing we've got right now. I'm tired of all this back and forth out here to the middle of nowhere. We can't keep it up. Sooner or later, we're going to slip up, and then it's game over."

"So, you want to go after Roselli at that fundraiser, because you're tired?" Rocco asked with exasperation. "Is that what you're saying?"

"I'm sick and tired of knowing Roselli's still alive and kicking," I said. "And you know as well as I do that we can't keep this up forever."

"Then what the hell do you suggest we do?" Rocco snapped.

"We can make it work," I insisted, turning to Julian.

"Use that big brain of yours. There has to be some way to isolate Roselli at the party."

"Without him seeing us," Rocco said, but at least he wasn't snapping at me now.

"We'll think of something," Julian finally said with a sigh.

"How do you know?" Rocco asked.

"Because we have to," Julian said simply. Then he downed his whiskey, and we started planning.

31

MAGGIE

AFTER BEING STUCK in this cabin for so long, things were suddenly happening. Rocco, Julian, and Slater rarely went to the city anymore now that they had a lead on where Roselli would be.

Instead, they went into full planning mode. I'd half expected them to do that out of earshot of me, but they didn't. I seemed to have become a kind of honorary member of the gang, though I wasn't sure when that had happened. Perhaps when I suggested that they destroy the drug lab?

But I wasn't complaining. It was fascinating to listen to them as they made their plans. One would propose an idea, then the other two would poke holes in the idea over and over until it collapsed. Then they regrouped and came up with the next idea.

They'd cuss at each other. They'd shout. A few times they looked close to blows. But somehow, they kept going. They knew each other as well as three men could, and this seemed to be their process.

I sat on the sofa, hugging my knees to my chest, as I watched them at the kitchen table. Rocco was standing up, but he kept pounding his fist on the table. Julian was hunched over a bunch of papers spread out on the table. And Slater alternated between leaning back in a chair, his long legs spread out in front of him, looking carefree and at ease. But looks could be deceiving.

Watching them made me think about the people in my life. Had I ever known anyone as well as they did each other? My mom, yes. Piper and Zoey? They were my best friends, but I couldn't claim that we knew each other as well as these three did. Sometimes they seemed to read each other's minds.

Still, I missed Piper and Zoey like crazy. I'd texted them a few times from a secured phone, but it wasn't the same as an actual conversation. Plus, Julian always hovered over my shoulder and examined every syllable, which was annoying as hell. It's not like I was going to slip up and say where we were.

Julian got up and got a bottle of beer out of the fridge, so it seemed to be break time.

"How's it going?" I asked in general, walking over. Rocco was closest, and he looked tense. I moved in behind him and started to rub his shoulders, but it wasn't easy to reach that high. Plus, they were just too massive. "If you sit down, I can do a better job."

"Thanks, sweetheart, maybe later." Rocco sounded distracted and stressed. I hated the toll this was taking on my guys.

"I'll take you up on that offer," Slater said, but when I walked over to rub his shoulders, he pulled me down onto his lap. He slung an arm around me, and I nestled against his chest, enjoying the closeness. He, Julian, and Rocco had been more focused on planning than on anything physical ever since Slater had gotten back from the city with his news.

However, other needs still needed to be met. "Are you guys ready for dinner?" I asked. We'd had so much takeout lately that there were enough leftovers in the fridge to keep us fed for days.

Rocco, who'd been staring at the papers on the table, looked up. Julian came in from the kitchen. Significant glances were flying back and forth between the men.

"Why are you guys acting weird?"

"We should discuss dinner," Rocco eventually said.

"Okay," I said, drawing the word out in my confusion. "Couldn't we discuss dinner over, you know, dinner?"

Slater laughed silently—I could feel his chest move behind me. "Not tonight's dinner," he said in my ear.

Now I was really confused.

"We want to take you out to eat," Rocco said. "The three of us. Like a date."

The thought made me smile. "I'd love that. How about after you three get rid of the man who wants us all dead, we'll do that."

"No." Julian shook his head. "Tomorrow night."

"Seriously?" Mr. Safety and Security wanted to go to a restaurant?

"Really," Rocco confirmed.

"But what about—"

Slater wrapped his arms around my waist, holding me tight as he interrupted me. "Life's short, and the future's never assured. So we want to do this now."

"Now? Like right now?" I was wearing yoga pants and a t-shirt with holes in it.

"Well, tomorrow night," Julian said.

"Is it... safe?" The precautions the three of them took had begun to rub off on me.

"Yeah," Rocco said. "We're going to have maximum security in place. Don't you worry about that."

Despite my unease, I couldn't help being touched that they obviously wanted this to happen, and they'd planned it to surprise me.

"What kind of restaurant is it?"

"A fancy one," Julian said. "Really fancy."

"It sounds wonderful," I said honestly. "But I don't have anything to wear."

Slater chuckled. "Hold that thought."

Julian got up and went to the small closet just inside the door. He returned with a black garment bag.

"What's that?" I asked. I tried to get to my feet to take it from him, but Slater held onto me for a little longer. He liked to do things like that to remind me who was boss. Which was both annoying and also, let's face it, hot.

When he let me go, I sprang up. Julian held the hanger up, and I unzipped the bag slowly.

Inside was an evening gown. A gorgeous evening gown—the most beautiful one I'd ever seen. The silky material was silver, and there were beads and jewels sewn onto it. The whole thing sparkled, and I couldn't wait to try it on.

"There are shoes and earrings in the smaller bag," Julian said, turning the hanger to show me the matching bag behind it. "Trust me, we thought of everything."

Reaching a finger out, I traced a line of beads sewn onto the bodice. "This is so beautiful. When did you guys get this?"

Rocco answered. "That's our secret."

"Thank you. All of you." I looked each man in the eye before turning back to the dress. I couldn't look away from it for very long. "And now I'm really curious about what kind of restaurant it is."

"I'll just say this," Julian began. "If you think you can be too overdressed at this place, you're wrong. So go all out—there's makeup in the bag, too, if you need it."

"And don't worry," Rocco said. "We're going to get dressed up, too."

I was a little bit worried on that point, though. The three of them looked hot as sin in t-shirts and jeans. If they were all decked out in bespoke suits, I might melt into a puddle of desire.

"Is there anything we've forgotten?" Julian asked, his eyebrow cocked.

"Nope," I breathed, still staring at the beautiful dress. Then I smiled like a schoolgirl. "Guess I have a date."

"Looks like you do," Rocco said with a smile.

The next day, I did my best to give myself a makeover. Not easy in a cabin in the woods, but I managed. I took a bath and shaved my legs. Anticipation about our date filled me, and it was hard not to sneak a few extra touches between my legs. But I hoped that tonight, someone else would touch me there. Hopefully more than one someone else.

I wore a robe while I did my hair and my makeup. I pictured the way Zoey did her hair and her eyes before a performance, and I did my best to recreate the look. In the end, I was pretty happy with the result. My dark eyes looked larger than usual, thanks to a combination of mascara, eye liner, and eye shadow. My lips were a dark red, and I'd gotten my skin so moisturized that it practically glowed. My hair was in an updo. Not the messy bun I often wore at the Rusty Bucket, but in a more sleek, elegant style.

And then it was time to put on the dress—something I'd been dying to do since I first saw it. I'd held it up to me the night before to make sure it would fit, but I hadn't allowed myself to try it on. Instead, I'd hung it on the back of the bedroom door and stared at it for nearly an hour this morning when I woke up.

It was so beautiful. And Rocco, Julian, and Slater had gotten it for me. That made it even more special.

I slipped the thin, sparkly straps over my bare shoulders. It was so low-cut in the back that I could easily zip it up myself. That was good. I didn't want any of the guys to see me until I was completely ready.

The bodice had a built-in bra, so that wasn't an

issue. For panties, however, I was hoping that there would be some sexy ones in the bag of things that had contained the shoes, the makeup, and the earrings. However, there weren't any panties.

That was disappointing. I only had regular panties, nothing pretty or special. I crossed over to the dresser and opened the top drawer. Inside were socks, bras, and t-shirts... but no panties.

I frowned. There were some in there this morning—I was sure of it. Looking around, I spotted the bag I was using as a laundry hamper. I bent over it, sorting through the dirty clothes—no panties. How was that possible?

Then I remembered that the ones I'd worn earlier today would be with the rest of my clothes in the bathroom. But this was such a gorgeous dress that I hated to wear ordinary granny panties.

Then a realization struck with such force that I nearly clapped my hand to my forehead. Those panties wouldn't still be in the bathroom. They'd be missing—just like the rest.

Because Rocco, Julian, and Slater had taken then.

They didn't want me to wear any panties tonight.

That knowledge made my pulse race and my thighs clench. It had likely been Slater's idea, but I bet Rocco and Julian hadn't had many objections.

My face flushed as I sat on the bed. I'd been looking

forward to our date for nearly twenty-four hours, but now I was really looking forward to it.

As I perched on the edge of the bed, trying not to wrinkle the incredible gown, I pulled the last item out of the bag, the shoes. I'd taken a look before but hadn't actually pulled them out of the bag.

When I did, a flash of disappointment filled me. They were pretty—silver and delicate. But they were flats.

I'd been sure that there would be sexy high heels to go with the dress. It had the kind of slit that showed a lot of leg. The guys had gotten me an amazing dress, but still, they were men, and they apparently didn't understand certain things.

Still, I wasn't going to let it ruin my evening. Nothing was going to do that.

My mood improved when I put on the earrings. They were big and dangly, and I loved the way they caught the light.

When it was almost time to leave, I spent a while longer fussing around with my hair and makeup, looking at myself in the mirror over the dresser from every angle. I'd never considered myself to be too hung up on clothes. When tending bar, I deliberately dressed down. It seemed to cut down on the number of patrons who hit on me, plus, it didn't make sense to wear nice clothes when they'd end up smelling like booze by the end of the night.

Zoey was always getting on me about wearing nicer things, but it hadn't seemed that important to me.

Until this dress.

I loved it. It was so elegant. It somehow made me look incredibly elegant. And possibly vain—after all, why couldn't I stop looking at the dress in the mirror? But then I realized that I was stalling. I was looking forward to this date more than anything, but I was also a little... nervous.

Not about safety. If the men said that we'd be safe tonight, then we would be. They always took security seriously. But I couldn't help being a little jittery. I was going on a date—a real date—with three masculine, virile men. I'd spent so much time with them in this cabin that they'd started to seem a little... domesticated? No, that wasn't the right word. But I'd gotten comfortable with them, at least to some extent.

But out in the real world, in a fancy restaurant, on a date... that was an entirely different situation. How would they act? What would we talk about? I felt almost as nervous as I had before my first date when I was a teen. And that had just been to Burger King with the boy next door.

Not even my nerves were going to ruin this evening, however. Slater was right. Life was short, and no one knew what the future held. Especially when a mob boss wanted you dead.

Taking a deep breath, I walked out of the room and went to find the men.

They were in the living room waiting.

All three looked up when I entered, making me stop dead in my tracks at the sight of them. My breathing halted entirely—my heart might have, too. My hand rose to my chest as I stared at them. And stared again.

Holy mother of god.

They looked as hot as sin. Hotter, even.

All three wore black suits that fit them like a dream. Julian's showcased his lean muscles, narrow waist, and powerful thighs. Rocco's suit seemed barely able to contain his muscles, yet it made him look incredibly classy. There was no other word for it. He looked sleek and powerful. They both did.

It was Slater who looked the most unlike himself. The cut of his black suit made him look like a million bucks, but the biggest change was his hair. He'd gotten it the bulk of it chopped off. It was short, almost like Rocco's. It made him look like a marine or something. Some kind of fit—and extremely hot—military man.

The men were still staring at me, and my nerves returned. Unsure of what else to do, I decided to indulge my curiosity about Slater's new look. I walked over to him and reached up to run my fingers across the shorn side. "Nice," I whispered.

He caught my fingers in his and brought them to his lips. "Right back at you," he said, giving my hand a kiss.

Out of the corner of my eye, I saw Rock shake his head as if snapping out of a trance. "You look gorgeous, Maggie," he said, and I gave him a huge smile. "Right back at you," I said, and he chuckled.

"She looks beyond gorgeous," Julian said, his eyes full of appreciation. "Told you that dress was the right one for her."

"It is." For once, Slater didn't have anything sarcastic to say.

"We should get going, Rock," Julian said, though he didn't move toward the door, his eyes fixed on me. "Don't want to miss our reservations."

"Right." Rocco held out his arm for me. "Ready, sweetheart?"

"Very."

Once outside, I found out that we were going in two cars. Julian and Slater left first in order to make sure it was still safe, they said.

Rocco opened my door and I very carefully climbed into the car. While the dress's high slit allowed for ample movement, I was careful not to let the gown catch on anything or rip.

Once he got in, his weight shifting the SUV, he

pulled out his phone. "We should give them a few minutes. Mind if I call Tommy?"

"Of course not."

It took a few minutes for him to get through. Evidently, Tommy's grandmother answered and wasn't too keen on handing the phone over to the boy. Rocco was patient and respectful, but I could hear a tinge of pain in his voice.

Finally, Tommy was there, his smile lighting up the screen. He was talking a mile a minute about how his grandparents had converted a guest bedroom into a game room. "There's a train table and everything," Tommy said enthusiastically. "There are three tunnels and two bridges."

"It sounds like a lot of fun," Rocco said.

"It is." Tommy hesitated. "I wish you could come here and play trains with me."

"Me too, son. I miss you so much." Rock cleared his throat, and for a moment, it didn't seem like he could go on.

"Can I say hi?" I asked.

He nodded and handed over the phone.

"Hi Tommy!"

"Hi Maggie," he said. The he proceeded to tell me more about the playroom, about the huge lawn behind the house, and about his grandparents' yappy little dog. Well, he didn't call it a yappy dog, but I could hear it in the background.

As pleased as I was that Tommy wasn't miserable, I knew that every enthusiastic word from him was painful for Rocco. I patted his leg as I talked to his son.

"Maggie?"

"Yes."

"Can you come visit me?"

My heart ached. "I wish I could. Your dad does, too. He misses you so much."

"I miss him, too."

A woman appeared behind Tommy and gave me a disapproving look. She said something to Tommy and then he turned back to me. "I have to go."

"Okay, but I'll give the phone back to your father first so you can say good-bye. It was nice talking to you, Tommy." Hastily, I gave Rocco back the phone, afraid that the snooty-looking woman would make Tommy hang up.

The pain was raw in Rocco's voice when he spoke to his son again. He kept telling him he missed him and that he'd see him soon.

I fervently hoped that last part was true.

Rocco was silent after the call ended. I took his hand and squeezed it. "You'll see him soon." They were empty words, but with sincere emotion behind them.

He shook his head, staring out the windshield in

front of us. "He's got everything he needs there," Rock said.

"No, he doesn't. He hasn't got you."

"Tell that to a judge. Any competent one would rule right away that my boy's better off there."

"Well, then, they'd be wrong." That kind of thing was why I'd always dreamed of being a lawyer. So I could help the people who needed it most.

For a big man, it was amazing how lost he looked right now.

"I'm sorry, Rocco."

He mustered a small smile for my sake. "Thanks."

"All of this should be over soon," I said. "Then you'll see him." "If it works."

"It will." I had no way to know that for sure, but I trusted these men. "Do you think we've given Julian and Slater enough of a head start?"

He smiled. "You make it sound like we're going to go hunt them down or something.

I shrugged. "Everyone needs a hobby."

Rocco gave a small chuckle, which I was hoping for. Then he nodded. "Okay, we can go. And I'm sorry. I didn't mean to bring you down right before our date."

"Never apologize for loving your child."

"I won't. But starting now, this night is all about you."

"I like the sound of that," I said. "And I'm getting pretty hungry."

"Then let's go." He backed up, made a sharp turn, and drove away from the cabin.

The roads were unfamiliar to me—indeed, this whole part of the state was unfamiliar to me—but it seemed like Rocco doubled back a few times. As I said, these guys took our safety seriously.

And then, in the middle of nowhere, he pulled onto a very small dirt road.

"The restaurants out here?" I said, trying not to use the phrase "in the middle of nowhere" in case it hurt his feelings. These guys had obviously put a lot of thought into this date.

"It is." He gestured ahead of us, and I saw Slater's car parked under a tall tree.

He pulled up next to it, and I squinted into the darkness. There were trees all around, but I could see some lights ahead.

Rocco opened my door for me, and when he took my hand, he kissed it, just as Slater had done. My confusion about our location faded, and anticipation returned. I couldn't wait to join Julian and Slater.

We walked along a dark, unpaved path. Rocco had my arm in his. For the first time, I was glad I wasn't wearing heels. I might've tripped on the uneven ground.

The lights ahead grew brighter, and we soon came to a small clearing in the woods. The sight that greeted me had me smiling from ear to ear.

Julian and Slater stood waiting, not at a restaurant. Not at a building at all. Instead, there was a table set up in the middle of the clearing. Poles with lights were placed at intervals around the clearing, with strings of lights stretching between them. Soft music played.

It was the most magical-looking setup I'd ever seen.

32

MAGGIE

My jaw dropped as I took a dreamy step toward the table. There was a tablecloth, candles, fancy china, and a half-dozen platters and bowls covered with silver domes. "You guys did all this for me?"

"We did," Julian said, with a smile almost as big as mine.

"All for you, sweetheart," Rocco confirmed, still holding my arm.

Slater pulled a chair out. "Come sit down, beautiful."

I felt like a princess as I sat on the chair. He pushed it in and then bent down to give me a light kiss on the side of my neck.

Julian poured wine for us as the others took their seats. The lights they'd set up only illuminated a small part of the surrounding darkness, but above them was a bright expanse of starry skies. Maybe after dinner, we could turn off the electric lights and enjoy the natural ones for a while.

The food was good—I think. Truth be told, I was too focused on Rocco, Julian, and Slater to pay it much attention. There were steaks, pasta, salad, and wine... and all of it paled in comparison to the men sitting with me.

We talked about this and that, whatever came up. They told me a few stories about Emilio. It was still hard to wrap my head around the fact that he was my biological father, but I appreciated learning about him.

Slater told a tale about Rocco breaking him out of the basement of a foster care family that had locked him in there. Julian talked about the time they'd tried to tunnel their way out of the group home they'd lived at for a while.

Slater, still looking very different with his short hair, laughed. "There were simpler ways to run away, but we'd just watched *Shawshank Redemption*."

Each story was illuminating—and heartbreaking. They demonstrated again how desperate these men had been for family when they were youths. I could understand that. I'd had my mom, but she worked such long hours that sometimes it felt like I barely saw her. And then she'd been taken from me far too soon.

It was strange how we'd all had difficult childhoods. Theirs was worse than mine, because at least I'd had one parent. It made me wonder if I would've turned to a life of crime if I'd been in their situation.

Julian asked me about my mom, and I shared a few of my happier memories.

"Sounds like Sheila was a nice woman," he said.

"Like her daughter," Rocco added.

After we were done eating, Rocco poured more wine. It was so pleasant, feeling the night breeze and watching the stars. The guys had made quite the oasis out here, and I told them that.

"Glad you like it," Slater said.

"I really do. And now I know why you guys didn't get me heels to wear with this dress."

It hadn't seemed like a controversial statement to me, but the three of them were exchanging significant glances, the way they sometimes did. It often made it seem like they were having a silent conversation when they did that.

"What?"

Still, the telepathic conversation continued. At last, Julian spoke. "We did get heels to go with the dress." He stood up and started taking dishes off the table, packing everything into a large box.

"You did?" That excited me more than I could say. But it was just such a gorgeous dress, and I was eager to have the perfect shoes to go with it. "Thank you. Now I can wear them next time if we're not going to be walking across the grass."

Slater looked me in the eye. "You can wear them now, if you choose to."

There was a note in his voice that I couldn't quite identify. I looked over at Rocco.

He grinned, pointing back at his buddy. "He'll explain."

Julian appeared again, topping off our wine before clearing more dishes off the table.

I turned to Slater. "Explain what?"

The gleam in his eye kind of ruined the wholesome military man vibe he'd had going, but it had me intrigued. "We'll make a deal with you," he said.

"What kind of deal?" I asked, but the sudden spike in my heart rate gave me a clue that Slater was about to go indulge his sexy, dominant side.

Julian set a cardboard box on the table and then sat down again. All three men stared at me.

"What kind of deal?" I asked again.

Slater lifted the lid of the box, and I gasped at the sparkly, strappy sandals. "You can wear the dress, or you can wear these shoes. But not both."

The throbbing between my legs intensified before my brain caught up. "What?"

He gave me an evil smile. "If you want to wear these shoes, then that's *all* you'll be wearing."

"That's—that's crazy," I gasped.

He shrugged nonchalantly. "That's the deal."

"But it's your choice," Rocco said. His words were for me, but his stern look was for Slater.

A dozen pros and cons filled my head, but the blood in my body was already pooling between my legs, making it hard to think. I reached out, wanting to touch the pretty heels, but Slater pulled the box back. "If you want the shoes, you have to give me the dress."

Heat made my chest flush. For weeks, I'd had idle thoughts about being with all three of them. Being stuck in a cabin with such sexy men made it all but impossible not to fantasize. But now, it was time to decide if I wanted the fantasy to become a reality.

My body wanted that. Hell, my brain wanted that, mostly. But actually doing it was another story. "I have a counteroffer."

Slater raised an eyebrow. "Yes, counselor?"

His form of address made me remember the day he'd spanked me in his apartment, and I could feel my face redden. "How about you let me wear the complete outfit, dress and shoes, for ten minutes." I took a deep breath. "And then I'll take off the dress."

"Deal," Julian and Rocco said at the same time, and Slater rolled his eyes at them.

"You two are softies," he said to his friends.

"Please, Slater. This dress makes me feel like a princess. I'm not ready for that to end," I begged.

He pushed the shoebox forward, and I kicked off the flats. I stood up and put one hand on Rocco's shoulder as I slipped the heels on.

"Let's see," Rocco said. I stepped back, nearer to the lights, and angled my leg through the slit.

"Fucking gorgeous," Rocco breathed, and the other two seemed to agree.

"It's going to be a long ten minutes," Slater said.

Julian swiped at his phone. "I know how we can pass the time." The soft music that had played in the background throughout dinner changed into something sultrier. He turned the volume up and then got to his feet.

He looked so damn handsome in his suit that I gulped when he held his hand out to me. "May I have this dance?"

Shit. These guys really knew how to turn on the charm.

"Of course," I said, my throat dry.

He took my hand and led me a few feet away from the table. It felt natural to go into his arms. We fit together perfectly. With his arms around me, he led me into a slow dance. The skirt of the gown swirled around my legs as he expertly guided me. I couldn't keep the smile off my face as I looked up at him.

When the song changed, Rocco appeared next to me. "May I cut in?"

Julian nodded, stepping back with a courtly little bow. These guys were good at this. They were excellent dates, and I was torn between appreciation for them for making this night special and, well, hormones. They were turning me on so much.

Rocco wasn't quite as smooth of a dancer as Julian, but it was still incredible to be in his arms. I rested my cheek against the crisp, white dress shirt he was wearing. I could feel his heartbeat through his sculpted chest.

And then Slater was there. Rocco handed me over and went back to the table to sit by Julian.

The new song was slightly faster, and Slater put his hands on my waist, lifting me off the ground, spinning me around before setting me down. I laughed, clutching his shoulders for balance as I regained my footing.

When the song ended, he held me tight, his lips close to my ear. "Three songs—that took about ten minutes, wouldn't you say?"

I knew what he was asking. And I wanted to play his game, but I wasn't sure I was brave enough. Finally, I stood on my tiptoes and whispered to him what I wanted him to do.

Immediately, his hand glided down my back, finding the zipper. He slid it down, and I could feel the cool night air caress my lower back.

Since I wasn't wearing panties, I assumed that Julian and Rocco were getting an eyeful as the fabric parted, but they didn't say anything. Clutching the front of my dress to my chest, I looked up at Slater.

He dipped his head and his mouth descended on mine. I moaned and reached my free hand up to stroke his short hair. His hands weren't still, either. They slid into my open dress, and he squeezed my ass, making shivers of desire radiate through me.

Then he picked me up again, not to twirl me this time. Instead, he set me on the table. Rocco and Julian were on either side of me, and Rock's big hand settled on the small of my back.

Julian slid his index finger under the strap of my gown. "Ready to take this off?" His voice was a soft whisper.

"Yes," I breathed back, and he tugged the strap down my shoulder while Slater stood over me with hunger in his eyes. I dipped my shoulder on the other side and that strap slid down my arm, too.

The only thing keeping the dress up was my hand pressed to my chest.

Slowly, I let go and the shimmery fabric fell to my waist.

Slater's eyes gleamed as he stared down at me. Then he took my hands and pulled me to my feet. The dress slid down to the ground, and my entire body flushed red. Slater picked up the dress and handed it to Julian who folded it loosely. I was glad. Even in my aroused state, I didn't want the dress they'd given me to get ruined.

Another kiss—this time, with Slater still wearing his suit and me almost completely naked. The only things I still wore were the earrings and the shoes.

My legs parted and he pushed his knee in between them, grinding his erection against my stomach. I hugged his hips with my thighs as I linked my arms behind his neck. His kiss was so all-consuming that I almost forgot Rocco and Julian were there—or at least I forgot to be nervous that they were watching me.

Then Slater picked me up, my legs wrapping around him. He stepped back, and a warm, hard body moved in behind me. From the size, I knew it was Rocco. His chest was bare now.

It was hot as hell being pressed between their two muscular bodies. Slater tilted his head and nuzzled the side of my neck. Rocco did the same on the other side. As I moaned, I reached my hand out, blindly groping for Julian's. When I captured his hand, I pulled it to my chest, pressing his fingers against my bare breast.

He got the message and began rubbing and teasing my already erect nipple.

God, it felt good. Slater and Rocco were completely supporting me—I wasn't even touching the ground. All I could feel were their powerful bodies and Julian's skillful touch.

My moans filled the night air as I clung to Slater's neck. Then, moving with synchronicity, the men switched things up. Rocco stepped to my side, and Slater carried me back to the table. Only this time, when he set me down, it was on someone's lap—Julian's. I could feel the huge bulge in his pants, and I ground my ass against it, making him groan.

His hands immediately moved to my breasts, caressing and kneading again. Then he bit my earlobe. "Do you want me inside you?" he whispered. At the same time, he reached down, dragging a finger along my slit. "I think you're ready for me."

"I am," I said. I looked up at Rocco and Slater. "Is that okay?"

I wasn't asking permission—not really. It was my body. But I wanted to make sure that they were okay with watching Julian take me.

"We know how to share," Rocco said.

Slater nodded with a wink. "And trust me, we're not going to let him have all the fun."

Rocco lifted me up by the waist, and a shiver of excitement shot through me. It was so hot how these guys were able to pick me up as if I weighed nothing. When he set me back down, it was on bare, warm skin. Julian's cock pressed lengthwise against my slit, and I moaned, writhing against it.

Slater grasped my thighs and positioned them outside of Julian's, spreading me wider. The cool air grazed over my heated skin, and I arched my back. Rocco's large hand slid along the inside of my thigh, stroking lightly, but not going where I needed it to go—yet.

"Are you ready?" Julian whispered in my ear.

"Yes."

"Then show me," he said.

Flushing, I reached between my thighs and took hold of his hard cock. It was hot to the touch, and I couldn't wait to feel it inside me. Lifting my hips, I positioned the tip at my entrance.

No one seemed to breathe for a long moment and then I sank down on his thick cock. The sudden stretch left me breathless but wanting more.

Julian let out a loud groan, his hands settling on my hips, guiding me as I lifted myself back up. I pushed back down, letting his cock go deeper each time. Soon, it filled me completely.

"Squeeze me," he said, and I did, tightening my inner walls as much as I could. While I was distracted with that, Rocco and Slater moved in. First one mouth, then the other, attacked my nipples. It felt so good that I cried out.

Julian's hands tightened on my waist, bringing my attention back to him. "Don't stop," he said, reminding me to keep myself as tight as possible around him. My pulse raced with all the incredible sensations.

Then he thrust upward, lifting my hips as he spread me so wide. Rocco's teeth lightly nipped at one nipple while Slater sucked in the other. I put my hands on the backs of their heads, marveling at how their short hair felt so similar now.

But then Julian pushed up again, and I lost all conscious thought.

Grinding my hips, I squeezed him and pulsed up and down. Rocco and Slater moved easily with me, continuing to tease my rock-hard nipples.

"Ride me, princess," Julian said in my ear, his grip tightening as he guided me up and down. The extra movement caused the other two men to release my nipples, but Rocco cupped them with both hands, making me moan again.

Slater slid his finger between my legs. He found my clit and my arousal level tripled. Arching my back, I moved up and down on Julian's thick cock, barely able to keep track of all the sensations. It didn't take long to get close to the edge as Slater worked my clit and Julian pumped into me.

My gasps filled the night as I made wordless pleas. Rock squeezed my breasts, harder than before, but it all served to turn me on more. I writhed back and forth, but Julian kept hold of me as he guided me up and down on his cock. "Oh please," I gasped, begging for the powerful release that was headed my way. "Please."

Slater rubbed my clit faster and Julian's engorged cock somehow grew even thicker. Then, with a sharp cry, I clamped down on it, my entire body thrashing as I came.

Rocco held me steady as I writhed around and cried out, as Julian's cock pulsed deep inside me. Slater didn't let up on my clit and the waves of pleasure seemed endless. Julian's gasps and grunts filled the air as he clutched my sides almost painfully. At last, I slumped back against his chest, and he cradled me against him. We were both breathing heavily.

Slater grinned and licked my moisture from his fingers. "You still taste good," he said. The bulge in his pants was massive. Rock, too, was hard.

I wanted them both. More than anything. Not just for another incredible orgasm, though I knew they could give me that. But because I wanted to feel as close to them as I did with Julian.

"I want more," I said.

Slater's eyes lit up as I reached for him, hooking my finger in his waistband. Julian gave me a quick kiss on the side of my neck and released me. I slid off his lap and turned around, my back to Slater.

He gave a low whistle of appreciation, and then I heard the sound of his zipper going down. I arched my back, balancing on those gorgeous high heels. He moved in behind me, his rock-hard cock smashing against my ass.

I looked over my shoulder at him with a teasing smile. "Think you can make me come again?"

He didn't even dignify that with a response. We both knew he could. Instead, he took his hard cock in his hand and ran the tip through my wet folds. Turning back to Julian, I placed my hands on his thighs, leaning forward. His hand plunged into my hair as his mouth met mine. He swallowed the cry I made when Slater drove inside me with one, long stroke.

God, it felt good. Slater's cock hit me from a different angle, and it was a whole new sensation. I clung to Julian, kissing him deeply, as Slater pushed into me with long, steady strokes.

The pleasure drove nearly every coherent thought

right out of my mind, but I held onto one because it was important.

He was important. Rocco.

I broke the kiss and nibbled on Julian's earlobe. Then I whispered to him what I wanted.

He got up from the table, and I pulled away from Slater. With Julian's help, I climbed onto the table on all fours, my sparkly shoes hanging over the edge. I angled myself so that I was diagonal across the table... and then I looked up and caught Rocco's eye.

Slater drove his rock-hard cock into me again as I reached for Rocco. I fumbled at the zipper of his pants, but I couldn't quite manage it and balance at the same time. But then Rock undid his pants, and his oversized erection sprang free.

I moaned at the sight. I wanted him so badly. Looking him in the eye, I licked my lips and gave him an inviting smile.

He moved closer, his cock bobbing in front of me, and I licked at it. Then he fed the tip into my mouth, and I sucked on it, moaning as Slater continued to pound into me. Rubbing my tongue on the underside of Rock's hard dick, I drew him in further. When he filled my mouth, I moaned again. I lifted one hand from the table, wrapping it around his waist as I sucked on his hard length.

All my fantasies hadn't done this moment justice.

The two cocks filled me, one at either end, and my muffled groans grew louder as they sped up. I was close to coming just from those sensations alone, but Julian wasn't content to leave it at that. His long finger zeroed in on my clit, and I cried out against Rocco's cock.

Slater took that as a cue to thrust into me harder and faster, and every nerve in my body trembled in anticipation. Julian stroked my clit rapidly while his buddies worked me into a frenzy.

My back arched and I screamed as I came. Slater held my hips steady as I thrashed around, nearly bucking off the table. He pushed all the way inside me and held himself there.

"Fuck!" he shouted as he came.

Despite the waves of pleasure shooting through me, I kept my mouth on Rocco's cock, sucking hard, until he grabbed my head and erupted into my mouth with a loud groan. The hot liquid shot down my throat as Slater's cock still pulsed inside of me.

Julian held onto me, making sure I didn't fall off the table as I cried out again and again. The orgasm seemed to last forever, and when first one man and then the other pulled out, I slumped against him.

He gathered me carefully into his arms, holding me against his chest.

Rocco's large hand rubbed my bare back and Slater found my hand and squeezed it.

The dual orgasms had been so intense that I felt close to passing out, but I forced my eyes open. I felt closer to these men than I ever had, and I wasn't ready for that feeling to end.

They pampered me as they tore down the makeshift restaurant. One was always touching me, holding me, stroking me as the other two loaded up the car. Julian helped me back into my dress, and then he and Slater and Julian followed when Rock carried me back to his car.

Rocco carefully deposited me on the passenger seat, and I reached my hand out to first Julian and then Slater. I almost didn't want them to leave, though I knew we'd all be back at the cabin soon. "Best date ever," I whispered.

The looks on all three of their faces told me they felt the same.

33

ROCCO

THE REMAINING days before our strike against Roselli were busy as hell, but I couldn't stop thinking about the date we had with Maggie. I knew my buddies were thinking about it, too. It had been incredible, seeing her come on our cocks. Hearing her cries in the night. Watching her naked body writhe in pleasure.

But the erotic aspects of the date weren't the only thing that filled my thoughts. It was the connection. I'd felt so close to her, especially when she comforted me after my phone call with Tommy. It felt like Maggie was meant to be mine, but somehow, that didn't lessen my conviction that she was meant to be with Julian and Slater, too.

It was hard to explain. We'd occasionally shared a

woman when we were younger, but that had been only about the sex.

This wasn't.

There was something more here, something that had the possibility to be amazing—but only if we could get through the next few days and take care of the threat that endangered us all.

And so we buckled down and perfected the plan. We enlisted Eddie, the hacker who'd been on board with helping us break into the bank in North Haven. He could get us into a hotel room, but he also had a bigger role to play. It was his job to lure Roselli there by posing as a bellboy. He was to hand Roselli a keycard for the room and say that one of the dancers was waiting for him up there.

There was no doubting Eddie's loyalty, but that didn't mean he was up for the job. The kid was just twenty-two. He'd just graduated from college, but that was not really the issue.

His awkwardness? Yeah, that was it.

Six feet tall, messy blond hair, pimples scattered across his face, and a typical geek behavior would make him stand out. Even to an average onlooker, he would seem out of place. Eddie was one hundred percent a nerd.

Shy. Withdrawn. And he stuttered every time he saw

a pretty woman. He was like the poster child of a dysfunctional human male.

The first couple of times he spoke with Maggie up at the cabin, it was fucking hilarious. And tragic. The whole plan would fall apart if he went weak at the knees every time he saw one of those dancers.

But Maggie was also the solution. While we coached him on the elements of the con, she teased him. Flirted, even. Eventually, he got more used to being around a beautiful woman. Or at least, it cut down on his blushing by quite a bit.

Julian joked that Maggie was giving him personal lessons, but that was more or less accurate. She got on him for staring and slouching. She made him speak up, loudly and clearly. We were paying him a small fortune for his role in the con, but he probably should've given her a big cut for making him into an actual human being.

She even made him look like one, too. He couldn't turn up looking like he'd just climbed out of bed. He had to look after himself, which meant brushing his hair and shaving off the ragged patches on his face that he'd claimed were a beard.

He looked like a completely different person an hour before the fundraiser started. Slater, Julian, and I were in the basement of the Ritz. Eddie's uniform, and his much-improved appearance, made him look like a convincing bellboy. As he paced and fidgeted with his bowtie, we went over the plan one more time.

"We know Roselli's going to have someone on the floor," I began. The room where the dancer was supposedly waiting was on the seventh floor. "I'll take him out when he comes in. Make sure you all stay away from the lobby, or you'll run into wise guys."

"I'll guard the door," Slater said, Eddie shuffling away from the mirror. "That fuckwad will definitely try to escape when he sees us in that room."

"Please, don't tell me you want me to chase after him," Eddie interjected. "I know I'll mess it up."

"For fuck's sake." I rolled my eyes. "How many times do we have to repeat this? All you have to do is tell us when he's on his way. Got it?"

"Yeah," he said with an exhale of relief. "I really hope I don't mess this up."

"You'd better not." Julian barely held onto his temper.

I sighed. If Maggie were here, I knew what she'd want us to do. "You can do it," I told the boy. "You're ready, and you know what to do." Then I kicked Slater in the shin before he could say anything negative.

"All right, boys," I said, clapping my hands to get their attention like a damned schoolteacher. "I'll be waiting outside the room, just in case the little prick manages to shake you. Let's do this."

Tension building within, I moved away from them.

The lobby was already bustling once I'd climbed the stairs. There were some really nice smells in the air, like molten cheese and bacon. Two waiters rushed past me, talking over each other. The red carpet underneath my feet was spotless as I stuck to the shadows. The hotel workers had to have been working overtime in order to welcome some of the worst criminals in the state.

In the elevator, I couldn't help smiling at the irony of what was going to go down tonight. Most of the men attending this party belonged in prison. I had a lot of respect for Gambini, but he wasn't all that much better than Roselli in some regards. Gambini just treated his crew better, like by handing out bonuses every once in a while. He was also much more polite to them. And he sometimes even recognized that loyalty was a two-way street.

Had he sanctioned murder?

Yep.

Had his men been dealing drugs?

Of course.

Had he broken people's fingers and legs for failing to pay their loans in time?

Sure he had—or more likely, he'd made his crew do it.

And those were just his lesser crimes. Soon, the

party would be filled with dozens of men exactly like him.

But I couldn't dwell on that stuff. I had to focus on the immediate, which was Nick Roselli. I wasn't going to be the one to purge New York of all criminal elements. I had no interest in becoming a vigilante. All I wanted tonight was to remove the man who had double-crossed me and my friends. The man who was determined to end the most amazing woman I knew.

I stopped at the eighth floor and rolled a cart out of the elevator, dressed as a maintenance worker. Julian and Slater should already be in the hotel room one flight down, waiting for Roselli. An elderly couple exited their room on my left, so I pulled out a screwdriver and pretended like I was fixing a light high up on the wall. The people who could afford to stay here would never notice a lowly maintenance worker.

After what felt like an eternity, Eddie's thin voice in my earpiece made me freeze.

"Guys, are you there?" he asked, the noise from the lobby faint in the background.

"Talk to me, Eddie," I demanded. "Where's Roselli? In the elevator?"

"No. I had to come to the men's room, because the lobby's just too crowded. The strangest thing happened when I told him that one of the dancers was waiting for him on the seventh floor."

My stomach did a painful flip flop. "What's that?"

"He said 'who gives a shit? I've got half a dozen of those bitches meeting me up on the roof later.' He said that's when the real party starts. What should I do?"

Shit!

"Did he say when?"

"No."

"Don't go anywhere. Your only job now is to let us know when Roselli gets on an elevator. Boys, meet me upstairs."

Fuck. Roselli hadn't taken the bait. But at least now we knew where he was heading.

I took the stairs, not wanting to risk running into someone who knew me in the elevator. Timing was going to be everything tonight. Roselli would have men up on the roof, his bodyguards and such. They'd be patrolling while he was conducting his own private orgy.

That meant we couldn't stake the place out now. If there was a shootout, word would get back to Roselli and he'd be out of here in a flash.

Julian, Slater, and I paced at the foot of the maintenance stairway that led up to the rooftop. Our guns were drawn, and our nerves were fried.

Finally, Eddie's weedy voice came through. "He's coming up."

That was good, but we still had to wait. If Roselli

arrived and saw any of his men were out of place, the gig would be up.

We waited five more minutes, pulled on our ski masks, and then crept up the stairs. I pushed the door open. We shouldn't be in the direct line of sight of anyone yet, but maybe we could get a bead on Roselli's location.

After a minute, I heard feminine giggling. Christ, Roselli must be paying those girls an amazing amount to feign that kind of enthusiasm.

We moved through the doorway at a crouch and split up. The new plan was to take out Roselli's men as quietly as possible. We had silencers, but a blow to the back of the head—and then catching the man before he crashed to the ground—would be better.

As I crept around the rooftop, my gun drawn, Gambini's words echoed in my head.

"Whatever you do to take out that motherfucker, it's got to work. You'll only get one shot at this. If you fuck up, Roselli's going to be so pissed that he's going to send every wise guy in New York after you."

The old man had a point.

Mistakes were not allowed.

Roselli could not be alive after our little encounter.

My heart was racing, and I forced myself to take some deep, steadying breaths. Some light was coming from the right. I eased around a wall and spotted light reflecting off the water of the first pool. A naked woman sat on the edge, her feet dangling in the water. I didn't have time to appreciate the view.

I waited a moment, hoping that Roselli would join her, but he didn't show up. While I was waiting, I spotted a guard off in the shadows beyond the pool. As I formulated a plan, he collapsed silently to the ground. That looked like Julian's work to me.

Roselli didn't show, but I could hear muffled giggles and shrieks. Just when I determined I was going to have to knock out the bathing beauty, she got up on her own, presumably wandering off to join the others.

Silently, I followed her.

That was when I saw Roselli.

That pervert was literally lying on the ground. A naked dancer walked up to him and straddled him, waddling past his head to his toes while he gaped upward with his mouth open.

Two more naked women lined up. To get their attention, I banged my gun against the wall behind me. The girls looked up and they screamed. I raised my pistol and fired one shot. A bodyguard who'd been rushing up behind them dropped to the ground.

"Clear the fuck out," I growled at the girls, my gaze staying on Roselli. He propped himself up on his elbow, an expression of shock taking over his face.

The girls ran toward the stairs, where Slater would

be waiting. He'd detain them as long as needed so that they wouldn't raise the alarm.

"What do you want?" Roselli said shakily. His cock had gone limp, and he looked pathetic as he struggled to his feet.

I pulled off my mask, and the fear in his eyes intensified.

"DeLuca!" he exclaimed, his squeaky voice thinner than ever. "You can't do this. Gambini will hang you up by your balls."

"That's not your problem," I said. Roselli's face turned even whiter.

"Rocco, wait! Please!" he begged as I strode toward him, towering over him. A rotten smell hit my nose and I realized he'd pissed himself.

"Are you scared, boss?"

"Please!" he begged once more as I grabbed him by the neck.

A movement on the left caught my eye. Julian was there, and he gave me a nod. I knew that meant all of Roselli's bodyguards had been taken care of.

I was free to shoot the prick who had made our lives miserable. Who'd threatened Maggie. And who'd been a shame to his family's name.

But instead, I stuffed my gun in my waistband. Then I dragged the squealing, naked man past the pools. Across the patio. And over to the ledge at the edge of the building. Hoisting him high up in the air, I smiled at him. "Any last words?"

"Go to hell," Roselli choked out in the weakest voice ever.

"Drop him," Julian growled, holding his gun so tightly that his knuckles were white. "Drop that motherfucker or I'll blow his fucking brains out."

I flung the little man out into the open air.

A deafening scream ripped through the night as I strode away, not even looking back.

From far below, there was a dull thud and the sound of a car alarm going off. I supposed it was too much to hope he'd landed on his own Bentley.

Slater jogged up. "Is he gone?" He pumped his fist when we nodded. "The girls are all tied up, and Eddie's long gone. Time to get the hell out of here."

As we retraced our steps down the back stairwell, I knew I wouldn't trade these last few minutes for all the money in the world. I just couldn't put a price on this mix of satisfaction and relief. At long fucking last, Nick Roselli was gone. The long fall had sent him where he belonged—to hell. He couldn't threaten anybody anymore. He couldn't lay a hand on my boys, me, or Maggie. The hits he had put out on us were history, just like he was.

34

JULIAN

Fucking beautiful.

The whole scene was a thing of beauty. The way Rock had hoisted that asshole over the side of the building would be etched into my memory forever.

I wished I could have stuck around and watched the ensuing mayhem for just a couple of minutes. But all I could do when we got out of that hotel was steal some glances in the direction of the blue and red flashing lights down the street.

I could imagine it, though. It was a wise guy's worst nightmare. Dons in their fancy suits and tuxedos, surrounding a smashed car and a ruined body, yelling at their lap dogs. Gesturing frantically. Making phone calls. Proving that they weren't as unflappable as they claimed to be.

Except for Don Gambini. I somehow thought that he might be taking this all in stride. Of course, since he'd sanctioned the hit, he'd had a heads up.

The drive back to the cabin was wild. We kept laughing and high-fiving each other like schoolboys. We wouldn't even wait to get to the mountain to celebrate properly. Or that's what we claimed. But I think that each of us were most eager to see Maggie.

Rocco even stopped to pick up more booze on the way back, so that we could enjoy our victory.

Victory... I repeated that word in my head several times over. I couldn't believe it. The powerful mob boss was gone, and we were still breathing? Up until a few weeks ago, I wouldn't have believed it. The odds had been stacked against us. We didn't have Roselli's resources. We didn't have his manpower or his connections. In the end, though, we had prevailed.

I hopped out the moment Rock parked next to the cabin. I picked up the bottle of whiskey, its top nudging my chin as I looked up ahead. The moonlight revealed a strange sight. Maggie was near the side of the cabin, leaning against the wooden fence that surrounded the yard. Even in the dim light, I could see the tear tracks on her face.

I dropped the whiskey and sprang forward, but Slater dashed past me, getting there first.

"Maggie, what's wrong?" Slater was quick to ask.

"We're all here. We made it. We're okay—and Roselli's dead."

"I know. His death's all over the internet. I just..." She sobbed and sucked in a deep breath. "I can't believe you did it."

"We did," Rocco bragged, a smug smile on his face. "He's gone. It's all over."

"Come here. All of you," she requested, unfurling her arms, more tears streaming down her face. We all wrapped our arms around her small figure, her subsiding sniffles the only sound my ears could pick up.

"Thank you," she croaked, her body shaking. "I'll never be able to repay you for what you did for me."

"Not just for you," I corrected her. "That fucker wanted to kill us, too, remember?"

"Yeah," she nodded, looking up at us. "Thanks for the reminder, but you still saved my life. *Again*."

"Enough with this sentimental stuff," I said, rubbing her lower back. "Let's go inside and drink our asses off. I think we deserve it, don't we?" If the whiskey had survived me dropping it, that was.

"You bet your ass we do," Rocco agreed, shooting me a grin.

"I'll get the ice," Slater stated, entering the cabin first.

"What are they saying online about Roselli?" Rocco asked, Maggie passing him by.

"I must have read the same article twenty times tonight," she claimed, turning to him. "Tragedy at the Ritz. Nick Roselli victim of a tragic accident."

"Accident," Slater chuckled, high fiving me and then Rocco when we entered the kitchen. "I couldn't have dreamed of a better way to end that bastard. Violent. Terrifying. And some rookie homicide cop called it an accident?"

"As far as we're concerned, it may as well be," Rock said. "It was a sanctioned hit. At least one mob boss authorized it, so we're off the hook."

Grinning, I poured amber liquid out of one of the bottles that hadn't smashed. We clinked our glasses together. I drained half of mine while Maggie just sipped hers. What we'd done tonight hadn't been easy, but she'd endured a special kind of hell waiting back here, hoping we were all right.

But even though she wasn't drinking a lot, she was still a bartender. "This is excellent," she said, staring at her glass. "Let's not ever go back to the cheap stuff."

"Whatever you say, Ms. Heir to the Throne," Slater teased with a smile. "Which reminds me, someone—possibly someone with aspirations of going to law school—should probably figure out what the next step with the Emilio's will is."

"I did take one pre-law class. Before I had to drop

out of school," she said. "Not that I know anything about the rules around inheritances."

"So we'll hire someone who does," Rocco said. "I know it's a little too early to ask, but what are you going to do with all that money?"

"You're right," she giggled, lifting her gaze up to his. "It *is* too early. Right now, I just want to get drunk."

"Don't we all?" Slater laughed out, holding his glass closer to his chest.

"I never enjoyed killing," Rocco confessed, the booze moistening his tongue. "But part of me wishes I could go back and throw Roselli off that fucking roof again. And again."

"I can almost understand why," Maggie said, nodding. "We went through a lot because of him."

"We had to go through *hell*," I corrected her. "But it's over now."

"Well done, Mr. DeLuca, Mr. Knight, and Mr. Winslow." Maggie's voice was somehow sincere and flirtatious at the same time. "I'm proud of you. All of you."

"You did pretty good, too," I said. "Call me sexist, but I never thought a woman could keep her cool like you have throughout."

She grinned at me. "Okay, you're sexist."

Rocco swung his arm around her. "I already knew that Maggie had nerves of steel. I knew it from the first moment when she pulled a shotgun on those two goons trying to rob her bar."

I downed my drink and laughed. This felt like my reward—to have us all here together. It made me remember what it took for us to get here. The pain and the agony we had to endure in order to get out of this ordeal alive. The weeks of uncertainty. The worry for ourselves, our friends, and our girl.

That's why I fucking loved every second of this tonight. How couldn't I? I had risked everything I had to get here, including my own life. We could spend the rest of the night laughing, drinking, and hopefully, having amazing sex. I was already getting into the way the three of us could drive Maggie out of her mind with pleasure. We'd earned our freedom, and now was the time to enjoy the fruits of our labor.

It was about damn time.

35

ROCCO

I woke up next to my buddies. *Naked* next to my buddies.

I sat up, shoving Slater's arm out of the way. Where the fuck was Maggie? She'd been a very integral part of our celebration last night. Grumbling, I made my way to the kitchen, stopping to get rid of what felt like a gallon of whiskey in the bathroom first.

Out on the table was a note. Maggie had gone to the drugstore for some medicine. She wasn't feeling well, the note said.

Well, she'd had a lot to drink the night before. We all had.

I glanced out the window as I put on the coffee. My SUV was gone, so she must've taken it.

We were all up and dressed, by the time I saw her pull in. Julian had even scrambled some eggs.

When Maggie entered the cabin carrying a white bag, I picked her up and spun her around. She hugged me back, but then she groaned. And not the same kind of groan I'd heard last night when we made her come for the third time.

She pushed against my chest. "Put me down—I'm still feeling a bit hungover."

Slater grinned at her from across the room. "And the spinning isn't helping?"

"Definitely not."

She walked over and gave him a quick kiss. Then Julian offered her a plate of eggs.

"No thanks," she squeaked, her face turning green. She sprinted to the bathroom, the pharmacy bag still clutched in her hand.

Unlike her, we were in good enough shape to eat. We were almost done by the time she emerged from the bathroom.

"You okay, sweetheart?" I called.

She nodded, but she still looked a little green around the gills.

Julian noticed, too, and pulled out a chair. "Here, have a seat."

She moved forward as if in slow motion. I couldn't figure it out. I'd seen her hungover before. Next time we had a wild evening, it would have to include more sex and less booze.

I could get behind that.

Slater reached across the table to cup Maggie's cheek. Then he frowned as he studied her face. "Do we need to take you to a doctor?"

"No," she said slowly, as if saying the word for the first time. "I mean yes. But not now."

I moved to her side, kneeling down next to her, beginning to get seriously worried. "What's wrong?"

In answer, she reached into her jeans pocket and pulled out a little white stick.

Julian gasped, but at first, I didn't know what it was and why she was showing it to me.

"It's positive," she said, holding it up in front of her. Slater swore in a shocked voice.

"What—" I began, but then I saw it. Two little lines. I'd heard something on a TV commercial about two little lines.

Holy.

Fucking.

Shit.

"You're pregnant?" I gasped.

She turned to me, biting her lip. Her face was pale now. "I—I think I am."

The shock in her expression overrode everything

else. I reached out and took her in my arms. My own shock could wait. Right now, she needed me.

36

MAGGIE

I BURIED my face in Rocco's broad chest as the tears flowed. The shock was still there, but they were happy tears. Of that, I was sure. What I didn't know was if my men would be happy.

We hadn't known each other that long. We hadn't expected this to happen. But then again, a week ago, we didn't even know if we'd be alive at this point.

That made it a miracle in my book.

Rock rubbed my back and made soft crooning sounds, likely the same ones he'd made when Tommy was a baby. That thought made me smile. Tommy was going to be a big brother—as long as Rock was willing to be a father again.

As long as all of them were. I'd spent my whole life

settling, and I didn't want to do it anymore. I wanted it all: Rocco, Julian, Slater, and the baby.

But I didn't know what they wanted, and it was time to find out.

I pushed away from Rocco, but I couldn't bring to take in the men's expressions. Not yet.

"Maggie?" Julian asked. There was concern in his voice. "Are you happy?"

"Yes." I answered in a small voice. "Are you?" I finally looked up to find three pairs of eyes on me.

"I don't think it matters," Julian said. "It's got to be Rocco's baby."

"It matters," I insisted. Then I turned to Rocco.

The affection I saw in his eyes hit me like a physical blow. He loved me. He wanted this baby. And he proved it by leaning down and planting the sweetest kiss on my lips. Then he turned to his buddies. "It matters," he said. "Because we're all in this together."

Another tear slipped down my face. That's what I wanted, and my heart filled hearing that that's what Rocco wanted that too. But did Julian and Slater?

"I'm in," Slater said huskily, staring into my eyes. "Whatever you need, Maggie. Whatever you and the baby need."

I reached across the table and squeezed his hand.

"I kind of love you, you know," he said, and my breath caught in my throat.

But this was Slater, and I knew he wouldn't want me to get overly sentimental. "I know," I said. "And right back at you."

We all turned to Julian. He still looked stunned as he stared at the table.

"Julian?" Rocco asked.

His friend raised his head. "Are you sure?" he said. "Because you two could just ride off into the sunset." He gave a brittle laugh. "Hell, I'll lend you my motorcycle."

Rocco chuckled. "We'd better take my SUV, because there are four of us. We're in this together."

Julian took a deep breath. "We are. And I think you counted wrong, because there are five of us. This baby has a brother."

Rocco's broad smile got even bigger.

"And before the year is out, there will be six of us," Slater said. "But who's counting."

I grinned at him. "I am." Then I turned to Rocco. "Are you sure this is what you want?"

"Absolutely. But are you sure, sweetheart?"

The warmth in his eyes made me start crying again. "I'm sure." I'd never had a real father, and now my child would have three.

"Good. Because I kind of love you, you know," he said, echoing Slater's words.

Julian gave a small laugh. "If you guys keep saying that, she's never going to stop crying."

"I've noticed that only two of us said it," Slater observed.

"Don't," I said in a rush as Julian opened his mouth. "You don't have to say it."

"Unless you really mean it," Rocco added.

"I mean it." The look Julian gave me melted my heart. "I love you too, Maggie."

"You forgot the 'kind of' part," Slater said.

Julian leaned back in his chair, looking smug. "No, I didn't."

"Good," I said. "Because I love you all, too. And Tommy. And this ridiculous little plastic stick with the pink lines."

Rocco laughed, plucking it out of my hand and tossing it on the table. "I prefer the real thing." He put his large palm on my stomach. Somewhere, deep inside, there was a tiny being, probably the size of a grain of rice, who was going to change our whole lives.

But change them for the better.

I, for one, was excited as hell to see what that world was like.

And I knew I wasn't the only one.

A NOTE FROM THE AUTHOR

Thank you for reading! I hope that you enjoyed the story of Maggie and her dangerous men. The next story features Maggie's friend Piper.

The next two books in the series are:

Mafia Bosses

Mafia Grooms

Please check out all of my ebooks, print books, and audiobooks at Amazon.

ABOUT THE AUTHOR

International bestselling author Stephanie Brother writes high heat love stories with a hint of the forbidden. Since 2015, she's been bringing to life handsome, flawed heroes who know how to treat their women. If you enjoy stories involving multiple lovers, including twins, triplets, stepbrothers, and their friends, you're in the right place. When it comes to books and men, Stephanie truly believes it's the more, the merrier.

Printed in Dunstable, United Kingdom